He saw Fallon ride  over the others. From the c_____ se rearing, rider preparing _____ y holding the fallen serva__

Fallon let go the _____rd with two hands. She swu__

For a moment, th_____ blocked his view, and when it passed, Anok saw the bandit's severed head spinning through the air, the horse charging away as its headless rider slowly slumped from the saddle.

Anok heard rapid hoofbeats behind him and turned, barely deflecting the point of a lance past his head with his sword.

He answered with his other sword, catching the rider as he passed, opening a wide, red gash between the bandit's ribs.

Anok did not follow as his attacker rode away, but turned and headed back into the center of the fight . . .

Don't miss the first adventures of Anok, Heretic of Stygia . . .

SCION OF THE SERPENT

Coming soon, the continuing adventures of Anok, Heretic of Stygia . . .

THE VENOM OF LUXUR

And don't miss the Legends of Kern . . .

BLOOD OF WOLVES
CIMMERIAN RAGE
SONGS OF VICTORY

Millions of readers have enjoyed Robert E. Howard's stories about Conan. Twelve thousand years ago after the sinking of Atlantis, there was an age undreamed of, when shining kingdoms lay spread across the world. This was an age of magic, wars, and adventure, but above all this was an age of heroes! The Age of Conan series features the tales of other legendary heroes in Hyboria.

AGE OF
CONAN™
HYBORIAN ADVENTURES

ANOK, HERETIC OF STYGIA
Volume II

HERETIC OF SET

J. Steven York

ACE BOOKS, NEW YORK

THE BERKLEY PUBLISHING GROUP
Published by the Penguin Group
Penguin Group (USA) Inc.
375 Hudson Street, New York, New York 10014, USA
Penguin Group (Canada), 90 Eglinton Avenue East, Suite 700, Toronto, Ontario M4P 2Y3, Canada
(a division of Pearson Penguin Canada Inc.)
Penguin Books Ltd., 80 Strand, London WC2R 0RL, England
Penguin Group Ireland, 25 St. Stephen's Green, Dublin 2, Ireland (a division of Penguin Books Ltd.)
Penguin Group (Australia), 250 Camberwell Road, Camberwell, Victoria 3124, Australia
(a division of Pearson Australia Group Pty. Ltd.)
Penguin Books India Pvt. Ltd., 11 Community Centre, Panchsheel Park, New Delhi—110 017, India
Penguin Group (NZ), Cnr. Airborne and Rosedale Roads, Albany, Auckland 1310, New Zealand
(a division of Pearson New Zealand Ltd.)
Penguin Books (South Africa) (Pty.) Ltd., 24 Sturdee Avenue, Rosebank, Johannesburg 2196,
South Africa

Penguin Books Ltd., Registered Offices: 80 Strand, London WC2R 0RL, England

This is a work of fiction. Names, characters, places, and incidents either are the product of the author's imagination or are used fictitiously, and any resemblance to actual persons, living or dead, business establishments, events, or locales is entirely coincidental. The publisher does not have any control over and does not assume any responsibility for author or third-party websites or their content.

HERETIC OF SET

An Ace Book / published by arrangement with Conan Properties International, LLC.

PRINTING HISTORY
Ace mass market edition / November 2005

Copyright © 2005 by Conan Properties International, LLC.
Cover art by Justin Sweet.
Interior text design by Stacy Irwin.

ISBN: 0-441-01345-7

ACE
Ace Books are published by The Berkley Publishing Group,
a division of Penguin Group (USA) Inc.,
375 Hudson Street, New York, New York 10014.
ACE and the "A" design are trademarks belonging to Penguin Group (USA) Inc.

PRINTED IN THE UNITED STATES OF AMERICA

10 9 8 7 6 5 4 3 2 1

Acknowledgments

This trilogy is the most massive undertaking I've ever been involved with, and it could not have happened without the assistance, support, and occasionally the patience of many wonderful people.

First I'd like to thank my agent, Jodi Reamer, for her able support and council.

As always, my deepest thanks to my wife, Chris, whose huge assistance proved not merely to be invaluable, but indispensable. Also for her eternal understanding and support. I hope I'm up to returning the favor as she faces her own deadlines.

My thanks to all the great folks at Conan Properties International who have participated in the project and guided it through its various stages, including Fredrik Malmberg, Matt Forbeck (with special thanks to Matt for tolerating my frazzled nerves, all the way to the end), Theo Bergquist, and Jeff Conner.

Special thanks to Ginjer Buchanan at Ace, who has stood with me through five novels now.

My thanks to all the friends who have offered encouragement, support, advice, and feedback through the project, including Sean Prescott, Dean Wesley Smith (yes, Dean, you told me so), Kristine Kathryn Rusch, Loren Coleman, Rose Prescott, the entire Sunday Lunch Gang, and my buds from the Sandbox who helped keep me sane when I ceased to have a life.

Thanks to my family, especially my father, Jim York; my mother, Martha York (secret sleuth of the Internet); and my brother, Tim, who all help keep me anchored through all the rough spots. Thanks to my kids, Shane and Lynette, for actually thinking something I do is cool.

Finally, my gratitude to Justin Sweet for some of the most breathtaking covers I've ever seen.

And of course, my appreciation to Robert E. Howard. Without him, we are nothing.

It is through the port city Khemi, located just south of the mouth of the River Styx, that the cursed land of Stygia conducts much of its congress with the more civilized lands to the north.

There outside traders and merchants are reluctantly welcomed, rarely traveling beyond the harbor, or Akhet, walled enclave of foreigners that nestles between the vast slums of Odji, and the walled inner city of Khemi proper.

The inner city is a citadel, protected by great black walls of stone, where those of Stygian blood retreat by night to feed their dark urges and foul desires. It is there that they perform unspeakable rituals of blood, torture, and sacrifice to appease their dark snake-god, Set.

Know, fellow traveler, that Stygia is foremost the land of Set. All power resides in his cults, and even their king is but a puppet in the thrall of his evil servants. It is clear to anyone who sees Khemi. For as the walled inner city towers over the Odji slums, so, too its fine houses are dwarfed by the tall palaces of the most rich and powerful families who have gained their station through service to Set. And towering over it all, the Great Temple of Set, its spire topped with a statue of Great Set. It is said his eyes burn like coals, even by night, and he looks down upon Stygia, master of all he surveys.

—THE SIXTH SCROLL OF VAGOBIS, THE TRAVELER

PROLOGUE

4,600 years before the Hyborian Age

THE MAN, OR sort-of-man, know as Graymoy the Sage,
limped to the mouth of the cave and looked down the rocky
side of the mountain. An icy wind whistled up the canyon to
the south, past the ruins of a great marble temple, now crumbling bit by bit down the side of the cliff.

Dark clouds rolled rapidly across the sky in an unbroken
stream, and flashes of lightning bubbled in their depths, filling the air with rumbles of thunder. It was a sky with no
promise save misery. It was the end of an age.

Far below, he saw two men like himself climbing up the
rocks.

To more modern eyes they would have looked bestial,
apish. They were short, hairy, thick of limb and body, their
faces wide and flat, dressed in animal furs and hides. To
Graymoy they were distant brothers, with faces little different than his when seen reflected in still water.

Yet all of them were descended of people who had once
been men, before the cataclysm brought down the world and
doomed them to slide back, generation by generation, till they

were little more than beasts. They would slide further still before they could begin the long climb back to civilization.

Graymoy was a sage, as were the men climbing up the rocks, a last spark of knowledge and wisdom in an age of darkness. Graymoy was wise enough to know that the world had fallen before and that it would fall again. He was wise enough to know that even his spark would soon be extinguished, and their like might not come again for a hundred generations.

Someone tugged at the fur cuff of his sleeve. He looked down into the dark eyes of a small boy, dressed in rough furs, hunched at his feet.

"Grandfather," said the boy, "is someone coming?"

He pointed to the back of the cave, past the fire and the many paintings of animals and men, to where a narrow passage led into blackness. "Go, Amet, and hide. Do not make a sound until they have gone."

The boy reluctantly nodded and scampered across the chamber, vanishing into the narrow maw of darkness.

As he did, Graymoy heard a clattering of rocks outside, and the wide figure of a man, bundled in furs, appeared in the cave mouth. The man stepped inside, put down his shoulder bag, bow, and quiver, and hunched beside the fire without a word. He warmed his hands as the second man entered and repeated the process.

Graymoy joined them at the fire, squatting on a flat rock, putting him a head higher than the others. Both men were younger than Graymoy, not much older than his son would have been had he not been struck down three seasons earlier by one of the great cats that sometimes stalked the canyon rim.

One man, blue-eyed, and golden-haired, looked up at him. "Why have you summoned us, Graymoy? Our time of wisdom is ending. We are the last sages of our people. What purpose can such a meeting serve?"

The other, of dark hair and dusky skin, nodded. "I have no wish to be away from home. My son's woman is large with child. I pray it will be a son this time."

"It will be, Kaleth," said Graymoy. "I have seen it in the

sacred flames. Each of you will have heirs, to carry your blood through the dark times to come. That is part of why I have summoned you. You know my only son was killed many years ago. There will be no heirs for me."

The fair-haired one scowled. "What matter is it to you that we have heirs?" He snorted in contempt. "Do you intend to steal our sons?"

"In a manner of speaking, Reloth" His eyes narrowed. "I have found them, all that are left. Two of the three golden scales."

Reloth's eyes widened. "The golden scales? Where?"

"On a mountaintop, three days south of here, amid the bones of two great demons who appear to have battled over them to the death."

Kaleth chuckled. "It is fitting justice. Death to all demons, gods, and creatures from beyond the veil, who have visited such ruin upon us."

Graymoy frowned. "They could never have done it without the aid of men. Were it not for the worship and service of men, our lust for power, such creatures would have little interest in our sphere."

Kaleth frowned, then nodded reluctantly. "It may be so, but they certainly warred over the three scales."

"Only," said Graymoy, "because the three scales gave them dominion over men. But now the necklace is broken, and I have learned that one of the scales is lost into the deep ocean, where no man can ever find it, and even gods will be humbled by the task. So until gods or demons return it to the world of man, only these remain—" He reached beneath his fur jacket and pulled out two leather cords. At the end of each, a shiny medallion of gold hung, each carved with a flaming sword and two inward-facing serpents. He held one out in each hand.

"I give these to you for safekeeping. In time, you must pass them to your heirs, and they to theirs, for the rest of time, or at least until the inevitable fallibility of men breaks the circle. Take them back to your native lands and let them be kept separate and lost to time.

Reloth held his over the fire, where the flicking flames reflected off its shining surface. "Why not just melt them down?"

"They were forged by powers beyond man. I don't think they can be destroyed, at least by such as us," answered Graymoy. "No hammer or axe or fire of man can harm them."

"Then," said Kaleth, "cast them into the sea as well, or into the sands of the desert, or into a mountain of fire."

"Such," said Graymoy, "would hide them from men, but not from supernatural beings, who would be drawn to retrieve them, no matter the cost. Just as someday the third scale may return, and must never be reunited with these two. Cast into the ocean, sooner or later they would be found and the war of gods would begin again. Only if they are always hidden by men may they remain safe from those who covet them. Perhaps not forever, for as we have seen, men are weak, but perhaps long enough that the wheel of time may make another turn." His eyes narrowed, and he studied the other's faces. "Do you see now?"

Reloth stood and nodded. "You speak wisely. I will take this back to my distant land, guard it closely, and charge its safety to my heirs when the time comes. Even if all we have learned is lost to history, perhaps they can still carry this burden through the long darkness ahead."

Kaleth stood, putting the leather cord over his head as he did. "Then I shall do so as well." He nodded to the other two men in turn. "We should make haste, for every moment these two remain together is a danger." He stood. "We will never meet again," he said. "Pray that the Scales never meet again as well." He turned and walked out of the cave.

Reloth reached out and clasped Graymoy's hand. "So it shall be. Perhaps I shall see you in the land beyond the veil." Then he turned and left also.

Graymoy crouched there by the fire, watching the empty entrance to the cave for a while, feeling a sense of great relief. They were wise men, these two, good men, but they were still just men. *Better they do not know. Better they never*

*be tempted as I have been tempted, for on another day, in a
moment of weakness, even I might have failed against it.*

He heard a rustling noise behind him. He looked over his
shoulder and saw the boy peering over the rocks. He signaled the boy over with his hand.

The boy trotted over and sat down in front of the fire,
looking into the flames.

"It is just us now," said Graymoy. "The two golden scales
are gone." He glanced over at the boy. "Now show me the
third."

The boy looked down, reached under his fur shirt, and
pulled at a leather cord. He drew out the golden scale and
looked at it in the firelight. He glanced up at his grandfather.
"What is it for?"

"It is for you and your line to keep safe," Graymoy said.
"It is the most important thing you will ever have and the
most important thing you will ever do. That is all you must
know, and all you must pass to those that follow you. If I told
you more, you would just forget, and if you remembered, it
would still be lost in the river of time. Or worse, you would
pass your knowledge along, someday to send men on dark
quests to wrest the power of the gods. Nothing but doom and
suffering could ever come from that. It is a thing, and you
must hide and protect it. That is all."

The boy hefted it in his hand.

"It is heavy," he said.

Graymoy frowned. "In time," he said, "it will become
heavier still."

1

"WELL," SAID ANOK Wati as he and his fellow acolyte, Dejal, marched up the marble steps to Great Temple of Set, "that was a poor excuse for a day, wandering the streets chanting praise to Set and frightening small children."

Dejal threw back the hood of his robe and glared at Anok, his eyes black as obsidian against his pallid skin. "Hush, brother, before one of the priests hears you! We serve Set in even our most humble tasks in his service."

You serve Set, Anok thought, *not I.* But he dared not even whisper his true feelings about Set or all his servants, for if it ever became known, he would be branded a heretic and killed by the slowest and most terrible means known to the High Priests of Set, and it was said that they could start killing a man on the night of one full moon and only end it on the next.

But heretic was what he was, a pretender in Set's temple, whose true intention was to bring down the snake-god, or at least to do him as much damage as possible before Set's followers could crush him.

As for Dejal, boyhood friend, and once comrade in battle,

there was a very personal score to be settled before Anok's final day came. *Dejal must pay for—*

He grimaced, and tried not to think about the beautiful Sheriti's murder. He pushed the rage he felt down into a deep recess of his heart, to fester with the almost infinite supply already waiting there. He had to maintain the pretense of friendship with Dejal, at least a little longer.

They passed the huge golden statue of a coiled serpent guarding the temple entrance, then through the doors to the ornate outer hall, with its gracefully tapered columns and wrought-iron chandeliers. They turned left and took a windowless corridor parallel to the main ceremonial chamber. Passing an archway watched over by four scarlet-sashed guardians of Set, they left the temple's public areas and descended a long staircase leading down into the catacombs beneath.

It was in this maze of ancient passages, many of which predated the construction of the temple itself, that the true secrets of the cult resided. The tunnels went on for leagues, extending far beyond the temple's foundations, and even beyond the plazas and gardens that surrounded it. In his time there, Anok had never come close to seeing their true extent. Some of the senior acolytes claimed they had no end, and others, that they led down to the flaming pits at the heart of the world.

Anok suspected these were mere tales concocted, like so much of the cult's doctrine, to create fear and confusion. On the other hand, he had seen terrors and wonders in these depths that prevented him from completely dismissing any claim, no matter how absurd it might seem, without firm evidence to the contrary.

He had seen forbidden caves filled with giant serpents, shrines to forgotten gods, pits filled with the bones of countless thousands, lakes of blood, glittering treasure troves, libraries full of ancient scrolls, and vaults brimming with artifacts both ancient and evil.

But these catacombs were at least one more thing. To the novice acolytes of Set, they were home. For it was in the catacombs that they lived in their humble cells, studying Set's evil works and seeking power in his service.

Their path took them back, beneath the great altar, where countless innocents had been sacrificed to Set through the ages, to a quadrangle of corridors that surrounded the cells.

Or should have. They turned the familiar corner, only to find themselves at the end of a long and unfamiliar corridor. Anok stopped short, as did Dejal a few steps later. They both looked around in confusion.

"Spell of deception," said Anok. "We've been tricked!"

Dejal quickly reached beneath his robe and extracted the short staff he had of late been building as his focus of power. The staff was as thick as a man's wrist and the length of a man's arm. Dejal had carved ancient runes and mystic pictoglyphs into the dark wood, and a fist-sized ball of crystal was held in the mouth of a metal serpent at the top.

He held the staff up in front of him and waved it back and forth. "Power of Set, protect me from my foes!"

Anok said nothing, produced no object of power. He merely raised his hands.

Suddenly, from the dimly seen end of the corridor, a ball of flame appeared, and with a roar began to rush toward them, like a charging bull.

"Flood of Flame!" shouted Dejal. "My ward won't defend against that!"

Anok planted his feet firmly on the dusty stone, held out his spread fingers, and shouted, "Deluge!"

From nowhere a wall of heavy rain appeared in front of him. The ball of flame struck the rain with a sizzle, and the combination instantly flashed into a thick, warm fog that flowed over them harmlessly.

"Clever, Anok Wati!" The deep voice seemed to boom from the air all around them. "Your elemental magic never fails to impress. Yet can it save you from a more subtle attack?"

Anok cried out in pain and grabbed his head. He felt as though a hand had reached inside the skull and was crushing his brain.

He struggled to resist, to summon some counterspell, but the maddening pain gave him no quarter. His power failed him.

He dropped to his knees, groaning in agony.

Dejal stepped in front of him, arm outstretched, staff parallel to the floor. "Ward of protection, to my ally as myself!"

The pressure instantly released, and Anok dropped to his hands and knees as though cut down from a hangman's noose.

"Quickly," shouted Dejal, "counterattack!" He waved the staff. "Peal of thunder!" With a mighty rumble, a visible blast of force shot down the corridor at their unseen enemy.

"Anok! Some help here!"

Anok struggled to stand, managing to get up on one knee and raise his hands. "Pestilence!" The air swirled, and a few cockroaches materialized on the corridor walls before the swirl faded out. Anok sagged, exhausted from the failed effort.

"Enough!" The voice boomed again, this time from behind them.

Dejal lowered his staff, and turned to face the footsteps approaching from behind.

Anok finally managed to stand. He saw three robed figures approaching them. The two on the outside wore dark, blood-colored robes similar to his own, though the yokes over their shoulders marked them as full acolytes and not just novices as Anok and Dejal were.

The man in the middle, taller than the others, wore the scarlet robes, trimmed with gold, of a priest of Set. As he approached them, he threw back his hood, revealing his pearly skin and white hair, identifying him as descended from one of the most ancient and revered of Stygian lines. Both Anok and Dejal knew him well. He was Ramsa Aál, the temple's Priest of Acolytes.

Ramsa Aál stopped and looked at Dejal. "Well done, acolyte. You've prepared your staff to store a useful assortment of spells and wards. However, as the Flood of Fire spell proves, you need to be prepared for simple, physical attacks as well."

Dejal bowed his head. "The staff of power is far from complete, Master. I'm preparing a jewel of reckoning to be mounted beneath the crystal. That should deal with such attacks."

He turned his attention to Anok. "That was—disappointing, Anok Wati. You carry the sacred Mark of Set on your left wrist. It is mysterious to me that such vast power should fail you."

"I'm sorry, master. As you know, I expended great energies when I went on my mission of vengeance. Perhaps my powers have yet to recover." This was no lie. Believing his friend and lover Sheriti to have been murdered by the gang lord Wosret, leader of the White Scorpion gang, Anok had hunted down and killed them all, finally calling down lightning that blasted their stronghold into rubble.

Yet it was also a lie, for he suspected he had tapped only the smallest sample of the power he now possessed. The trouble was not in tapping the power, it was in keeping it in check once released. Only after killing Wosret had he learned that Dejal was Sheriti's true murderer, and now his anger, and his power, had a new natural target. It took all his will to keep that power in check, to keep from vaporizing Dejal with but a thought, and to direct the power elsewhere.

It was that effort which had brought him to his knees, not the summoning of energy for a counterspell.

Ramsa Aál studied him. "Perhaps it is time for another test. There are many aspects to a sorcerer's abilities—power, yes, but also skill, knowledge, and of course, will. Let us see if you still have the will to be an acolyte of Set."

Ramsa Aál gestured for the two novices to follow him. The senior acolytes remained behind. Doubtless it had been they, not Ramsa Aál, who had performed the practice attacks and the spell of deception. A priest such as Ramsa Aál would never waste his great powers on such a trivial task.

They rounded a corner and instantly were back in their

familiar home, the corridor outside their cells. Anok glanced back and found only a solid corridor wall behind them.

Ramsa Aál led them past their individual cells to a common room often used by the novice acolytes for discussions or games of chance. He went to a locked cabinet in the corner and, extracting a brass key from under his robe, unlocked it.

He glanced back at them and pointed at the round, wooden table in the center of the room. "Sit," he said.

Anok and Dejal pulled up benches and sat across from each other at the table. Anok watched, curious, as Ramsa Aál extracted an unfamiliar metal object from the cabinet.

It was round, as wide as a man's body, shaped like two shallow bowls, or perhaps two shields, joined lip to lip. It was made of bronze, inlaid with polished copper, and intricately engraved with ancient hieroglyphs in concentric bands that circled its circumference. At the extreme bottom of the object was a small, bluntly pointed, projection.

Ramsa Aál put the object on the table between them, holding it balanced on the bottom point. "This," he said, "is a wheel of Aten. It is a simple device, powered by its own mystic energy. It responds not to power, but to will. I will spin it, thusly." He gave the disk a rapid spin, which caused it to balance, wobbling, on its point.

"Anok! Focus your will on continuing the wheel to your left!"

Anok stared at the spinning object, pictured its movements in his mind, then tried to imagine it spinning faster. To his amazement, the wheel responded, the hieroglyphs turning into a blur. The wobbling ceased, and the wheel spun smoothly in the center of the table.

"Now," continued Ramsa Aál, "Dejal. Focus your will on the wheel also, but I want you to focus your will to spinning it to your *right!*"

Dejal leaned forward, his dark eyes narrowing. His brow furrowed with concentration.

The wheel wobbled slightly, then lurched.

In an instant, it was spinning as rapidly as ever, but now to the right.

Ramsa Aál stood back and smiled. "This is a contest of wills. Let us see which of you will be the victor."

Anok lowered his head, felt the spinning wheel in his mind, and willed it to spin to the left.

Nothing happened.

Harder!

Anok smiled as the wheel reversed direction, spinning ever faster.

Dejal frowned, his lips pressed tightly together in concentration.

Suddenly the disk was spinning to the right.

Anok strained, again reversing the disk.

Then Dejal.

Then, with great effort, Anok.

Dejal leaned closer to the spinning disk, putting his palms flat on the table at his sides. He seemed to tap some deep reserve.

The disk reversed, spinning ever faster to the right. Dejal smiled, then laughed.

Anok struggled to reverse the disk, but without result.

Dejal laughed louder.

Anok looked into Dejal's face, ivory-pale like the priest's. The black eyes sparkled with malice. Again the laugh.

That laugh! Anok imagined that laugh as Dejal slit Sheriti's throat. That face, cruel and utterly lacking in kindness or mercy—

There was a snapping sound, and the disk again spun to the left, faster now.

Anok remembered seeing her body, the bruises on her alabaster skin, the blood caked on her wounds—

Something howled, a long, rising note. The disk spun faster, no more than a blur now.

Ramsa Aál's eyes widened with concern. "Anok!"

But Anok thought only of Sheriti. He now admitted to himself what he had never been able to when she was alive.

He loved her.

He had always loved her, since he first met her in the Great Marketplace as a child. Since he had saved her life and returned her to her mother, and they, in turn, had given him a place to live, and a new purpose.

The howl turned into a shriek, growing in volume. The wheel spun furiously, and wisps of smoke curled up from the wood under its supporting point.

Why had he never admitted it to himself? Why had he never told her? He had shared, in the end, his bed with her. Why had he never shared his heart?

The disk weaved from side to side, tracing curling lines of charred wood on the tabletop as it moved. The shrieking grew louder, becoming almost unbearable.

"Anok!" Ramsa Aál shouted.

What he could give, what he would pay, an eternity of torment, for but five minutes in her company, to show her his heart, to pledge to her his love!

But that would never happen.

Never.

Betrayer!

Defiler!

Murderer!

A deafening crack echoed through the room.

The disk shattered, fragments flashing through the air.

Wood splintered.

Pottery shattered.

Chips of stone flew through the air.

Anok blinked, stared at the empty table, with a startled Dejal cautiously peering over the edge.

Anok looked up at the priest, who in turn was calmly contemplating the long, jagged, shard of metal half-embedded into the stone wall next to his head.

The priest licked his lips. "Well," he said, "that was unexpected. This isn't usually such a hazardous exercise. Clearly, Anok Wati, you are not lacking in will." He reached out and touched the metal with his finger, then looked back at Anok.

"In one week's time, you will be promoted to full acolytes, and it will be time for you to take the next step in your studies. Especially for you, Anok Wati, I will have to consider how you may best restore your powers."

The priest turned to leave. "I think, perhaps, a journey may be in order."

2

IF KHEMI WAS actually three cities in one—the slums of Odji; the enclave of foreigners, Akhet; and the inner city of true Stygians—then Anok's life had wound through all of them.

He had been born with the name Sekhemar, in Akhet, the product of an arranged marriage between an Aquilonian merchant and the daughter of a Stygian noble. His mother had been killed by bandits when he was an infant. He had been raised in isolation by his father until his twelfth year, when his entire life changed.

Strangers had come to their home late one night, dressed in concealing robes. His father had greeted them with familiarity, and so it was with shock and horror that Anok had seen the men murder his father before his eyes.

As his father lay dying, he had given Anok a mysterious iron medallion and instructed him to flee Akhet. He should not seek revenge. Instead he should seek out his sister, a sister Anok had never heard of before, and give her the medallion. She would know what to do with it. Anok had fled the house as the robed men were burning it to the ground, and left Akhet forever.

Orphaned and alone, living in fear of the men who had killed his father, he had gone into the slums of Odji, taken the name Anok Wati, and learned how to survive.

He made friends there: Teferi, the dark-skinned giant of a warrior with a surprisingly gentle heart, beautiful Sheriti, daughter of a whore, pledged never to follow her mother's path, and Dejal, runaway son of a Stygian noble, seeking, or so he claimed then, to escape his father's influence and the corruption of the Cult of Set.

He had lived in the old horse stalls beneath the Paradise brothel, where Sheriti's mother plied her trade. His friends gathered there. They called themselves the Ravens, and Anok's humble dwelling the Nest, and together they had made a reputation for themselves on the street.

They were hired by merchants, tradesmen, and the gang lords who ruled the streets. They served as couriers, guards, bouncers, and negotiators. They developed a reputation for honesty and honor that had served them well. Anok was known for his negotiating skills, and he had settled many an intergang or business dispute without spilling a drop of blood.

But they were also known as fighters, swift, agile, and fearless, a force to be reckoned with if blades were ever drawn. Anok, who could fight as well with his left hand as his right, and always carried two swords, became known as the "two-bladed devil."

There were other Ravens who had come and gone, and a few who had died, but it was the four friends, Anok, Teferi, Sheriti, and Dejal, who had stayed together and been there for all their adventures. For years, they were princes of their tiny world.

But Anok's life had changed again. Despite his pledge to his father, he had never gotten over the murder or his thirst for revenge.

Of his supposed sister he had never found a trace, but he

had learned one secret of the medallion he had been given. It could be opened with a hidden catch, and inside was hidden a golden charm that he later learned was called a Scale of Set.

As they reached adulthood, the Ravens began to crumble. Teferi developed a wanderlust and wished to leave Stygia behind. Trained to read and write by Anok, Sheriti had been accepted as an apprentice scribe, a position that would allow her to escape both Odji and her mother's fate. Worst of all, Dejal reconciled with his father, embraced his dark Stygian heritage, and joined the Cult of Set as a novice acolyte.

As for Anok, he was being aggressively recruited by the gang lord Wosret, leader of the White Scorpions, who feared the adult Anok would turn from hireling to rival.

Lost, troubled, and running out of options, Anok had taken up one of Teferi's people's traditions and gone on Usafiri, a sacred journey into the wilderness to seek wisdom and purpose.

Anok had only half believed, yet he hoped to lose his father's medallion in the shifting sands of the desert and finally put his past behind him.

It wasn't to be. After many trials where he nearly died, Anok had an encounter—be it vision or real he still could not say—with the skeleton of a giant snake. The snake talked to him and claimed to be Parath, a lost god of Stygia. Once friend to the gods Set and Ibis, Parath was betrayed by both and cast into the desert for eternity.

In return for his aid in gaining revenge against Set, Parath promised to help Anok take revenge against his father's killers and to find the answers to all the secrets of Anok's past. But to do this, Parath told him, he had to join the Cult of Set as Dejal had, learn its secrets, and strike at it from inside.

To find his destiny, Anok would have to become one with the very thing he hated most.

He would have to become an acolyte of Set.

LATER THAT EVENING, Anok sat alone in his cell, studying yet another ancient scroll from one of the temple's archives. The cells were small and sparsely furnished, making the Nest, his old quarters under the Paradise brothel, seem positively luxurious. There was a table, a narrow bench for sleeping, a bench for sitting, a cupboard for storage, and a small scribe's desk where he could conduct his studies.

He spent hours each evening with scrolls spread on the desk, as he took notes or copied mystic symbols on sheets of papyrus for later reference or study.

Study of ancient scrolls and texts was part of his training as an acolyte, but he had his own agenda as well.

First, he was looking for references to Parath, the self-professed lost god of Stygia. In that he had been less than successful. He had found not a single reference to Parath in any of the texts.

He was uncertain what to make of that. It could mean that Parath had deceived him, but it could also be confirmation of the god's story. Parath claimed that he had been trapped in the body of one of Set's great serpents, and that Ibis had led him into the desert and exiled him there for all time. A god without followers is no god at all, and there can be no followers, no cult, for a forgotten god.

His other purpose, more recent, but even more urgent, was to learn about the mark of power that had been joined to his wrist during his trial in the Maze of Set. There, he had found only scattered references, and they did little but confirm what he had already been told by Ramsa Aál.

The texts said that the mark, which had appeared to Anok in the form of a tiny snake known as the son of Set, could only bond with those of rare potential, and that it conferred on them almost limitless power. The snake had wrapped itself around his arm, and burned its way into the flesh, appearing now as nothing but an elaborate tattoo of a snake. The head of the snake lay across the back of his hand, and the body coiled three times around his wrist. The tail pointed back up his forearm, toward his heart.

As far as he could determine, the mark had not been conferred on a mortal for at least five hundred years. Yet for a mark that supposedly granted such power, little was written of its bearers. Anok had a grim suspicion why.

Sorcery always extracted a price of those who wielded it. Sorcerers inevitably became corrupted by their power, and great magic often eroded even a man's sanity. Many of the most powerful sorcerers were said to be mad, or at least subject to episodes of madness after casting their spells.

One reason powerful sorcerers, such as the priests of Set, sought followers and acolytes was to have them do most of the spell casting, thus saving the master from his own power. Only when there was no other choice, and his greater power was required, would the master act directly.

Anok had no desire to experience this, and he suspected the Mark of Set was as much a curse as a gift. When he had first called upon its power in the stronghold of the White Scorpions, it had sent him into such a bloodlust that he had very nearly killed his friend Teferi and himself. Only Teferi, his courage and friendship, had pulled Anok back from the brink.

He had no desire to repeat the experience, and yet Ramsa Aál kept expecting him to use the power. If his master wished to corrupt him, he suspected it was only so that he could use Anok as a weapon.

Like an arrow, he was being carefully prepared for battle. But once fired at Ramsa Aál's enemies, he was expendable and disposable.

He pulled back the sleeve of his robe to examine the mark. It continuously troubled him, itching and burning. The skin around the mark remained red and inflamed, and there were times when it made even sleeping difficult. It was as though the mark itself wished its power to be used, and even more so than Ramsa Aál, it would not be denied.

Frustrated with his lack of progress and the nagging influence of the mark, he stood rapidly, knocking the bench over as he did, and nearly spilling his inkpot. If he had to use magic, he would use it in his own way and for his own purposes.

He went to the cupboard, and extracted his notes, a stack

of sheets now almost too thick to wrap his hand around. He put them on the table and began to flip through them. He had, in the writings of an ancient Shemite mage, seen reference to a spell called the Walk of Shadows.

He found the page. On it, he had traced a symbol, somehow key to the spell, much like the old-Stygian hieroglyph for "seeing," a stylized eye with a long, curling, lash. The Walk of Shadows was not an invisibility spell, but it supposedly granted the user the ability to travel unnoticed by the unaware. Hopefully, that would be enough for his purposes.

He held out his left hand and, focusing on the power of the Mark of Set, traced the symbol in the air before him. He felt a warm tingling run out through the mark and up his fingertips. The air seemed to ripple and bend where his fingertips traced.

As the power flowed through him, he immediately felt better, stronger. The itching and burning around the mark lessened, and he felt strangely invincible.

He tried to shake off the feeling, lest it make him reckless. The spell would not protect him from his own clumsiness. One trip, one dropped object, and he could be revealed to anyone nearby.

He opened the door and stepped into the narrow corridor outside. A broad-shouldered guardian of Set stood at the end of the corridor, leaning on his spear and half-dozing. He would make an effective test of the spell.

Anok moved toward him, walking carefully and silently. The guardian blinked sleepily, but managed to keep his eyes open and dully looking straight ahead. In fact, he was looking directly at Anok, but Anok could see no sign that the man was focused on him. His eyes did not move as Anok moved, and indeed, seemed to be locked on some fixed point behind him, perhaps one of the oil lamps that illuminated the walls.

Anok was close enough to study the man closely now. His skin tone was dusky, not unlike Anok's own, but his blue-black beard suggested he carried Shemite blood as well as Stygian. His face was wide, and his cheekbones high and angular. He wore a bowl-shaped helmet with guards that jutted down over the ears, but what Anok could see of the man's scalp suggested he shaved his head, or perhaps was naturally bald.

Anok was only a few arm's lengths away from the man, and it seemed he was unseen.

The sensation was both intoxicating and disconcerting. Anok found himself tempted to wave, or dance a little jig, and yet he knew that such attention-getting moves might well shatter the spell. Yet it was also disturbing not to be seen, as though through his lack of visibility he had ceased to exist. Part of Anok wished for even the slightest acknowledgment of his existence to make him feel real again.

It was in the middle of that thought, that the guardian began to move. He walked rapidly and purposefully toward Anok, and for a moment he thought the guardian had seen him.

Yet the focus of the man's gaze still seemed to go right through him. Paralyzed by confusion, he almost let the man run head-on into him, but at the last moment, he stood aside and pressed himself tightly against the cool stone wall.

The guardian brushed past him, so close he could feel the breeze as he moved, yet he never actually touched Anok, which was probably fortunate. Anok watched the guardian walk as far as the door to Anok's cell and stop.

Again, he wondered if he'd somehow been discovered. But the guardian wasn't interested in his door, but rather the oil lamp on the wall next to it. The lamp sputtered and flickered. The guardian studied it for a moment, before pulling his dagger from his belt and using the point to draw out a bit more of the wick.

The lamp was restored to its proper brightness. The guardian smiled and proceeded on down the corridor, turning left at the end of the hall and vanishing from sight.

Anok looked at his hand, half-expecting to see nothing. The spell worked, almost better than he could have hoped. He was free to wander the temple, and he had a good idea where he was going.

He wound his way out of the novice's living area, toward

the front of the temple. He passed the guards along the corridor undetected, then climbed the stairs to the main level of the temple. Near the front of the temple, he climbed a pair of staircases, a curved one near the front corner of the building, then a straight one up from the mezzanine to the area where the priests' private chambers were located.

He avoided the chambers themselves, suspecting they would be equipped with magical wards or traps against which his simple deception spell would be ineffective. Instead, he went to a closet at the end of the hall, where certain magical objects used in the training of acolytes were kept.

Nothing kept here was of great value or significant power. Such objects were kept by the priests themselves, or returned to the vaults in the subbasements of the temple each night. These were lesser items, which he suspected were not as carefully protected.

As he expected, the closet was locked, but he was prepared for that. Upon returning to the temple from his mission of revenge against Lord Wosret, he had smuggled in a few small items, including a set of picklocks.

He removed the small kit, tied in a roll of oilcloth, from under his robe and unwrapped it. He selected a pair of thin brass tools and knelt in front of the door. Though his skills were rusty, it took him only a minute or so until the lock clicked open.

He smiled. *Sometimes the old ways are the best.*

It was dark inside the closet, so he reached into his pocket and removed a smooth, translucent crystal sized to fit in his palm. Using the point of one of the picklocks, he pricked a fingertip and squeezed out a tiny drop of blood, which he touched to the crystal. At once it began to glow with a soft, blue light rather like the light of the moon.

Using the light of the crystal, he carefully examined the contents of the closet. The shelves were cluttered with various items, sacrificial knives, bottles of magic powders and potions, minor spell books, shrunken heads, several human bones, and other oddities.

He ignored them all. His interest was in a shelf of crystal

balls. He bypassed the larger ones, intended to be used on a table, and examined only the smaller ones, sized so that a sorcerer could keep it on his person and comfortably hold it in his hand.

Even those, however, were not what he was looking for. At the end of the shelf he found a number of oblong wooden boxes, covered with ornate carvings. He selected one and lifted the lid. Inside there was not one crystal, but three, a large one in the middle, about twice the size of a man's fist, and two smaller companions, each the size of a plum.

The larger crystal had many uses, the most common one being to invoke a vision spell, to observe persons or events at a distance. But the smaller crystals had a special function. They could be used by the holder to communicate with the sorcerer in possession of the large crystal, even over great distances.

Such crystals were often used by priests to communicate with their agents and underlings over distance, be they acolytes or guardians of Set. Their function had been demonstrated to the novices only a week earlier, and Anok had coveted a set ever since.

Anok didn't have underlings, but he did have his friend Teferi, who acted as his surrogate outside the temple walls. They had devised a system to bribe guards, but there were many difficulties, not the least of which being that Teferi was almost totally illiterate. They could sometimes communicate simple concepts using the few symbols and hieroglyphs that Teferi was familiar with, but for anything more complex, Teferi had to take the additional step of hiring a scribe. This was both expensive and risky, as some scribes were also followers of Set.

He slipped the box into a hidden pocket inside his robe, quietly closed the closet, and put the Jewel of the Moon away. Then he retraced his steps through the temple.

Once again, he was able to walk right past all the guards he encountered without them giving him a glance, and he was feeling quite smug about it by the time he rounded the last corner to reach the his cell.

He was but a few feet from the door, when the air in front of him seemed to twist and shimmer. He blinked, and Ramsa Aál appeared from nowhere. He leaned his back against Anok's door, his arms crossed over his broad chest. He smiled slightly, but the expression was as cold as one of Set's serpents.

"Anok Wati," he said. "I see you've been out for a stroll." He put out his hand. "Now, why don't you show me what you've brought back?"

3

ANOK STARED AT the priest leaning casually against his door. "Ramsa Aál, master, I . . ." He found himself at a loss for words.

Ramsa Aál bobbed his hand urgently. "Let me see."

Anok saw no other choice. He had been caught. He reached into his robe and extracted the box.

Ramsa Aál took it in one hand and removed the lid with the other. He regarded the crystals inside for a moment. "Good choice," he said. "A good compromise between size and portability."

He lifted the larger crystal and held it up to the lamp light. "Nice clarity. No flaws. The companion crystals of voice and vision are a bonus." He put the crystal back in the box and replaced the lid, handing it back to Anok.

"It would be wise, acolyte, to remember that any spell that you can use, so can another sorcerer, especially one more skilled than yourself. And as you desire your own crystal ball, you should know that one can just as easily be used to follow your activities as well."

"You used a crystal ball to discover that I'd left my cell."

He considered with some alarm what that might mean. "Have you been watching me all along?"

Ramsa Aál put back his head and laughed. "Acolyte, I have more important matters to concern me than watching you day and night. I have set magical snares along the exits from the acolytes' quarters. By leaving under the influence of your cloaking spell, you triggered one of these snares, alerting me. Only then did I go to my crystal ball and use a vision spell to see what you were doing."

He bowed his head. "I'm sorry, master." The priest didn't seem angry, but Anok had once seen him kill a sacrificial victim with a smile on his lips. Ramsa Aál's mood and intent were maddeningly difficult to read.

"Don't be. You were quite clever, actually, and used great initiative. Of course, if you'd tried to raid one of the vaults, or the treasure troves, or even my private chambers, you'd likely be dead by now. But you merely went looking for humble sorcerer's tools to add to your kit. You could have merely asked, but"—he smiled slightly—"where's the fun in that?"

The door next to Anok's swung open, and a groggy and confused Dejal peered out. He looked at Ramsa Aál, seeming not to even notice Anok. "Master, is there a problem?"

"None, novice. Anok is merely undergoing some special sorcerous training."

Dejal blinked, seeming finally to notice Anok. "I wish to learn too, master."

The priest sighed. "Then you would do well to spend more time on your studies and less on trying to curry favor with the priests."

Dejal looked hurt. "I only wish to please, master."

"That you do. You did bring us a golden Scale of Set." His fingers brushed the front of his robe over his breastbone.

The gesture was familiar to Anok, as he had often done the same when wearing his father's medallion with the Scale of Set hidden inside. Anok noticed for the first time the glint of a heavy gold chain worn around the priest's neck, vanishing beneath the folds of fabric. *Does he wear the Scale of Set there? Or even two of the three Scales?*

Ramsa Aál continued addressing Dejal. "And your father has just made another sizable tribute to the cult. I doubt even his coffers will last long at this rate." Ramsa Aál raised an eyebrow knowingly. "I hear rumors he had a small fortune in blood emeralds stolen from him not long ago."

Anok tried not to let his reaction show. Dejal had secretly given those gems to the Ravens in return for securing the Scale. Anok had wondered how Dejal had gotten them. Stolen from his father? Then perhaps, things were not as good between them as Dejal let on. His anger with the man was not gone, merely buried.

As is mine with Dejal. For the merest moment, Anok cracked open the dark box where the glowing embers of rage always dwelled. For that moment he felt them, almost *savored* them.

The old and familiar grief over his father's death, his murder before young Anok's eyes, and the fresh and agonizing hurt of Sheriti's murder.

But only a moment, and, lest it overwhelm him, he snapped the lid shut on that dark place, back to where it could sit and fester until the day when he brought them all down.

Far from being unsettled by the mention, Dejal seemed to compose himself. He smiled crookedly. "A setback, master, nothing more. A business deal gone sour, as they sometimes do. My mother's family, left without an heir, turned the business to my father, but it is not in his blood. Rest assured, when it is my turn, I shall do far better and enrich both myself and the cult."

And there, Anok saw an inkling of Dejal's plan. The Cult of Set was the main center of power in Stygia, true, but there were others, namely the hereditary wealth of the old families and the modern wealth of commerce and trade.

The cult had its way of serving each. They all depended on the cult's guardians, coastal navy, and slave armies to defend Stygia's borders against the constant threat of invasion, and to keep the caravan roads and sea-lanes open despite the threat of bandits and pirates. The guardians kept the mongrel hordes of the underclass in control as well. Important, as they outnumbered full-blooded Stygians by twenty to one.

The cult in turn depended on the taxes and tribute provided by the wealthy, but the alliance was always an uneasy one. If Dejal could obtain some measure of status in the inner circles of the cult, then take charge of his father's business holdings, he could become a formidable power. By bridging the two worlds, he stood to gain status he could obtain in neither alone.

I taught you something after all, "brother." It was just the sort of ideal compromise Anok had become known for arranging on the streets of Odji. *But now that I know your plan, what to do?*

What he wanted to do, of course, was to crush Dejal's plan, to ruin his former friend's fragile aspirations in the cult, and step on his face as he himself climbed to power. But for now, that could not be. Dejal might have his uses, and there would be time for vengeance later.

Ramsa Aál seemed to consider Dejal's words for a time. "How," he asked, "will you gain control of your father's wealth? Perhaps wait for him to grow old and die? To my eyes, he seems . . . distressingly healthy."

Dejal's smile grew slightly. "When I am ready, master, I will persuade him to cede power to me—by whatever means necessary."

Again, the priest considered, then nodded slowly. "I was impressed tonight with your friend Anok's initiative. I see now that you also have initiative, perhaps more than I gave you credit for."

"Then I can stay for the lesson, master?"

"The lesson is done, but you may stay. I was about to deliver some news to Anok. I had intended to give it to him on the morrow, but since we are here—"

"Yes, master?"

"Tell me, Anok, have you traveled beyond the city?"

Anok's mind raced. He didn't want to offer any clue to Ramsa Aál about his Usafiri, the spiritual journey into the desert that had put him on his path to destroy Set. Yet there seemed little reason to be directly untruthful. "I have made the journey down the coast a ways, to some of the villages and towns there, and a bit into the desert, to the edge of the Sea of Sand."

Ramsa waved his hand. "That's nothing. A sorcerer's power grows with knowledge and experience. You've effectively lived your whole life within this city. It is time for you to see more, learn more. In one week's time, I am sending you to Kheshatta to study in the city of sorcerers. There, you will encounter many forms of magic from across the known world. You will learn that there is much to our cult beyond what you have seen here at the temple. And if you are very lucky, you may have an audience with Lord-master Thoth-Amon, Lord of the Black Ring, High Priest of the Cult of Set."

Anok had heard of Thoth-Amon, of course. Who had not heard of the mightiest wizard in Stygia? His name was spoken in fear throughout the civilized world. It was rumored that only Conan, the mighty barbarian-king of Aquilonia, had stood against the wizard and lived to tell the tale. "I thought his palace was in Luxur, master?"

"Good, you've been paying attention. You would do well to learn as much as you can of our great lord-master. But to answer your question, yes, his main palace is there. But our lord-master has ever suffered from wanderlust, and his stays in Luxur are infrequent and usually short. He often travels within Stygia and beyond. He has an apartment in the black tower of the temple, though he has not visited here in many years, a keep at the foot of the Mountains of Fire, and a great palace in Kheshatta as well. I have it on good authority that he will soon come again to Kheshatta."

"But I'm only a humble acolyte, master. Why would Thoth-Amon take audience with me?"

He smiled. "Because of the mark you carry on your wrist, Anok Wati. Oh, yes, he has heard of it, and while others in the cult may doubt its importance, such things never escape the attention of our lord-master. It is not for this that he returns to our shores, but I doubt he will let it escape his attention."

Dejal again leaned into the conversation. "Will I go to Kheshatta as well, master?"

"Perhaps, but not yet. If you truly wish to serve, then there is another duty I may have for you, one closer to the temple but no less important. If you think you are equal to the task—"

"Yes, master. Of course!"

"Good, we will speak of it later." He turned back to Anok. "You will leave in a week's time. I will arrange for you to travel by caravan across the Sea of Sand. There is no temple such as this at Kheshatta, so you will be provided coin to secure your own place of lodging."

Anok was delighted with this news. His plans against Set had thus far been hampered by his living at the temple, with little freedom and constant scrutiny.

Ramsa Aál continued, "Kheshatta is also a very dangerous city for such as we. I will assign you an officer of the guardians as a bodyguard."

In an instant, Anok's hopes for freedom faded. Then he had an idea. "Master, if it could be permitted, I would prefer to bring the Kushite servant Teferi as my bodyguard."

At the mention of Teferi's name, Dejal shot Anok a sharp glance. The three had known each other since boyhood, and he was more than aware that Teferi was no man's servant. He suspected Anok was engaged in deception, but he showed no more than interest, saying nothing.

Anok continued his plea. "He may be stupid," another untruth, as Dejal well knew, "but he is fearless and skilled with a blade. He would work for a few slips of silver, far less, I'm certain, than you pay your officers." When Teferi had burst into the temple recently to deliver news of Sheriti's death, he had nearly been killed by the guardians of the temple. In order to save him, Anok had been forced to mislead Ramsa Aál about his friend's intelligence and their relationship. Perhaps he could now use that to his advantage.

Ramsa Aál frowned. "The Kush? Is he still alive?"

"He was wounded during my battle with the White Scorpions, but I hear he is nearly recovered."

Ramsa Aál sniffed in contempt. "Very well, if you can have him for two pieces of silver per day. I'll pay no more for the services of a savage."

Anok hid his anger at hearing this abuse of his friend. Like many Stygian nobles, Ramsa Aál held all non-Stygians in contempt, but especially the dark men from the lands south of their borders. *Let his hatred blind him, then, if it serves my needs.*

"As for you, you shall not want in your travels. I will be generous." He glanced aside at Dejal, as though to make sure he was listening. "It seems that in the past few days, all of the surviving gang lords of Odji have arrived at the temple bearing tribute, a prince's ransom in total. They have all seen the smoking hole that was the stronghold of the White Scorpions, and they have all heard that it was a follower of Set responsible for the deed."

Anok blinked in surprise. "I had no idea, master."

"Who knew your little adventure of revenge would turn out so valuable to the cult? More than you know, for their gold may soon be spent, but their fear"—his lips formed a twisted smile—"will serve us for years!"

4

AWAY FROM THE temple and outside the walls of the inner city for the first time in weeks, Anok felt free. It was a sunny day, cooled by a steady breeze off the harbor below. The fresh salt air kept the smoke from stoves, kilns, and forges from pooling over Odji and diluted the cloud of human and animal stink that usually hung over the place.

He'd never realized just how foul that smell was until he'd spent time in the inner city, with its garbage-free alleys, lack of food animals, and dung collectors cleaning the streets after the horses and donkeys. How had he lived in this place all these years and never really smelled it?

Yet he was glad to be back wandering the narrow streets of the slums. He smiled, pushing back the hood of his robe, and he hardly noticed the angry, fearful, stares of strangers, or the way people steered clear of his acolyte's robe. They were responding to the robe, he told himself, and knew nothing about the man within.

His destination was the Green Lotus Tavern, an inn located in his old neighborhood, where Teferi had been living these last few months. Though he'd spent some time recovering from his wounds in a back room at the brothel, he was reportedly back at the Green Lotus.

The streets were busy, full of shoppers, merchants, tradesmen, and livestock, all jostling for a place on the street. These were the lower classes, most descended of slave stock. Most had dark skin, brown or black, though almost any race and creed of the known world could be found here in some number.

He saw several familiar faces but no close friends, and nobody seemed to recognize him in his temple garb.

He was recognized at least once though. As he climbed up the stairs on the potters' street, past shop windows filled with stacked pots, cups, plates, and cookware, he spotted two hulking, blue-bearded Shemites, whom Anok recognized as enforcers for Lord Nakhti's River Rat gang.

The men wore heavy broadswords and carried bows and quivers of arrows slung over their backs. They walked as though they owned the streets, and with the White Scorpions gone, they probably did.

But when the men saw Anok, they stopped and pointed. He saw them lean in and whisper to each other as they watched him. Then they turned and hurried away in the other direction, doubling their pace to get away from him.

Anok smiled. *They fear me. Good.* If he had succeeded, even for a while, in throwing the street gangs of Odji into fear and uncertainty, then he had done the people there a service. It was a small thing, but perhaps something to be proud of.

Anok rounded a corner and found himself looking at the entrance to the Nest, the converted stables under the Paradise that had been for many years his home. It was a sliver of daylight basement under one side of the two-story building, with tiny, high windows and a single wooden door near the back corner of the basement.

The main entrance to the brothel was around the corner and up the hill from where he stood. Even from here, he caught a hint of exotic perfume on the breeze. He knew that on a day like this, colorful silk awnings would be blowing in the breeze, and naked whores would lounge in almost every window, beckoning passersby.

But from down here on the side street, the building looked plain, almost utilitarian. Weeds had grown up around the door to the Nest, and the door looked dusty and disused. The sight of it filled him with a profound sense of sadness. Sheriti was dead, and with her all that he had once held dear in life.

The Ravens were no more. His friendship with Dejal had turned rancid, like old milk. Only Teferi remained to give him any true connection with that part of his life.

He walked up to the door, his fingers tracing around the doorframe, finding the hidden catches that would unlock the door. For a moment he considered going inside, but there was nothing for him there but ghosts and lost yesterdays.

He turned his back on the brothel and walked around the corner. Just up the hill he could see the Green Lotus, with its elaborate green flower, carved from wood, hanging over the door.

He walked up and glanced through the open shutters in front. Business was slow. Several men sat at scattered tables, drinking, eating, and ignoring each other.

Anok slipped into the tavern. The barkeep was unknown to him, a short man, brown-skinned, with a round, hairless head that somehow reminded him of a coconut. Anok strode purposefully up to the bar. "I seek Teferi, a tall Kushite. I hear he has a room here."

The barkeep eyed him warily, but after a moment's consideration, nodded. "Up the stairs, at the end of the hall on the right."

He climbed the narrow, rickety stairs in the back of the room, not much more than a ladder really. The corridor wasn't much wider, lit by only a tall, narrow window at the end. Most of the doors along it were open and dark. One on the left was closed, and judging from the moaning and thrashing inside, was well occupied at the moment. The only other closed door, as promised, was on the right at the end. A tray with an empty tankard and a bowl showing traces of some kind of stew sat just outside.

He tapped on the wood, and the whole door rattled.

"Who's there," yelled a deep voice from inside, "friend or dead man?"

Despite himself, Anok managed a little grin. Despite his injuries and their shared grief over Sheriti's death, his old friend had lost none of his spirit.

"A little of both," he answered. .

There was a moment's hesitation, then a shout: "Anok Wati! About time you came to see me! Get in here!

The door was unlocked, and Anok pushed it open. He found Teferi stretched out on a sleeping bench, dressed in simple loincloth. Even sitting up with his back against the wall, Teferi's feet hung off the end, and Anok couldn't imagine how the big man managed to sleep there.

He looked a little thinner than the last time Anok had seen him, though not unhealthily so. Teferi had always carried a few stone of extra weight. Now he looked lean and even more dangerous, if that was possible. The only thing distracting from that impression was a linen dressing tied around the middle of his chest. Anok was relieved to note that it appeared clean and unbloodied, on the outside at least.

There were few furnishings in the room, a table, a small bench, a few storage baskets. If anything it was even smaller and more austere than his cell back at the temple. But at least this one had a small window looking out over the street, and fresh air, or as fresh as air got in Odji, anyway. Anok pulled the bench over next to the bed and sat down. "How are you feeling."

Teferi glanced down at the bandage. "Oh, this? I hardly need it anymore. The wound oozes sometimes, but I'll probably take this off for good in a day or two. The women at the Paradise cared for me well."

Women? The word was somehow surprising. Anok, in all his years, had never heard them called anything but whores. The word was so ingrained into Stygian culture that he'd always spoken it without thinking. Yet they were women, too. One of them had been Sheriti's mother, had shown him kindness, and for years provided him a place to live.

Teferi saw the look on his face. "For years I've known the keepers of the Paradise, without really *knowing* them. They are good women, Anok, on whom life has forced hardship and difficult choices. I should have treated them better."

Anok smiled sadly. There was a soft side to Teferi's warrior heart that he admired, even if he questioned its utility in this hard world in which they lived. "Perhaps I should have as well, old friend, but I fear I'll not again have the chance. I'm to travel to Kheshatta to continue my studies of sorcery."

Teferi's eyes widened, and he pushed into a fully upright sitting position. Anok saw him flinch just a little as he moved the wrong way. His wound still troubled him, at least a little. Anok felt guilty for that, though he knew that without his magic, Teferi would be dead.

Anok had—somehow, he still wasn't sure how—transformed a sword into water even as it was piercing Teferi's chest. *I should have been faster.* But that was self-deception, and he knew it. Teferi shouldn't have been there at all. They'd invaded the White Scorpion gang's lair, killed them all. Anok had killed their leader, Lord Wosret, himself, all in vengeance for the murder of Sheriti.

But while there had been much innocent blood on Wosret's hands, they'd been wrong about his killing Sheriti. It had been Dejal who murdered her. He'd as much as admitted it to Anok.

And poor Sheriti. In his mind, he'd come up with a thousand ways he could have prevented her death, come to her rescue, seen Dejal's intentions and killed him first. *Be thankful, Teferi. Your wounds will heal. Mine never will.*

Yet here he was, about to ask Teferi to follow him into danger again. Here he was, maintaining the fiction that Sheriti's death had been avenged, while her killer still walked free and unmolested, all because it served Anok's purposes.

He realized that Teferi was staring at him. "Kheshatta? From the look on your face, you treat it like some sort of death sentence."

"No, it's just that—I was hoping you'd agree to come with me."

Teferi smiled. "You don't even have to ask. Of course I'll come with you. It will be an adventure!"

"Don't be so quick to decide. It's the kind of adventure where people can end up dead."

"Fah! I fear boredom more than death, and I've spent too many days trapped in little rooms like this feeling miserable. When do we leave?"

"A week. You'll be paid, though not enough. Ramsa Aál wanted to assign me a guardian as protection on my journey. I told him I wanted you instead."

"He agreed?"

"Reluctantly. You'll be paid two pieces of silver a day."

Teferi chuckled. "A princely sum. I'll be able to eat poorly at least three times a week."

"We still have some money of our own left, and it sounds like I'll be more generously provided for. What's mine is yours. You know that."

"Well," he said, grinning, "if you didn't give it to me, I'd just steal it anyway."

He grinned back. "You're an honest man, Teferi. You wouldn't take a bent copper from a stranger. It's your friends that need to watch out."

Anok glanced down and noticed an object sitting on the edge of the bed that he hadn't seen before. He frowned and pointed. "What's this?"

Teferi glanced down. "A scroll," he said.

"I've seen one before," he said sarcastically. "What is it?"

Teferi shrugged. "I don't have the first idea. I bought it from a man down in the tavern for five silvers. I've been trying to make sense of it."

He laughed in surprise. "Teferi! You've been trying to read? I tried to teach you once. That lasted—what—a week?"

"Two, but only because you insisted. I never saw the use in it."

"And now?"

His expression turned somber. "Sheriti saw value in it

when I couldn't. She's gone. Maybe it's time I gave it another try. Will you help?"

"Of course I will! I'm proud of you, old friend." He reached for the scroll and unrolled it. "Let's see what you've got here."

He looked at the crumbling parchment and frowned. "Teferi, this is some merchant's inventory ledger, and I'll bet it's a hundred years old if it's a day!"

Teferi frowned. "Well, I guess I got took then. If I'd known how to read, that wouldn't have happened I guess."

"We'll go to the Great Marketplace later, and I'll find you something more appropriate. We'll need provisions anyway, and desert clothing. And if we don't find him today, I have something I need you to give to Rami."

Teferi frowned. "That little weasel? Why him?"

"Because we're leaving, but Dejal is staying here. Ramsa Aál has some mysterious mission for him, and I want Rami to keep an eye on him for us."

"We'll have to pay him, you know. He does little or nothing for friendship and loyalty. Why we ever let him call himself a Raven—"

"Because then, as now, he has his uses despite his flaws. And frankly, I don't know who else we could ask that I don't trust even less." He reached into his bag and extracted a sphere of crystal small enough to conceal in one's hand. He passed it to Teferi, who stared at it curiously.

"What is it?"

"Magic," he answered.

Teferi started and almost dropped the crystal. Hurriedly, he put the crystal on the bed, found a scrap of black silk, and scooped the offending object inside, wrapping it away. With some disgust he tossed the object on the table. He glared at Anok. "You know how I feel about magic."

"That's why I warned you. I won't even tell you what it does."

"Then how am I supposed to tell Rami?"

"I'll tell him myself."

"But if you aren't going to see him?"

Anok chuckled. "Just give it to him and tell him to keep it with him. Warn him that if he sells it, or loses it, or bets it in a game of dice, I'll know about it and put a curse on him that makes his man parts shrivel up like a raisin."

Teferi looked shocked. "Rami has man parts? Who knew?"

THEIR FIRST PURCHASE at the Great Marketplace was a small handcart in which to collect their purchases. They then headed directly to the stall of a merchant who serviced the caravan trade.

The booth was run by an old woman, by her dress and appearance one of the desert nomads who largely ran the caravan routes. Her skin was tanned and deeply wrinkled by long exposure to the desert sun, her hair thin and white, and her nose long and hooked as with many of her people. The nomads were a fiercely independent people, an ancient mix of Shemite, Kothic, and Stygian blood. Sometimes their elderly came to the city for comfort in their declining years, but they always returned to their sacred desert to die.

The woman eyed them skeptically as they entered her stall.

Anok addressed her. "We join a caravan bound for Kheshatta. We will need proper attire and whatever else a traveler may need."

"You worship the snake-god. Many of your kind take this journey, and they wear"—she reached out and tugged rudely as his sleeve—"their temple robes."

"Then," said Anok, "they are stupid. A man would cook in the desert wearing these robes. He would have to carry twice as much water just to account for his sweat."

"You are a city boy. What do you know of the desert?"

"More than you imagine, and far less than you, I venture. Tell me what I need to know."

The woman walked over to a table covered with clothing

made of white and cream-colored linen. She glanced back at him. "You will not miss your temple robes, snake worshiper?"

He couldn't help liking the woman. It took courage to say such a thing in the presence of an acolyte of Set.

He lowered his voice a little and leaned closer to her. "I would do well to be rid of them."

Her eyes twinkled, and she smiled just a little. She turned away from the table and headed toward the back of the stall. "That trash is for gullible city folk," she said. "I have better for you."

She told them how to pick a proper circlet, and to wear it and their headcloth in proper nomad style. She gave them each a bag of honey-and-sesame candies said to be much favored as treats by the camels, and told them how to pick the best ones in the caravan. They were warned which caravan leaders were honest and which could not be trusted.

Anok paid her with only a little bickering, and then, with a bow of thanks, placed an extra gold sovereign in her leathery palm. They left the booth with their cart well loaded, not just with clothing and a proper desert kit, but with something more valuable, *information*.

As Anok and Teferi walked to the scriber's shop, Teferi took one of the candies from the bag and cautiously licked it. He made a face. "I see why they give these to the camels," he said, dropping the candy back into the bag.

"Maybe it's an acquired taste."

"I hope the desert isn't that wide." He looked thoughtful and a little glum. "There's one part of this I'm not looking forward to, brother."

"You agreed to go. Have you changed your mind?"

"No, of course not. I look forward to the adventure. I look forward to leaving this cursed city behind, at least for a time. It's just that Kheshatta lies close to the border with Kush. Closer than I have ever been to its lands."

"The homeland of your people, yes. I'd think you'd be glad."

He frowned. "The sorcery-cursed land from which my

tribe long ago fled in exile. It is my people's land no more. It belongs to demons and evil gods. Some say they keep the true gods of our people in chains, all but Bovutupu the betrayer, and Jangwa, because they could not find him in the wilderness."

"Then perhaps one day we'll go there, kill the evil gods, and restore order to your people."

Teferi grunted. "You fancy yourself a god-slayer, Anok. It is a dangerous conceit. Men do not slay gods. Gods toy with men."

"Perhaps I can't kill gods, Teferi, but gods are still worshiped by men. Without followers, gods are nothing. Men can be killed. Men's hearts can be won. Gods do not fall easily, but like kings, they can still fall."

The scriber's shop was located on a narrow alley off the market. The wooden sign was small, and unlike most of the signs in the market, which were designed to attract the illiterate populace of Odji, it had no bright colors or pictures or carvings, just writing. It said, "The Word," and nothing more.

They slipped into the dark, cramped interior, with its stacks of clear papyrus, quills, reeds, and pots of ink. But Anok's interest was in the back wall, where scrolls and books were to be found.

The shopkeeper, a thin, pale man of Hyborian blood, watched them intently. "I know you," he said. "You were Anok Wati, of the Ravens, the street urchin who could read and write."

Anok glanced at him. "I am still Anok Wati."

"You serve Set now."

"I serve truth," he said.

"We have no scrolls of Set here."

Anok examined a basket of dusty scrolls. "I already have some, thanks. We seek something for my friend here. He wishes to learn to read. Something simple, but with lots of words. Stygian is fine, but Aquilonian would be good as well."

The shopkeeper raised an eyebrow but reached under a

counter and pulled up another basket of scrolls. "These are all the Aquilonian scrolls we have. I have some books over in that cabinet, but books cost much more."

Anok pawed through the scrolls. The first one he looked at recorded the adventures of some lost prince of Gunderland. It would do well. There were even illustrations, which Teferi would doubtless like. He put it aside to purchase.

He was about to return the basket to its place when one particular scroll caught his eye. It was darker than the rest, the wooden handle on one end scorched and blackened, the paper dark and crumbling at the edge. He carefully lifted it from the basket.

He looked sharply at the shopkeeper. "Where did you get this?"

"That? I don't know. It's been here for a very long time. Some boys brought it in, I think. Young foreigners from Akhet, selling what they could to buy beer. Probably stolen from their fathers, I suppose, but what business is that of mine?"

Stolen? Or found in the ruins of a burned-out house? "How much for these two?"

The shopkeeper named an outrageous sum. Anok slapped the coin on the counter without dickering and rushed out into the sunlight.

Teferi ran after him. "Anok, what's wrong?"

Anok held up the scorched scroll. "This," he said, "belonged to my father."

5

ANOK WAS UNREADY to return to the temple, and so they went back to the Green Lotus Tavern. For a little silver, the tavern keep agreed to let Teferi store the cart and its contents in his back room.

Anok looked at Teferi. "Do you want some beer?"

Teferi shook his head. "It's a fine day, and I'm starting to feel like myself again. There's a courtyard behind the tavern where I can enjoy the sun."

Anok shrugged and followed Teferi through a rear door and outside.

The courtyard was small and paved with flagstone. A stunted and scruffy-looking mulberry tree grew through a break in the center of the stone. Drying laundry hung from poles across the far corner, and empty beer jars were piled against the near wall. There were a stone table and two benches, but little otherwise to recommend the place.

Anok was unsure why Teferi had wanted to come here, until he heard the sound of the big man's sword being drawn from its scabbard.

Anok instinctively reached over his shoulders and

grabbed a sword in each hand, drawing them from the scabbards strapped to his back.

Already Teferi was swinging his sword toward him in a horizontal arc, a vicious two-handed blow that could cut a man in half. It was too late to draw and deflect the blow, even if he dared try with his much lighter weapons, so he released his swords and dived into a shoulder roll.

Teferi's blow slashed over him as he rolled just out of reach, springing to his feet and drawing his swords.

Teferi recovered quickly and slashed again. Anok jumped back, arching his back so that the blade just missed his stomach.

Another swing, and he ducked under it, knees bent, bringing his left sword up toward Teferi's throat.

Teferi's left hand swung up, something white trailing from the end of it. Something wet hit his left arm and whipped around it, tangling in his sword's guard.

Laundry! The clever devil had grabbed some wet laundry!

He tried to release the sword and pull his hand free, but he was caught. Teferi used his superior size and strength to sling Anok in a semicircle, until he slammed into the trunk of the scrawny tree back first.

Leaves and berries rained down, and Anok saw stars as his head hit the tree.

He finally managed to extract his hand, and tried to bring up his sword to block the inevitable blow. The big sword clanged into his own with such force that his hand went numb.

He dropped his guard just long enough to leave himself open for the next blow. He staggered back and ducked, so that Teferi's sword took a deep bite of a tree limb instead of his skull.

Then his right sandal caught on something—maybe a loose stone—and down he went. Again he hit his head. He tried to raise his sword but found the tip of Teferi's sword against his breastbone.

He lay back and sighed. "I yield!"

Teferi grinned down at him, then tossed back his head

and laughed. "You were too easy on me, brother! Not on my best day have I ever bested the two-bladed devil in a fair fight." He swung his sword away from Anok and returned it to its scabbard. He reached down and offered Anok his hand.

Anok took the hand and let Teferi haul him to his feet. His whole body ached, and he wasn't moving too well on his own just yet. "I'm not sure how fair that trick with the wet laundry was, but as for me"—he frowned—"I wasn't being easy at all."

Teferi laughed again. Then he saw Anok was serious, and his smile faded.

"I haven't touched my sword since that day at the Scorpion's lair, and Ramsa Aál had them before that. I'm getting soft at the temple. I'm out of practice. I don't like that. I don't like it a bit."

Teferi hobbled over and sat down on one of the stone benches. Anok watched him hold his hand over his chest and saw a spot of blood on the clean dressing. "It's nothing." He smiled weakly. "It was worth it to beat you for once."

"We used to spar like this almost every day."

Teferi grinned just a little. "We used to use sticks, so we didn't kill each other."

Anok rubbed his numbed hand, which still tingled. "Maybe we should go back to the sticks for a while."

Teferi chuckled. Then his expression turned serious. "You never told me what was on that scroll."

"You saw it."

"I can't read, remember?" His tone was sweetly sarcastic.

"Well, it doesn't make much sense to me either, so we're about even on that score."

"You can read it though?"

"I can read the words. It's written in Aquilonian."

"So, what does it say?"

"It's a temple scroll of some kind, from the Cult of—" He looked around to see if anyone else was near. "The Cult of Ibis. Obviously the shopkeeper never actually read the scroll, or he would have finished burning it."

"Ibis? I've heard you mention Ibis, but I don't know that cult."

"The worship of gods other than Set is forbidden in Stygia, yet we both know it goes on. Many gods are quietly worshiped in Odji, and I hear even more are worshiped in Kheshatta. Even in the catacombs beneath the Great Temple, shrines to ancient and forgotten gods are maintained, and the High Priests sometimes have ceremonies there, cheating on Set as a man might cheat on his wife. But while such is usually tolerated by the High Priests and guardians of Set, worship of one god, above all others, is forbidden in Stygia, and that is Ibis."

"Ibis must be one of Set's enemies."

"From what I've heard, blood enemies, ancient and deep. Yet Parath, the god I spoke to in the desert, claimed to be an ancient enemy of both Set and Ibis, and he claimed that my father, that all of my bloodline, worshiped him back to ancient times."

"But if that's true, why would your father have a scroll of Ibis?"

"Exactly why I'm puzzled. But this scroll is important somehow, I just know it. My father set me on a mission when he died, to find my sister and give her the Scale that he left me. Yet I've never been able to do it, never found any trace of a sister. I had no clue where to look. It was years before I dared return to the ruins of my father's house, and by then there were only ashes."

Teferi looked thoughtful. "So what kind of temple scroll is it? Maybe that will tell you something."

"It doesn't make sense, none of it. It's written in Aquilonian, yet Ibis is mainly worshiped in Nemedia these days. And near as I can tell, it has something to do with the initiation rites of a priestess of Ibis."

6

RAMSA AÅL'S PRIVATE chambers were located high above the main entrance of the Great Temple of Set, as were those of the other ranking priests in the temple. The temple looked west, and from this vantage point one could look down across the inner city and its towering black walls, out across Odji, to the harbor of Khemi and the Western Ocean beyond. The view was spectacular, and an expanse of large windows gathered the cooling ocean breezes.

Anok stood in front of those windows, hands behind his back, watching the ships bobbing at their moorings, triangular white sails flying on merchantmen and the swift coastal warships of the Stygian navy as they came and went past the stone breakwater.

To the north he could see the broad expanse of the mouth of the River Styx, with its many delta islands extending out to the horizon, its muddy brown waters spilling out into the dark blue of the sea. To the south, sandbars and barrier islands both protected the farming villages of the coast and provided hiding places for the scattered pirates that often raided non-Stygian vessels, often under the noses of the Stygian fleet, who cared little about outlanders.

Above all, he thought, he would miss the sea. He had never been far from it for long. He would miss it like a parted friend.

Ramsa Aál stood behind him, and he could feel the priest's eyes staring at him. Anok continued to look at the sea.

"Again. What did you say?"

"I said, Aken Anu is a thief and a cheat. He's been charging the temple too much for his camels for years, and he robs the pilgrims on his caravans blind. He's not the worst caravan leader you could have chosen for my journey. He hasn't murdered anyone—yet—that I know of. But he's not far up the list."

"You question my judgment?"

"Perhaps I should rather question your motives. Why send me with such an unreliable guide? Perhaps you wish some harm to come to me on the journey? Perhaps you are testing me, or hoping he will goad me into using my sorcery in anger, so that it will overcome the weakness that I have suffered of late."

Ramsa Aál seemed to relax a bit. He smiled and stepped forward to lean against the windowsill to Anok's left, as though drawn to the mark of power burned into Anok's left wrist. But he smiled, and his demeanor was no longer that of a stern elder but of one equal dealing with another.

Anok glanced at him out of the corner of his eye. *He likes to be challenged, at least by those he hopes to influence.*

"You're right. He isn't the best caravan leader I could have found, and I had considered, even hoped, that you might have trouble with him. Your last guess was correct. I thought he might anger you into using your powers without thinking, avoiding the fear that currently binds you."

"I fear nothing."

He laughed. "All men fear. Only fools deny it to their equals—or their betters. You carry the sacred Mark of Set on your wrist. The power has not deserted you, it never will, and so it must be the will that is weak."

There was truth to that. He feared the power, what it could do, what he had done to the White Scorpions in a misguided attempt at justice, and what he had nearly done to Teferi in the heat of battle. At some point he had ceased to wield the power. The power had begun to wield him. It was not something he wished to experience again. But he wished to admit none of this to Ramsa Aál.

Yet Ramsa Aál seemed to anticipate this and did not wait for him to speak. "You should know that it is the nature of sorcery to be inconsistent in its gifts. The power of all sorcerers, even the greatest, will wax and wane over time. If that were not so, how could a barbarian, even one as talented as the false king Conan of Aquilonia, have defeated our master Thoth-Amon? He was fortunate enough to encounter our lord at times of weakness and profited from his fortune. But a great sorcerer is always patient, and one day Conan will not be so lucky. One day he will meet his doom at the hands of our master."

Anok glanced at the priest, raising an eyebrow. There was something he had long wanted to know and yet not dared to ask. "Master, why do we speak openly of Thoth-Amon's defeats? Why are they recorded and spoken of often in the temple?"

Ramsa Aál's smile grew. "You have asked an important question, and I will tell you the answer. We record them because a great sorcerer is defined by his enemies. One cannot become a great sorcerer without great enemies, and Conan has proven worthy of our master in many encounters.

"Through each defeat, our master was challenged to expand his powers, to engage in even more ambitious schemes of conquest, to seek out more followers and proxies to use against his enemies. Our master has become greater, and in challenging him, Conan has become greater as well. Now he sits on the throne of a mighty nation, with vast armies at his command. And still he will one day fall to our master, and he will seek out an even more worthy foe. Do you see what that means for you?"

Anok blinked in surprise and confusion. Did Ramsa Aál's words have some double meaning. Could Anok, in his wildest dreams, be the "more worthy foe" that Thoth-Amon would one day need? It was prideful madness, and yet, with the powers he might yet command— *Stop. Assume he knows nothing, until otherwise proven. This is only the power, trying to free itself, trying to corrupt my soul.*

Anok tried to look innocent. "How can such important matters be the concern of a humble acolyte, master?"

"In great mountains, the form of anthills can be seen. Where is the adversary worthy of your power, Anok Wati? Where is your Conan? I sense that you have had enemies, yes, but none truly worthy of you. You thought this gang lord Wosret was such an enemy, but though it was not without cost, you destroyed him with little more than gesture, with no more than a fraction of that which is yours to command. That is, as much as anything, why your power fails you. You have no target worthy of its release. What say you to this?"

"I don't know, master. I have destroyed all my enemies, and none stand to replace them." That was a lie. He stood not against a Conan. It was as though he stood against an army of barbarian kings. He had the murdering betrayer, Dejal. He had Ramsa Aál himself. He had the entire Cult of Set. And thus by definition, he had Thoth-Amon himself. Enough great enemies for a dozen lifetimes.

"That is part of why I send you to Kheshatta. It is a place of great mystical learning, true. But it is also a lawless place, where the Cult of Set holds only nominal power. Many gods and demons are openly worshiped there, and their followers move in open opposition to our cult. But in Kheshatta, knowledge is more precious than gold, and the greatest power at any moment resides with the greatest and most learned sorcerer in the city. When our master is in Kheshatta, it is he who fills this role, but when he is elsewhere, many powerful sorcerers struggle for dominance. There, perhaps, you will find an adversary worthy of your talents.

Khemi is too tame, too controlled by Set. You will never find your adversary here."

That isn't true, but my enemies live in Kheshatta as well. They live throughout Stygia, in every city, town, and empty place. Here, Set is all, and Set is my enemy. "Then I will go and seek my adversary, master, if you think it for the best."

Ramsa Aál laughed. "You do not find your adversary, Anok Wati. He will find *you!*"

LATER THAT DAY, Anok went to the acolytes' dining hall, an austere room located behind the temple kitchens. There were oak tables and chairs enough to seat over two dozen, and when Anok had first arrived at the temple, it was generally near full at mealtimes. Now less than a dozen remained of his group.

Some had apparently been killed, or simply vanished, during trials, though the priests were never forthcoming with details when things like this happened. Some had been expelled, or left the temple of their own accord.

Others, who Anok suspected were the sons of the very rich, the very powerful, or even the priests themselves, had been given the yoke of a full acolyte and sent home early. For them, becoming clerics of Set was a matter of appearances, a stepping-stone to power and respect for those who could afford it. It was an elite status that apparently even Dejal's father's wealth was not sufficient to buy, or that, perhaps, he was not generous enough to bestow on his only son.

The food was spread out on a long table near the kitchen door. There were steaming bowls of spiced beef, baked sole, smoked clams, boiled yams, and grape leaves stuffed with crab. Beyond this were platters of flatbreads, olives, fresh and dried fruit, sweet cakes dripping with honey, and small jugs of wine.

His stomach rumbling, Anok grabbed a heavy earthenware plate and heaped it with food. Grabbing a jug of wine, he headed for one of the many empty tables. At first the other acolytes had shunned him because of his late entry into the group, because of his favored status with Ramsa Aál, and because of his mixed Stygian blood and poor upbringing.

Now they still shunned him, but he suspected it was more out of fear. They had all heard rumors of his destruction of the White Scorpions, and of the other, fearful, warlords arriving at the temple with carts of tribute for the temple. They had seen the mark upon his wrist and at least heard rumors as to its significance.

Though most of those remaining were said to be competent sorcerers, none besides Anok had distinguished themselves in that regard. One, a tall, angular young man with exceptionally dark skin, even for a full-blooded Stygian, now wore a jewel on his forehead (Anok had heard whispers that it was embedded in his skull) that was a mark of exceptional second sight, but it carried with it no other special power of sorcery.

And though Dejal aspired to great power, his success had been only moderate in that regard. Of the other acolytes in Anok's group, he was doubtless a bit more powerful than the rest. But though he threw himself into great magics with reckless abandon, his ambition always seemed to exceed his talent. The great spells eluded him, and with each failure, his anger and resentment grew.

Anok sat at the bench, skillfully uncorked the bottle with his dagger, and threw some meat and yams onto the flatbread, which he folded and bit into hungrily. He washed it down with a deep draw from the bottle. He knew that his eating manners seemed crude to the eyes of his more refined company, and the thought that he might be offending them gave him a bit of secret pleasure.

He shoved a grape leaf into his mouth, letting the juice roll down his chin before wiping it with his sleeve. He glanced up to see three acolytes at a nearby table staring. *Good.*

Then someone stepped up behind him, put his plate down on the table, and sat down in the chair next to him. He glanced over. *Dejal.*

Anok's appetite immediately faded. Still, he couldn't let

his displeasure show. He forced himself to continue eating. The meat had lost all flavor, the bread gone dry and crumbly in his mouth as he chewed slowly.

"Greetings, Anok." Dejal stabbed a boiled yam with his knife and lifted it to his mouth.

Anok's eyes were drawn to his meaty fingers wrapped around the knife, his neatly trimmed nails, a golden ring with the crest of his father's house on his middle finger. He watched the muscles in his hand flex, imagined them tightening around the knife handle as they drew the blade across Sheriti's throat—

He realized he was no longer chewing, and swallowed. It felt as though he were swallowing gravel. He focused on his plate and saw the pink juices from the meat pooling there. On his left wrist, the Mark of Set burned his flesh, seemed actually to writhe beneath his skin.

Stop it! He cursed his own anger. Very soon he could leave the temple, wouldn't have to see Dejal every day, wouldn't have to lie awake every night with a dagger in his hand, thinking of Dejal sleeping in his bed only a wall away.

Dejal glanced at him curiously. "You seem distracted, brother."

He composed himself, pushed the anger away, pulled over it the curtain of false calm and civility that had become so familiar. "I was only thinking of my impending journey to Kheshatta. It's an honor to be trusted on such a solitary quest for knowledge."

Dejal smiled slightly. He spoke quietly, so the others wouldn't hear. "You will have Teferi with you, a brilliant deception to avoid being monitored too closely by the priests. I hear the whores of Kheshatta engage in depravity that the whores of the Paradise could scarcely dream of, that there are exotic blood sports from the East, intoxicants from every far outpost of the caravan trade, and from the famed prisoners of Kheshatta themselves."

"You wish you were going in my stead."

"I am envious, yes, but to gain power, one must keep the company of the powerful. While you are exploring distant fleshpots and the dusty scrolls of scholarship, I shall be at Ramsa Aál's right hand."

Dejal dropped the yam, knife still embedded in it, on his plate. "He is a rising power in the temple, and it is said he could be High Priest of the Temple if he only wished it. But his ambitions run far higher than that. I have seen letters arrive for him from Thoth-Amon himself, and I suspect they are planning some great spell involving the very Scale of Set that I delivered to him. He is sending me into the desert in search of— I should not say. But know that I will play an important role in this thing, and as Ramsa Aál rises in power, so shall I.

"Am I supposed to be jealous?"

Dejal chuckled. "You were ever lacking in ambition, brother. Dusty scrolls and ancient books, and perhaps a whore or two. That is a better life for you. I wish you the joy of it."

Having heard enough, Anok pushed back his chair and picked up his plate. "I have preparations to make. Ramsa Aál has given me permission to hire my own caravan. Best I get to it."

He scraped his uneaten food into the slop bucket and tossed the plate on the table just inside the kitchen door. He really did have things to do, and the sooner he could arrange to leave this place, the better.

7

IT WAS WELL before dawn when Anok and Teferi pulled their little cart through the empty streets of Odji, headed for the camel barns near the southeast corner of the inner city's walls. A torch lashed to the front of the cart lit their way, and each of them carried another.

Teferi had spent the evening engaged in serious drinking and making farewells to several female friends. He looked groggy, and Anok suspected he was nursing a hangover. He was quiet, and that suited Anok, who was in no mood for conversation.

What, Anok wondered, had he been expecting? He'd told Ramsa Aál yesterday that he'd secured passage on a caravan leaving two days earlier than his original departure, meaning that he would miss the ceremony graduating the novices to full-acolyte status.

Most likely, he'd expected that Ramsa Aál would refuse him, insist that he remain for the ceremony. That didn't happen. Once again, the priest seemed pleased with his eagerness and initiative.

Failing that, perhaps Anok had expected some private

ceremony, some ritual, or even one last trial. Instead, Ramsa Aál had simply unlocked a chest, removed the golden yoke of a full acolyte, and placed it around Anok's neck. Then he'd gone immediately back to the scroll he'd been studying when Anok arrived. When, a few minutes later, he'd noticed Anok was still standing there, he'd actually seemed slightly annoyed.

Anok remembered his words: "This is no grand passage, no great accomplishment. The difference between a novice and an acolyte is simply a small bit of trust and that small symbol of respect. The rich patrons who send their sons to study here expect something more ostentatious, and we give it to them, but you do not need it. You know just enough to know how little you really know, have learned just enough to know how much you have yet to learn. Go, get on with it. We will meet again soon."

Anok shifted his grip on the little cart's shaft so that he could reach up and examine the yoke with his fingers. It was a band of gold, made of overlapping plates crafted to look like Scales. A finger's length wide, it draped loosely around his neck and shoulders. Hanging from the front, a round medallion was deeply engraved with the writhing serpent that was the symbol of Set. The medallion, he noted, hung directly over his father's medallion, which Teferi had returned to him this morning, and which he now wore under his robes.

The camel barns were built around a small plaza in an unusually neat and orderly neighborhood of Odji. The nomads who dwelled there were a careful and frugal people. They did not waste, and they did not spoil what they considered to be their own territory, even if most of them actually lived here only for days or weeks at a time.

Anok's dealings with them had mostly been occasional and brief. They kept to themselves, and only dealt with city dwellers on matters of business. He knew a few of the camel drivers who traveled with the caravans by name, but they were not true Stygian nomads, merely hired drivers of other races and creeds. He was looking forward to at last having a chance to learn about these mysterious people.

They reached the barns just as the eastern sky was beginning to pinken and found a caravan already assembling in
the plaza. Anok left the cart with Teferi and walked over to
greet the man who seemed to be in charge.

The man was old but moved with the spring of a much
younger man. He was loading a camel, and he hefted heavy
bundles with seeming ease. His skin was dark and leathery,
his nose long and hooked, even for his people, and his eyes
were intense and fearsome-looking. His pointed, curly beard
was mostly white, but a few of the blue-black hairs common
to men of his race still showed here and there. He wore loose
white robes, and the circlet holding his headcloth was ornately embroidered with threads of colored silk, silver, and
gold.

Anok bowed in respectful greeting, as he had seen nomads do on occasion. "Pardon, but are you Havilah? I spoke
with Havilah's son Moahavilah about securing passage on
this caravan for my companion and me."

The man's eyes zeroed in on the medallion around
Anok's neck. He glared at it for a moment, then turned his
head and spat upon the sand. "Moahavilah is my youngest
son and has no right to speak for me. There will be no passage for you." He turned and went back to his camel.

"Pardon, but I gave your son fifty pieces of silver as a
deposit."

Havilah did not look back at him. "Then I will give it
back to you."

Anok had heard that among the nomads, a man's word
was a matter of some importance. "Pardon, Havilah, but
promises were made to me in your name. If Moahavilah is
your youngest son, he is still of your blood, and I now see
him across the plaza watering your camels. I hold you to
your word and beg passage as it was originally promised."

Havilah turned back and glared at him. "You Set worshipers are all the same. You think you own Stygia, but you
do not own the sands where we dwell. Beyond the bounds of
this city, your cult is weak, and the gods of the desert are

strong. I have seen your kind die of thirst or in a storm of quicksand just like any other man."

"Pardon, honorable Havilah, but I ask for nothing more than any other man, safe passage at a fair price. I was told by a woman at the Great Marketplace, I believe her name was Setarah, that you were an honest and honorable man and that I should seek you out. I have been promised passage in your name, and I only ask that the promise be kept."

The old man looked back at him over his shoulder, his narrow lips twisted into a scowl. "I do not like snake worshipers. It would not be a pleasant trip."

"Perhaps you would find me different than other snake worshipers."

"Perhaps the sun will rise from the Western Ocean this morning." He considered a moment. "Setarah was wife to my older brother until he was killed by bandits almost ten years ago now. She has great wisdom and perception for a woman. If she sent you here, she must see something in you that I do not." He sighed. "Have you ridden a camel before?"

Anok smiled a bit, knowing he had won. "No, honorable Havilah. I have rarely traveled beyond the city, and then only on foot, or by boat."

The old man shook his head sadly. "You will take those two camels over there." He pointed to a pair of camels just behind his own. "They are well trained and hardly need driving. Find Moahavilah and have him show you how to mount the camel and stay in the saddle. You are his doing, I will make you his responsibility. Now go, I have things to do, and we leave when the sun is full."

Anok bowed again. "Thank you, great Havilah. You are a man of your word."

Anok heard a rude snorting sound, but he wasn't sure if it came from the man or the camel.

HAVILAH SEEMED SURPRISED when Anok and Teferi briefly disappeared into the barn and returned dressed in nomadic dress. As they passed him, he glanced up and grunted in a way that Anok suspected passed for grudging approval.

Anok had removed every sign of the Cult of Set and packed them away, even his new acolyte's yoke, and he was surprised how much it lifted his spirits. He felt almost—*clean.*

But there was one reminder of his association with the cult that he could not remove. He pulled back the loose sleeve of his long shirt to see the mark there. The nagging redness had faded, as though his flesh had finally accepted the invader, but it remained warm to the touch. At times, he swore that he could feel it *moving,* though he hoped that was only an illusion.

More disturbing was the twitch he had developed in his hand. Sometimes the fingers seemed to wiggle of their own volition or would inexplicably clench into a fist until his nails cut into his palm. It didn't happen often, but it always disturbed him when it did. He suspected it was only the beginning of his troubles with the Mark of Set.

Often he found himself rubbing the little silver ring Sheriti had bought for him. He wore it constantly now, and it gave him comfort, especially when the mark troubled him. The memory of her pure heart and fierce spirit helped keep him centered.

Anok and Teferi found Moahavilah loading their camels when they returned, hanging their sacks and bundles from the corners of the tall, curious-looking saddle. He was the runt of the family, his characteristic blue beard little more than a scraggly patch on his chin. But his ready smile and his eyes, with much of his father's fire and none of the malice, made him a difficult man not to like. Anok hoped that his decision to book passage for him and Teferi didn't cause conflict with his father.

Anok had ridden horses and mules a time or two in his life, but never a camel, and he was somewhat daunted by the prospect. The youngest son of Havilah made introductions to their camels, demonstrated a few simple commands (kneel, stand, go, and stop). "Most of the time," he explained, "there will be a rope between your mount to one of our camels, so there will be little to do but sit and enjoy the ride, if you can. Many city dwellers do not appreciate the beauty of the desert."

"I'm not one of those people," replied Anok, "though I find it easier to enjoy the view when the desert isn't trying to kill me."

Moahavilah raised an eyebrow but resisted following up on the comment. Instead, he showed Anok how to climb into the saddle. First he ordered the camel to cush—that is, to kneel until it was resting on its belly. Once it was down, Anok climbed into the saddle. Camels were curious creatures, and his mount turned her long, flexible neck to watch him with large, brown eyes.

He returned her gaze and tried to be reassuring. "Easy, girl. Let's be friends here."

He found himself high on her hump, straddling the tall, wooden saddle horn in front and leaning lightly against its twin behind him. Moahavilah showed him how to hold himself in place by crooking one knee around the horn and locking his foot under the other leg.

He felt off-balance, and awkward, and was totally taken by surprise as Moahavilah patted the camel on its flank and shouted, "Up."

The camel stood up with startling speed, lurching violently. Anok tried to hold on, but found himself tumbling through the air. He landed hard on his shoulders, his fighter's instincts keeping him from hurting anything but his pride.

The camel lowered its head and nuzzled him, giving him a faceful of putrid breath in the process. Teferi roared with laughter, as Anok tried to pat the big animal's muzzle and push it away at the same time.

"You must lean with the camel as it rises," said Moahavilah, "or you will surely fall."

"I'm glad," he said, pulling himself up out of the dirt and brushing off his robe, "that you told me that *before* I got on the camel."

His second try was more successful, and having learned from his mistakes, Teferi seemed to have little trouble at all.

Though the camels were large, smelly, and fearsome-sounding, they seemed to be curious and intelligent beasts. To Anok their temperament seemed more like that of a large and somewhat friendly dog than a skittish horse.

By the time they'd gotten accustomed to their mounts, the sun was well above the eastern hills, and Anok wondered what they were waiting for.

From the far end of the plaza, a trio of camels appeared. The lead two were ridden by men with pointed, neatly trimmed, beards. They were tall and slender, dark, of Turanian blood most likely. By their dress, they were servants, but high servants of some noble. Their clothing, though subdued in colors was elaborately embroidered in bands around the sleeves, collars, and hems. Everything about their camels was ornate and expensive-looking. Tassels woven with gold thread hung from the reins and saddle, and their saddlebags were ornately embroidered.

They led the third camel with a rope, and it was unusual in several ways. First, it was white, an expensive rarity, and the largest camel Anok could recall ever seeing. On its back was not a saddle, but a platform surrounded by four outward-facing corner poles draped with colorful silks, forming a tent of sorts.

Through the translucent silks he thought he could see a variety of pillows, and a reclining woman inside. He couldn't see her clearly, but she seemed to be asleep.

As he tried to get a better look, one of the Turanians rode between them. "Do not disturb the mistress. She sleeps off too much celebration."

Teferi raised an eyebrow. "Celebration of what?"

The Turanian's mouth twitched slightly at the corner, as though he suppressed a smile. "The mistress does not need a reason to celebrate." He rode on past to speak with Havilah.

Teferi grinned at Anok, and he grinned back.

The caravan was soon under way, twenty camels total, eight paying travelers, including Anok and Teferi, Havilah and his three sons, and two young Shemite boys who both drove and tended the camels.

As they climbed the winding road up the hills that separated the ocean from the desert, it was all familiar to Anok, who had traveled this road once before not long ago. He recalled that day, wistfully, when he had gone on what Teferi called Usafiri, a journey into the wilderness to find one's purpose.

He'd only half believed, if that much. His greatest purpose had been to cast his father's medallion into the desert, to be rid of the curse he believed it had become. But as Teferi had predicted, his Usafiri had taken Anok's life in a totally new direction. He had returned with the medallion and a new purpose, to seek the very heart of Set and destroy his cult from within.

"I think she's a princess." Teferi's camel pulled up next to him, and at his command, took pace with Anok's.

Anok glanced at the camel, curiously. "You seem to be learning very quickly."

Teferi shrugged his broad shoulders. "I have heard that my ancestors rode camels. Perhaps it is in my blood." He nodded toward the white camel with its elaborate cargo. "So, a princess? Wandering granddaughter of Stygia's puppet king?"

Anok chuckled. "I will give you this, Teferi, you have a vivid imagination. Probably some fat noblewoman returning to her husband in Kheshatta after a month's shopping in the Great Marketplace and a quick dalliance with an Argossean trader in Akhet."

It was Teferi's turn to chuckle. "And you accuse me of imagination!" His expression turned more thoughtful. "But I do not think so. See that bundle on the side of the white camel?"

Anok looked. Though it was bundled in colorful silks, its size and shape suggested that it might contain a war sword. "It might belong to one of the servants."

"The Turanians wear scimitars, by their style more for show than battle. I do not think they are strong fighters who would wield such a blade."

Anok considered this as they crossed the hills into the

desert highlands beyond, and the beginnings of the caravan road proper. There were few dwellings here, small farm buildings clustered around wells, with herds of goats and skinny cows searching for anything edible among the rocks and dry brush.

Finally, he had considered enough. Following Teferi's methods, he urged his camel forward. The beast charged right past the white camel, attracting a curious glance back by Havilah, who evidently decided it was no concern of his.

But as Anok managed to slow his camel enough for the big white camel to catch up, again the servants rode up.

"I told you, the mistress sleeps!"

Anok smirked. "I'm sure she does." He leaned around the nearest servant. "Fallon! Wake up, barbarian!"

There was stirring behind the silks and a throaty moan.

To Anok's surprise as much as anyone, he was able to guide his camel around the servant and pull in close to the white camel. "Fallon! Wake up, trollop!"

There was a rustling behind the silks, and he caught the outline of a woman, tall, broad-shouldered, and bosomy. The silks parted a bit, and strong hands grabbed his sleeve, pulling him right off his saddle. He could only imagine the look of surprise on the servants' faces as he was yanked up to vanish behind the flowing silks.

He found himself spun around, a supple arm crooked around his forehead to pull his head back, a dagger held to his throat.

It wasn't quite the greeting he had been expecting.

He couldn't see much of the powerful woman holding him, and not much of what he did see reminded him much of Fallon of the Smoke Clan. The nails of the hand holding the knife were filed and polished red in the style of Stygian noblewomen, and the sleeve of the garment she was wearing was multicolored silk woven through with silver thread. A thin and elegant golden bracelet hung loosely over her wrist, and the fragrance of some exotic perfume filled his nose.

It was almost enough to make him think that he had wrongly identified the woman.

Then she spoke.

"Anok Wati," a familiar voice roared, "you Odji gutter trash! Do you not know that only a suicidal fool would waken a hungover barbarian woman with his bellowing!"

There was a silent pause, then she began to laugh, deep and hard. The blade parted company from his throat, and he was abruptly pushed away, twisting so that he landed sitting with his back against one of the carved wooden corner posts.

Fallon was immediately up on her knees. She leaned forward and planted a hard kiss on his lips.

It was not unpleasant, and he felt a sudden pang of guilt.

Somewhere in the middle of the kiss, which went on rather for a time, Teferi rode up next to them. As Fallon's lip briefly left his, Anok glanced over and saw Teferi watching them through the now-parted silk drapes, a bemused look on his face. "Do you require rescuing?"

"I can handle it," said Anok, just as Fallon kissed him again.

Then she leaned back and looked at him. She plucked at the sleeve of his nomadic robe and smiled. "This looks good on you. Certainly better than those foul cult robes I heard you were wearing. Surely you've given up that madness by now?"

"Not exactly," he replied.

She frowned.

He really didn't want to talk about it, especially not here where anyone in the caravan might listen in. Havilah certainly had no love of the cult, but he really had no way of knowing who could be trusted. He decided to change the subject.

"You accuse me of madness? Look at yourself! Perfumed, dressed in fine silks, face painted— Are those *flowers* in your hair?"

She reached up and touched a slightly wilted blossom woven into the ornate braids in her long, dark hair. Her lips pouted slightly. "You don't like this?"

"Well . . ." In truth, she looked rather fetching, if a little incongruous, in her new finery. He merely found it difficult to reconcile her delicate dress with her coarse barbarian mannerisms and his knowledge of what the woman could do with a sword. "It's lovely. Really."

She laughed. "Well, don't get used to it. As a rich woman, I'm merely trying new things."

"Rich? What happened to your scheme to—" He hesitated. Realizing that this subject was no safer than his own plot against the temple, he lowered his voice, and leaned closer. "—smuggle poisons out of Kheshatta?"

"Abandoned for lack of need. While you were off playing with your *snake-god,* I was in the back rooms of Odji gambling with the gems your friend Dejal paid me to deliver his magical trinket. Luck favored me well, and over several days, I doubled my stake several times over." She spread her arms dramatically. "And so, the proud barbarian plays at being a noblewoman." She leaned forward, and whispered mockingly, "It is overrated."

Anok frowned slightly but said nothing. There had to be more to the story than that. There were few men in Odji with that kind of money to gamble, and most of them were gang lords. An outlander, especially a woman, who won that kind of money . . . Well, even if she won it fairly, it was doubtful she'd simply be allowed to leave with her winnings.

Still, it was a long trip across the desert, and he would let her tell it in her own time. In fact, they had nothing *but* time, and he was not without his own secrets.

"But you're still going to Kheshatta?"

She shrugged. "I'd heard so much about this so-called city of sorcerers, I grew curious. I thought I'd see it myself."

He raised his eyebrows skeptically. "You're going to Kheshatta—because you're curious?"

She frowned. "I am a wanderer, an adventurer. I have traveled from the Cimmeria of my childhood, through far Aquilonia, through many other places to get here, and I will travel farther yet before I am through. I need no reason to go to a new place. I just go."

"And you aren't afraid to go to a city full of wizards and dark magic?"

She tsked. "I have no fear of magic. It is all smoke and trickery, trickery and smoke."

The Mark of Set on Anok's wrist itched. "If you say so," he replied.

8

IT WAS A long day in the desert. Before the sun was high in the sky, they passed the Black Pyramid. He could sense the dark magic in the ancient place, and as had happened last time he was here, the Scale of Set began to call to it, even from within the iron prison of the medallion. He was relieved to know that only he could hear the metallic ringing sound, evidently a result of his enhanced sensitivity to magic.

But he had not expected that the Mark of Set would respond to it as well. As they came closer to the pyramid, it began to itch and burn, and he suffered the uncomfortable illusion that the snake tattoo that circled his wrist was actually squirming, like a living snake.

His left hand began to twitch as well, much more powerfully than ever before, and he was finally forced to jam the offending appendage between his thigh and the saddle, literally sitting on it to keep it still.

It was with great relief that he watched the Black Pyramid disappear behind the jagged hills behind them. As soon as it disappeared from sight, his hand relaxed and returned to his control, though the mark continued to tingle for hours afterward.

They stopped several times through the day to eat, drink water, and rest both themselves and the camels. To Anok's surprise, their pace was a leisurely one, and he suspected he could have walked just as fast. He said so to Moahavilah at one point.

The young nomad just smiled. "Camels can run quite quickly, but here in the desert, they pick their own pace. Yes, you could walk as fast, but you would use three times as much water as you do now and need more food as well. The camel need not drink at all until we reach the next oasis, and can live without food as well, if need be. A caravan is not about speed, it is about water. In the desert, *everything* is about water."

The caravan road had, for several hours, run just along the edge of the Sea of Sand. They were usually within sight of at least of a few of its towering dunes.

Anok could not help but reflect on his own journey there. He asked Havilah if had had heard of the great spiders that hunted in packs, like wolves.

Havilah had laughed. "Of course I have! Tales told by old women to scare children! Where did a city man such as yourself hear such a thing?"

Anok was not amused. "I *saw* them."

The old nomad just roared with laughter. "And what bottle did you drink from to see such a thing? Did you see some pink camels also?" He rode on ahead, still laughing.

Anok frowned after him. He *had* seen them.

Hadn't he?

He had been delirious when Teferi and Rami had pulled him from the desert. What if it had all been a fever dream? The spiders, the giant skeleton of the snake, the voice of the Parath, all of it—

No! He'd seen the spiders, fought them, killed them, eaten their bitter flesh and drunk their foul blood to survive! That was why he'd been delirious: the poison in their flesh. It had all been real. He was sure of it.

Almost.

He hung his head. What was truth? Was there even such a thing? Was truth what you believed, what you experienced, or what others told you was real? He had seen things, done things, experienced things, all so unbelievable. He immersed himself in lies, deceptions, and half-truths. Was it any wonder he could no longer separate fancy from reality?

And if he drove himself into madness, what of it? But he dragged his friends along with him; Teferi, Fallon, even Rami. And beautiful, sweet, Sheriti. His folly had cost her her life.

He tried to convince himself that it wasn't so. Dejal had killed her in the name of the cult, and Dejal's decision to become an acolyte of Set had nothing to do with Anok, nor did his bloody betrayal of Sheriti's trust. Yet if Anok had been there, instead of at the Great Temple getting this cursed mark on his wrist, he might have stopped Dejal, might have saved Sheriti.

Perhaps.

But the most bitter notion, the one that haunted his nightmares, was that Dejal had used Anok as bait to lure Sheriti out of the safety of her home on Festival night.

He imagined Dejal arriving at her door. "It is Anok, Sheriti! He has been injured at the temple! He lies dying, and he calls only for you."

How else had he lured her onto the streets that night? How else had he lured her to her doom?

IT WAS LATE in the day, and many times along the road, Anok had seen Havilah eyeing him from a distance, an enigmatic half smile on his face. Finally, the old man dug his heels into his camel and trotted it over to ride alongside Anok's mount.

"Perhaps," he said, "I was too hard on you today when you spoke of the spiders. I have seen you brooding over it, and I meant only sport. It is our way to tease those new to the deep desert, to test their knowledge and will. Most men would have simply become embarrassed at their tall tale, or angry at my jabs, but in you, I sense I have touched a deeper nerve."

Anok looked off at the red rock formations in the northern distance, carved by wind into strange and twisted forms. Nearer, outcroppings of blindingly white chalk pushed their way up through the sand. Yet strange as this landscape was, he was sure it was real.

He glanced back at Havilah, who waited patiently for his reply. He had no desire to discuss his sanity, or lack of same, with this relative stranger.

Finally, seeing that no reply was forthcoming, Havilah again spoke. "Though I have never seen these spiders of which you speak, or heard of them from credible men"—he grinned—"yourself excepted, of course, I know there are many strange things in the deserts of Stygia. Things both fantastic and terrible, natural and unnatural. This sand"—he swept his arm dramatically—"hides countless secrets of the past. Once this land was green and wet, home to great civilizations long gone. Relics of the forgotten past are everywhere." He pointed at a low, rounded hill just ahead. "Come, I will show you."

Anok trotted his camel along after Havilah, as they ranged ahead and slightly south of the rest of the caravan. Amid the splendor of the desert, the hill looked drab and uninviting, a rounded heap that seemed to be made of gravel and loose stone. He couldn't imagine what Havilah hoped to show him.

Then, as they grew closer, he realized that the stones that made up the hill were strangely formed, round, even spiral in shape. Havilah spurred his mount ahead, reaching the base of the hill and quickly dismounting. He bent down and began to pick through the stones, picking some up and throwing them back, gathering others in a fold of his robes.

Anok pulled up next to him and stopped, bending over to examine the rocks more carefully. At first the shapes confused him. They seemed strangely familiar, but he couldn't place them in this context. Then, at once, he realized what he was seeing and exactly how strange it was. "Shells! This whole hill is made of shells from the sea!"

It was as though they had come upon a beach after a storm. There were shells in the forms of spirals and twisting points, cowry shells shaped like nut meats, sand dollars, and fluted clams, some as big as a camel's foot. Their numbers were countless. It would have taken a thousand camels many lifetimes to bring them all from the nearest ocean shore. How, then, had they gotten here?

Havilah grinned up at him. "You ask yourself the question we all have asked ourselves. How can this thing be?" He handed his collected shells up for Anok to examine.

He rolled them over in his hand. They were rough and heavy, colored in tans and browns rather than the off-whites and pale colors more typical of shells.

"They are made of stone," Havilah said, "perhaps transformed by great age, or some ancient magic we cannot hope to understand. The stories of our people say that this place was once more than wet and fertile, it was part of the sea. The waters receded, and it became first grassland, then desert. It is said there is a cycle to all things, and over time, the mountains are all ground down by wind and until that are but basins for the ocean, and the oceans all fill up with sand." His eyes twinkled. "You see?"

"It is hard to believe."

"Stygia is very old. Older than the Cult of Set. Older than the age of men. Older, perhaps, than the gods. Some say it has always existed, mountains into sea, sea into mountains, on and on back to the dim beginnings of time. So if you tell me you have seen pack spiders, who am I to tell you it is impossible? In Stygia, *all* things are possible."

THE CARAVAN ARRIVED at a ruined stone building just before nightfall. There was a well, Havilah explained, but it had dried up in his grandfather's time. "It is still a good place to camp," he said.

They set up tents in and around the walls of the old building. The young boys tended the camels and built fires, using what sticks they could gather and dry camel dung as fuel.

Fallon's servants set up a splendid tent for her, white with gold roping and tassels around the edges. Streamers of brightly colored silk streamed from the center pole and rippled in the slightest breeze.

They fussed over her, preparing to cook her dinner from their own private stores, fetching her water, and waiting on her constantly. It clearly grated on her, her rage growing until she exploded, bellowing at them in a most unladylike fashion to go away and tend their own business.

She vanished into her tent and emerged lugging a basket filled with wine jugs. One of the servants ran back to help, but she glared at him until he cowered and scuttled away.

She carried the basket over to where Anok and Teferi were warming themselves against the growing night chill.

"May I join you? I come bearing gifts." She dropped the basket in the sand next to them.

Teferi took one of the jugs, removed the stopper, and sniffed the contents. "City wine," he said. "Good stuff."

She took a jug for herself, and plopped down cross-legged in the sand between them.

Teferi passed Anok a jug.

They sat, drank, and watched the fire for a while.

At their own fire, just a little way away, Havilah and his sons sang songs in Shemitish, while the camel boys kept time on hollow wooden drums struck with mallets.

As she started her second jug of wine, Fallon plucked at the translucent purple silk of her sleeve. "Am I not fine? I wear garb fit for a princess. Fit for a queen!" She got a distant look in her eye. "I could be a queen, you know. You know of Conan, proud Cimmerian king of Aquilonia? Who will he take for his queen? Some soft, *civilized,* Aquilonian woman? I think not! Such women might be fit for a dalliance, but to be his queen? No! King Conan needs a woman who understands barbarian honor, a woman who can share his bed without breaking like pottery, a woman who can take up arms and fight with him back-to-back, match him blow for blow!"

She again looked down at herself and fell silent.

Anok finally turned to Fallon. "You don't seem happy."

She snorted. "Happy? Happy? Let me tell you, it was madness to seek wealth. Wealth is a curse."

Teferi just laughed. "Is that so?"

"So," said Anok, "what really happened back in Odji?"

She glowered at the fire. "As I told you, I won a great deal of money from a gang lord. Truth be told, I didn't expect to walk away with it, at least not without a fight. But it turns out there were rumors that I had been seen with you, Anok, and your name is apparently something of great significance to the gang lords of Odji these days. I didn't fully understand it, but I thanked my good fortune and left."

"But your good fortune didn't last?"

"I didn't wait to find out. I suspected that someone would come for me, and at best, I had made powerful enemies in Odji. Best to make myself unseen and seek to leave as soon as possible."

Anok reached out and touched her silken sleeve. "Who did this to you?"

"Whores," she said, matter-of-factly.

Teferi sniggered, and Fallon shot him an angry look.

"It wasn't like that, but I needed to change my appearance. What better way for a warrior-woman to hide than dressing like this? Truly, you didn't suspect me at first, and you know me well." She glanced directly at Anok. "*Very* well. But who to show me how?

"Then I had the idea. I went to one of the finer houses of Odji. Not the Paradise brothel, as, knowing your connection to it, they might have looked for me there. The women there were more than happy to take my gold for nothing more than a game of dress-up. Truth be told, I think they enjoyed it far more than I." She scowled.

"Then they helped me buy new clothing and to find these servants and camels. Enough gold has a way of silencing all questions, easing all transactions."

She drank more, and as she did, her mood turned darker. "Look at me," she finally said with a tone of disgust. She stood and yanked at her silken clothing. "Dressing like a trollop, riding on soft pillows, fussed over by servants. This is not a woman worthy of Conan! This is no way for a proper barbarian to live!"

Abruptly, she grabbed her silk blouse with both hands and ripped it apart. She broke into a growling fit, ripping her garments away until she stood before them naked but for a few tatters of silk. She panted and glanced over at them, unashamed of her nakedness.

Teferi smiled broadly, but she ignored him.

"I am a Cimmerian! I will not become soft and weak!" She stomped back to her tent, her shapely flanks looking pale in the moonlight.

Still, Teferi grinned, and Anok kicked him in the ankle.

Teferi gave him a hurt expression, then, the affront seemingly forgotten, took another drink from his jug.

After a time, Fallon returned. The braids were gone from her hair, as were the flowers. She wore simple warrior's garb, a leather kilt, leather tunic, and sandals. Her arming sword was belted proudly around her middle, and a large knife was tucked into the other side of her belt.

She looked more comfortable to Anok than since they had begun the journey. She sat down heavily and a little clumsily, immediately finding another jug of wine.

"Wealth," she said, "is a poison. You're better off without it."

"Then," said Teferi, "give me yours!"

She stared into her wine for a moment, then laughed knowingly. "Spent," she said. "All spent. The last of it on these silks and camels and servants, and"—she hoisted the jug high over her head—"on this fine wine. I am once again free of its taint." She took another drink, then chuckled. "Until next time, anyway."

They all laughed.

Yet Anok's thoughts were darker. The wine had not dulled

the tingling of the mark on his wrist. If anything, it had made it stronger, opening his mind to its dark whisperings.

As he listened to Fallon, all he could think was, *If only it were so simple for me.*

9

ANOK THOUGHT HE had experienced the desert, but the next morning showed that it still had harsh lessons to deal him. The sun blazed as they broke camp. It was already hot, and he could tell it would soon be hotter still. A wind from the east brought with it nothing but more heat and blowing sand.

He had thought that the cooling effect of the ocean air had ended on the hills above Khemi. But he saw that until now it had continued into the desert. They would experience the desert's true heat this day.

Fallon's servants seemed utterly perplexed by her transformation. They watched, speechless, as she ripped the silk coverings from her camel's canopy, threw away the soft pillows, and cut loose tassels and ornamentation from its tack. She growled at them when they approached, and she made her own breakfast despite their protests.

They were soon under way, though their pace was even slower than the day before. The camels seemed to sense the impending heat and paced themselves accordingly. There was little chatter among the people in the caravan. With the

camel's soft feet, there were long stretches where they
moved in eerie silence, broken only by an occasional moan
or roar from the beasts themselves.

They stopped more frequently for water, which Havilah
personally doled out in tiny portions. It was at one such stop
that a buzzing of flies caught Havilah's attention. He walked
over behind a nearby rock outcropping, returning a few minutes later with a frown on his face.

He saw the curiosity in Anok's face. "Can you fight, city
man?"

Anok quickly motioned for Teferi to come over and listen
as well. "We can fight," Anok replied, as Teferi arrived.
"Why?"

"Behind the rocks, horse droppings and tracks, no more
than a day old, and from more than one horse by my eye. No
one uses horses this deep in the desert but soldiers and bandits, and there are no armies on the march here that I've
heard of."

Anok nodded. "Horses would need water."

"Perhaps they've found a lost spring or well, or maybe
they have a large camp, and bring in water by camel." He
looked suspiciously at Teferi. "Will you fight your own kind,
Kushite? Bandits in these lands almost always come across
the border from Kush."

Teferi pulled his broad shoulders back. "I was born in
Stygia. I will fight any who attack us, and I will not care for
the color of their skin."

Havilah seemed satisfied. "Keep your weapons close and
your eyes open."

"Fallon can fight, too," said Teferi. "We will tell her."

Havilah frowned. "The rich woman? That she now
dresses strangely and hauls a sword does not make her a
fighter."

"She is a barbarian from the north," explained Anok, "a
Cimmerian."

Havilah shook his head. "I have not heard of this place."

"Have you heard of King Conan? He is her countryman,
and in their land, the women fight alongside their men."

His eyes widened slightly. "We will see. Tell her then."
He gave his sons a few simple hand signals, which seemed
to convey to them all the information he had spoken to Anok
and Teferi. They immediately began scanning the horizon,
and the middle son strung his bow.

Anok considered their forces. He had no doubt that Havilah and his sons knew how to fight. He had gained considerable respect for the old man and his family.

Teferi, Fallon, and he would fight well, of course, but this
was not their kind of battle, and they were not good enough
riders to fight from camel-back. They would likely have to
dismount and that would put them at a great disadvantage
against mounted attackers. He had no confidence that Fallon's servants would be of any help at all, and the other travelers were older traders of mixed Stygian blood. He saw no
sign they would be useful. Perhaps the camel boys would
surprise him, as boys sometimes did in war, but they were
too small and weak to be of much good.

Seven fighters, protecting six against—how many? He
considered asking Havilah what he thought, but it would
likely just be a guess. If what the old man said was true, their
opponents were a large and well-organized group. He
doubted they would even consider an attack unless they
thought the odds were strongly in their favor.

Given that last thought, perhaps they wouldn't attack at
all. But it was a faint hope. If they were so organized, they
would have resources, and he doubted they'd be out here unless they could mount at least a dozen men.

The long day became longer as the caravan advanced
slowly along the road in the oppressive heat, searching for
any sign of bandits. The country was varied and broken, offering many places to hide. Great spires and arches of red-
and-orange stone, shaped by wind, stood along the road like
forgotten sentinels from the time of giants, and the blowing
sand stung the eyes and made it difficult to see.

The bandits appeared, finally, in the most unlikely place,
after they had emerged from the badlands into an open plain
of rolling ground and yellow sandy soil, dotted with flower-

ing cactus and dry scrub. It was here, where the visibility was good and hiding places nearly nonexistent, that they saw the line of horses standing against the sun-bleached sky.

Havilah pulled the caravan to a halt, and the seven who would fight gathered their camels together at the front of the group.

"There are a dozen," said Anok. "Unfortunately, I guessed correctly." He looked around at the open land. "This is very bad, isn't it?"

Teferi frowned. "What do you mean?"

"They didn't attack us when they had the chance to hide. They don't think they need to hide. They're more concerned that we'll hide from them."

Havilah scanned their surroundings. "There," he said, "to the north of the road. See that light-colored spot? It's a small basin, perhaps a dried-up pond where the sand will favor our camels more than their horses."

Anok nodded. "It's as defensible as anything we're likely to get to. Do we hurry, or take our time?"

"Both," said Havilah. He signaled the camel boys over. "You and the rest go to that white spot over there. Cush the camels in a circle, and get behind them. We will come later. Go quickly!"

The boys urged their camels, turning back to herd the remaining camels and their riders toward what small safety the depression offered.

"We ride after them," said Havilah, "but taking our time about it. Rush only if they attack, and it seems advantageous."

As they began to move, a black stallion and its rider separated from the line, trotting down toward them.

Teferi drew back his mighty bow. "I can get him."

Havilah gestured for him to lower his weapon. "He comes to talk. All the while they are talking, they will not be attacking us. Let them talk."

The horse that approached them was thin, seemingly by its breeding rather than hunger, with ropey muscles and fierce eyes. Its bridle and saddle were decorated with elaborate tassels made of some plant fiber.

The rider was also thin and muscular, shorter than Teferi by a head. He was clothed only in a small loincloth, his dark skin burned almost the color of charcoal by the desert sun. He wore a headdress surrounded by a broken fan of red feathers, and many fine loops of gold wire around his neck, wrists, and ankles. His face, shoulders, back, and arms were covered by a tracery of rough, pinkish brown, scars, forming complex patterns and symbols in his flesh, some vaguely familiar to Anok, though he couldn't place them. The Kush warrior carried a light lance, a long, curved knife, nearly as large as a sword, hung from one side of saddle, and a painted wooden shield carved with a demonic face hung from the other.

The horse pulled up a spear's throw away from them. The man looked at them for a moment, then he smiled broadly. Anok was surprised to see that his upper teeth were filed to sharp points. "You speak Stygian?"

Havilah nodded. "We speak Stygian. What business have you with us, horseman?"

The sinister smile grew even wider. "You know our business, nomad. We are bandits! Give us all your goods, your weapons, your camels, your woman, and boys, and we leave you enough water to walk to the next oasis. Save yourselves."

Teferi leaned closer to Anok and whispered, *"He's fair. I'll give him that."*

Anok shushed him, lest Teferi accidentally provoke something.

Havilah grunted. "And if we lay down our weapons, what promise is there that you won't put that lance through our backs? I think probably you would."

The bandit chief laughed. "Perhaps I would, but it would be quicker for you then." The horse shuffled in place nervously, and his smile disappeared. "Choose your own way of dying, but die you shall." He slapped the side of the horse and rode back to his companions.

Teferi frowned. *"Now, can I kill him?"*

Havilah shook his head. "They have bowmen as well, shields and perhaps even a sorcerer to protect them from your arrows. Even if you kill their leader, you will only enrage the rest. Wait till they are close and make your arrows count."

Anok's eyes narrowed as he heard the mention of sorcery, but he said nothing. He remembered now the symbols carved into the Kush bandit's flesh. He had seen them in scrolls at the temple, among the most ancient Stygian texts. Teferi had long claimed that the people of Kush had been corrupted by ancient Stygian magic. It did not seem so implausible now.

Their chief rejoined the line of horses, but they did not charge.

Teferi scowled. "What are they waiting for?"

"For our fear to grow," said Havilah grimly.

"These are men used to being feared," said Anok. "I know their kind well."

"*We* will teach them fear," said Fallon, drawing her long sword.

Havilah chuckled. "I like your spirit, barbarian. You could have been one of my people."

"I hear you keep your women hobbled in tents. I will keep my tribe, desert man. Watch me, and know what your women could do, given half a chance!"

Havilah grunted skeptically, then flashed her a smile.

The horsemen began to ride.

"Here they come," said Havilah. "Make ready! Fight hard! Die well if you must!" He waved his scimitar in salute to his offspring. "You will live always in my hearts, my sons, as may I in yours!"

The raised their blades in answer, and rode into the charge. The others came after, Anok and Teferi struggling to stay on their rushing camels. Fallon stood in a half crouch on the platform of her white-furred beast, hanging on to the corner poles for support, sword in hand.

The horsemen charged on, and Anok's party looked straight down the muzzles of those lean, dark, horses. Then, suddenly, the charging horses veered off sharply to the left.

Havilah pulled the camels up short, and their party struggled to regroup. "We have been tricked!"

"Those devils," shouted Teferi, "they seek defenseless prey! After them!" Suddenly it was he leading the charge, urging his camel on ever faster.

Havilah rallied the rest after him. Anok following close behind the nomads, and Fallon and her white camel, the great creature not trained or saddled for speed, brought up the rear.

They watched in horror as the horsemen came to the edge of the dry pond and split into two groups, a smaller party leaping over the circled camels, while the rest circled, shooting arrows into the fray.

To their credit, the two servants were waiting, with swords drawn, standing between the two camel boys and danger. They engaged the horsemen with courage, if not much skill.

The merchants had blades, too, but they held them up weakly, cowered behind the camels, and waited to die.

Before the sons of Havilah could reach them, one of the servants had fallen, an arrow through his heart. One of the boys climbed up from behind him and picked up his bloodied sword.

Then the battle began, as Havilah's brood charged into the outer group, swords flashing in the sun.

Anok mustered his courage, not against their attackers, but against his mount. Now he had to trust the strange beast and what he had learned in less than two days.

He tightened his knee around the horn, made sure his foot was firmly locked under the other leg, then dropped the reins and drew both swords.

The Kush horses were skittish and easily spooked, but Anok's mount was well trained, and seemingly fearless. She roared as they rode in among the bandits. As he passed through the line, each bandit managed to deflect his blows, with swords or shields, but he broke their line and put them on the defensive.

He saw Fallon ride past, her camel practically stepping over the others. From the corner of his eye, he saw a Kushite horse rearing, rider preparing to stab with his lance, below him a boy holding the fallen servant's sword.

Fallon let go the corner posts and took up her long sword with two hands. She swung, *hard*, as she rode past.

For a moment, the white camel's body blocked his view, and when it passed, Anok saw the bandits severed head spinning through the air, the horse charging away as its headless rider slowly slumped from the saddle.

Anok heard rapid hoofbeats behind him and turned, barely deflecting the point of a lance past his head with his sword.

He answered with his other sword, catching the rider as he passed, opening a wide, red gash between the bandit's ribs.

Anok did not follow as his attacker rode away, but turned and headed back into the center of the fight.

The white camel was back in the middle of things, becoming a nearly stationary tower from which Fallon could fight. The bandits seemed not to want to harm the camel, probably because of its special value.

As he watched, Fallon reached down and grabbed the other camel boy by the wrist, tossing him onto the platform behind her. He crouched there, trying to stay away from her sword and the flying arrows.

He spotted Teferi nearby, kneeling behind his fallen camel, pulling off one arrow after another, keeping the horsemen on the defense. As long as they had their shields up, it was difficult for them to attack with their lances, costing them at least one advantage.

Anok slipped past one rider's lance and got close enough to sink his left blade into the bandit's heart. A spray of blood cascaded over Anok's arm, and he hissed with pain. It burned like fire where blood touched the Mark of Set.

"Blood is the food of dark sorcery," Ramsa Aál had once told him, *"and blood of the living heart is sweetest of all."* He felt the Mark of Set call to him, but still he resisted. He

remembered what had happened when he and Teferi had gone against the White Scorpions. He feared that the corruption of magic would betray him and have him slay his friends as well as his enemies.

Anok rode on, trying to hold the blade in his left hand and ignore the trembling that was working its way up to his elbow.

He turned and went at another horseman, but he was forced to pass on the right, and his left arm would not serve him. The blade thudded ineffectively against the bandit's wooden shield and fell from his hand. He cursed.

Another rider slipped up on him. He managed to fend off the point of his lance, but the horse bumped his camel and the rider's shield slammed into him, throwing him to the ground.

Anok scrambled to his feet, finding some cover behind a dead camel. There lay one of the merchants, dead across the fallen animal, an arrow protruding from his back.

A few paces beyond, he saw the other merchant, lying in a pool of blood from his own severed throat.

A few paces beyond that, he could see Moahavilah also to ground, an arrow through the flesh of his upper left arm. The young nomad reached down and with a roar broke the shaft off a finger's length from his bloodied robes, then kept on fighting.

Only Fallon still seemed to be on her camel now, and the horsemen took turns running circles around her, keeping just out of sword's reach.

We're losing! Anok realized that it was only a matter of time now. They were pinned down, outnumbered, and Teferi was down to using arrows pulled from the dead camels. They could never prevail by force alone.

He saw the lead bandit riding at him and started to raise his remaining sword in desperate defense. Then he thought better of it.

Anok stood, open and vulnerable, and planted his sword point first into the sand in front of him. He spread his arms wide, made eye contact with the bandit leader, and shouted, "truce!"

Among the defenders, all eyes turned to him.

But on the bandit captain rode, his lance pointed at Anok's heart.

His wrist burned and tingled, his fingers twitched uncontrollably, but Anok stood his ground. He waited for the point to pierce his chest.

The horse charged up, and just as it would have struck, the lance was lifted, the horse sliding to a stop just in front of him, swallowing them all in a cloud of dust.

When the dust settled, Anok was still standing, and the leader grinned down at him. He shouted a command in Kushite, and the riders fell back, circling at a safe distance from the defenders.

He looked down at Anok. "You wish to surrender, Stygian?"

"I wish to challenge. You and I, man-to-man. Our sides have both taken losses. Let it end here. If I fall, all I ask is that you give the others water and a head start. If you fall, your men will withdraw and trouble us no more."

The bandit chief stared at him for a minute, wide-eyed, then threw back his head and roared with laughter. He dug his heels into the horse, and it started to turn away. "Let us finish this!"

"Coward!" It was an act of desperation, but it seemed to work.

The leader hesitated, turned back.

"You heard me, coward! Let your men see that you are afraid to face one, lone, Stygian city man! You are old, and weak, and one day soon a true man of Kush will slit your throat as you sleep and rightfully take your place!"

His horse danced restlessly. The leader looked at him and sneered. Then he said, "I will fight you, but when you die, I will kill all, save the camels and the woman that I keep for myself."

"Good luck with the woman," muttered Anok, under his breath.

The bandit raised his eyebrows. "What did you say?"

"I said I will still fight you," he shouted back, retrieving his sword.

"Do not do this," shouted Havilah. "If you lose, you die for nothing, and if you win, they will never keep their word."

Anok spat on the ground and trudged forward. "But he will still be dead!"

The bandit leader trotted his horse fifty feet or so away then turned. Anok hoped that honor would force him to dismount, but he did not. Instead he raised his lance and heel-kicked his horse into a charge.

Anok stood his ground, feet apart, knees bent, ready to move in any direction. He faked to the right, and the lance point followed.

Then he dived left at the last minute, using the numbness in his left arm to his advantage as he rolled on it, unable to feel the pain, and landed on his feet as the horse thundered past.

The bandit immediately wheeled his horse around and charged again.

Anok feigned movement to the left, but the bandit captain was having none of it. Anok moved right, and the lance anticipated it. He ducked, but the point of it slashed across his arm, cutting a deep gash in his flesh and nearly knocking him off his feet.

He staggered, trying to fend off the pain. *I'm better than this!* Better yes, on a good day, with both swords and a left arm that obeyed his commands.

Again the charge. Anok tried to duck inside the lance and was successful, but the shaft knocked his sword back before it could find its target, and the horse's shoulder struck him, spinning him around so that his sword flew away, and he landed chest down in the dirt.

He tasted his own blood, felt ribs grating in his chest as he struggled to breathe.

He heard the bandit leader laughing as he circled back. "Pray to your god of snakes, Stygian! He will not help you now!"

Anok lay there, feeling the burning running up his left arm, like blood poisoning reaching for his heart, ancient voices whispering to him out of unseen mist.

The chief rode up, and his horse whinnied and reared.

He means to trample me to death!

For weeks on end, Anok Wati had struggled against the Mark of Set. Now he set it free.

Magic washed over him like a warm wave at the beach. Pain faded, as did the taunting cries of the bandits, the sound of their horses replaced by the rhythmic pounding of his own blood in his ears. His heart slowed, and he was gripped by a calm resolve, as hard and cold as iron.

Anok rolled over and held up his left hand, fingers cupped.

The horse towered over him, front legs pawing the air, sharp hooves ready to slam down on him.

"Away!"

The horse's eyes widened, the pawing of the legs now somehow desperate, and it staggered backward, then toppled, falling over.

With the skill of a master horseman, the bandit chief leapt from his saddle and dived to one side, barely avoiding being crushed by his own mount.

He came up quickly, his long, curved, knife in his hand, easily the equal of Anok's fallen sword. He smiled, and those sharpened bestial teeth glinted in the sun.

The bandit charged with a roar, great knife held high.

Anok saw his fallen blade in the sand a short distance behind his left foot. He held out his left hand at it. *"Sword!"*

As though pulled by invisible strings, the sword jumped from the sand and flew through the air toward Anok. But it did not come to his hand. It spun through the air, and he guided it with his gestures, sweeping it past him, so that it flashed past over the chieftain's head.

The bandit ran two more steps before he saw his hand, still holding his knife, fall in front of him.

The bandit stopped, screaming, and clutched at his spurting wrist with his remaining hand. He looked to Anok, eyes wide, searching for some sign of mercy.

The sword spun past the chief again, making him flinch. But it merely returned to Anok's hand, and he replaced it in its sheath on his back.

A look of relief crossed the bandit chief's agonized features.

Then Anok extended his hand toward him. *"Die!"*

The bandit's eyes went wide with agony, his mouth open in a gurgling scream, arms extended wide, his severed hand now of little consequence.

There was a wet crack, a liquid ripping sound like a small tree being uprooted in a swamp, and the chieftain's chest burst open, his still-beating heart flying to land with a *plop* in Anok's hand, where he crushed the life out of it before the bandit's dying eyes.

Then he threw the heart on the ground, stomped it beneath his sandal, and stood over the fallen body of the chief. He looked around at the horsemen, his bloodied hand extended, and roared, *"Who will be next!"*

The horsemen stopped; their horses bucking and rearing, they looked at each other, then turned and ran at full gallop.

"Run!" Anok screamed after them. *"Run, dogs, or I will rip your heads off and feed them to your necks!"*

And run they did, until nothing could be seen of them but fading clouds of dust.

Anok watched them go.

Then his legs began to tremble. He glanced down at the Mark of Set. There was more power there, much, but he had no strength left to wield it.

He staggered and fell to his knees.

"Anok!" He heard Teferi's deep voice, but he could not see from where. He could see the others though, Havilah, his sons, the camel boys, even Fallon, looking at him with shock—and fear.

"Anok!"

It is better this way. They will be spared—

His eyes grew dark, and he felt himself falling. He did not feel himself land.

10

ANOK WOKE TO see the sun, low and red in the sky. He was disoriented. It took him a while to realize that the sun was in the east and that he was looking at morning, not dusk, through the open flap of a tent.

Then he heard several unusual sounds. One, was a slow, irregular, clanking of stone against stone. The other was the sound of singing. He did not recognize the language, but it sounded as though a man was singing a prayer.

He pushed aside the blanket—already it was too hot for it—and found clean clothing in his bags. To his surprise, he moved easily and without pain. He took a moment to inspect his side, and his shoulder where he had been wounded, but they were already nearly healed. *How long have I slept?*

His dirty and torn clothing from the battle were there, too. He inspected them and found some of the blood not completely dry.

He inspected the mark on his wrist. There was no redness, no irritation, the skin around the mark of the serpent pink and healthy. Moreover, the mark itself seemed to have changed. It was still outlined in black, but the fine pattern of scales seemed filled with an iridescence that shimmered as it moved in the sunlight. It was a small difference, but he noticed.

Anok finished dressing, realizing as he did that he was parched and hungry. He stepped out of the tent and saw that they had moved from the site of the battle, though the surrounding hills and terrain seemed similar. Then a movement to the west caught his eye, and he saw many vultures circling near the horizon.

The surviving camels, including the white one, were tied up nearby. The rest of the tents were already taken down, assuming they had ever been set up. He followed the sound of the singing around the back of the tent and up a low rise, where he saw Havilah, Moahavilah, Teferi, and Fallon standing around a mound of stones that could only be a grave. Moahavilah was the one singing.

Three other mounds of stones were nearby, the last of which was still being added to by Havilah's two unwounded sons, the clanking of stones he had heard from the tent.

Anok started walking up to join them, but before he had gone far, Teferi spotted him and hurried down to meet him.

He took Anok by the arm, and steered him back toward the tent. "You should not be out, brother. You are injured and ill."

He shook off Teferi's hands. "I'm fine!" He pulled back his robe to show him the nearly healed shoulder.

Instead of being pleased, Teferi scowled. "Magic, I suppose."

Anok nodded. "The same thing happened when I brought down the White Scorpions, though you were in no shape afterward to notice. Unleashing the power of the mark seems to heal my wounds almost instantly."

"This will not sit well with the others. We pulled a piece of arrow from Moahavilah's shoulder as long as my hand, and he will be long in healing."

"What do you mean by that? Sit well with the others?"

Teferi leaned closer. "They fear you, Anok, now that they have seen with their own eyes what you can do. Even I fear you. I fear *for* you." He looked away at the vultures and shook his head sadly. "I have seen now, too, what I had only heard before as tales, my kinsmen corrupted by evil magic. There was no mercy in them, no honor; only cruelty and malice."

"They were men, Teferi. It takes no magic for men of any land or bloodline to be evil and cruel. It is only a wonder when they aren't."

"Before the Sikugiza, the dark time, our people lived in peace, with themselves and with their land. This is what has become of them, those who did not flee their land forever as my forefathers did." He looked at Anok. "Sorcery did this to them, brother. Now what is it doing to you?"

Anok found himself annoyed. "Nothing. Nothing is what it is doing. I'm learning to control it. I saved us all, yesterday, if you didn't notice." He nodded up the hill. "If I had only failed to hesitate, if I had acted sooner, I might have saved their lives."

Teferi only frowned and looked at the vultures.

"They didn't bury them?"

"We were battle-weary, and shorthanded, with our own dead to bury. Havilah said they deserved to be left for the vultures."

"You don't think so?"

"They were evil creatures who deserved to die, but they are also of my people."

Anok nodded and put his hand on Teferi's shoulder. "Come then. I will help you bury them, and to do whatever it is your people do for the dead."

Teferi smiled sadly and nodded. "Perhaps I have not lost my friend Anok to darkness. Not yet."

THAT NIGHT, ANOK sat alone at the fire. Teferi had been there for a while, but neither had been in a talkative mood, and Teferi had finally retired to their tent.

Anok wasn't sleepy, and he was having vague memories of dreams from the night before, troubling dreams, doubtless brought on by the Mark of Set.

Yet today, at last, he wasn't sorry he had the mark. Whatever he'd done, he had saved them all. Magic had won out when blade, skill, and muscle had failed him. Was that so bad?

If the others feared him, what of it? Back in Khemi, he had seen how a fearful reputation could be an effective tool. It had served the temple, it had kept the gang lords at bay, and it had even served Fallon, merely by her slight association with him. It could serve him as well. In fact, should it not serve him *first?*

He was alone, but it suited him. He poked at the fire, watched the dancing flames, and kept company with his own thoughts.

So lost was he that he did not hear Havilah's approach until the old nomad sat down on the stone next to him.

Anok glanced over at him. The old man looked into the fire, shadows dancing across his craggy face in the light of the flickering flames.

"Don't you fear me, as the others do?"

The old man did not turn to face him. His eyes did not move at all. But after a time he spoke. "I fear your power, yes. Only a fool would not. But I do not fear *you.*"

"Then you are wise. You and your sons are honorable and brave, and have served us well. I mean you no harm, and offer only my service and protection."

Havilah did glance at him finally, from the corner of his eye. "What you mean is of little consequence. Magic serves the passions of the heart more than the will of the mind."

Anok chuckled, that this old nomad should lecture him about sorcery. "What do you know about magic?"

Havilah looked insulted. "I have traveled the caravan roads of Stygia all my life. I have traveled with countless wizards, sorcerers, and priests. I have even escorted Thoth-Amon himself through the wilderness three times, once half-dead after an encounter with the barbarian king of Aquilonia. Though I pray each time that it will be the last, I have seen dark sorcery many times before yesterday."

Anok blinked in surprise. "Forgive my arrogance, then.

My father taught me to respect my elders. I shouldn't have forgotten that lesson."

Havilah smiled slightly. "You defer to your father's wisdom. That is not something one often hears from a sorcerer, much less a priest of Set."

"I'm only an acolyte, not a priest, and barely more than a novice at that."

"But you have power."

"That I do."

"Then you must know that in the Cult of Set, that is a better coin than gold and even more tempting to those who would steal it."

"What do you care? And you still haven't told me why you don't fear me. You have experience, yes, but I would think it would make a reasonable man *more* fearful of magic, not less."

He chuckled. "True. Why do you think I was so angry at Moahavilah for offering you passage with us? But as I said, magic serves the heart, and your heart is true. For now."

"What does that mean?"

"I come to offer you advice, because I feel I owe you a debt. I have taken countless seekers of knowledge to Kheshatta, some, powerful wizards like Thoth-Amon, others, eager students of learning, seeking only pure knowledge for its own sake. And many of these same travelers I later take away. I warn you, that none come back the better. Some return mad, some are corrupted by forbidden knowledge, some consumed by blind lust for power."

Not I! But Anok said nothing.

"Your pure heart will not serve you there, for in each man there are the innate seeds of evil. We are flawed by our nature, and your goodness will be undone."

"If you think me doomed, then why bother to tell me this?"

He smiled sadly. "I could tell you to turn back, to stay at the oasis tomorrow, and return to Khemi on the next caravan, but you would not. I know that. But you are different from any other seeker I have seen in my long years, and so perhaps your fate may be different. I only tell you this: Seek only power, and it will be your ruin. Seek only knowledge, and it will be your ruin. Seek first redemption, and perhaps you will not be consumed by the first two." His eyes narrowed as he watched Anok.

"When I said 'redemption,' you touched that ring."

Anok looked down, startled, realizing that he was unconsciously turning the silver ring Sheriti had given him.

"Do you know what it is?"

"A man at the marketplace said it was a carving of a demon worshiped by some"—he glanced at Havilah in realization—"nomads."

"It is Jani, and indeed, he has his cult among our people. We believe he is more than a demon but less than a god. A spirit of the desert, who travels the sands by riding the whirlwind. He is many things, Jani, but he is best known for rescuing fools from peril."

"Fools?"

Havilah smiled. "We are all fools, in our own way, especially in matters of the heart. Who has not been blinded by love, driven helplessly by anger, or misled by pride? Yet fools often survive their foolishness. We are more aware of this in the desert, where even a simple mistake can kill, and so we see Jani where city men may see only chance. Yet Jani is everywhere. Did he not lead you, an unbeliever, to this ring?"

"It was a gift, from someone important to me."

"It is written, an honest man is not honest for himself, he is honest for others. Did your father give you this ring?"

He shook his head. "A woman, dead now."

Havilah's eyes were sad and knowing. He nodded, clearly a man who had known grief. "But she is with you still?"

Anok nodded. "Always."

"Then for *her,* save yourself." He stood. "Jani often saves those in peril, but he always fails those who come to depend on him. Ultimately, you must save yourself. That is all I have to say." He walked away into the night.

Anok turned the ring, and for a moment there was clarity. "Help me, Sheriti, to find my way through the wilderness."

But he knew she would not be enough.

11

BY RIDING LATE under a bright moon, they reached a large oasis the next evening and spent one day there watering and fattening the camels and tending the wounded.

Word was sent to the nearest garrison of the Stygian army, who would doubtless seek to hunt the bandits down. The caravan trade was the lifeblood of Stygia, and in turn, the Cult of Set. Perhaps the bandits would be caught and killed. Perhaps they would pull up their camps and return to Kush. Either way, they would be gone.

Moahavilah was doing well. Anok had learned that the bandits often poisoned their arrows or dipped them in dung to cause infection, but not this time, and the wound had been clean, without damaging anything vital. His arm would be sore and weak for some time, but he would recover.

More gratifying to see was the new respect with which Havilah and the older brothers now treated their youngest. As he watched them, Anok felt something so strange it took him a moment to recognize it.

Jealousy.

He would have given anything to have a living father,

even to be a least-favored son. He had lost so much when his father had been murdered. There had still been so much to learn. So many good days ahead of them. Stolen. Stolen from them both.

Leaving the oasis, they traveled for three more days. On the third day, the land began to change, with stretches of greenery along dry stream- and riverbeds that must occasionally flood. It was still hot and dry, but there were occasional farms, with herds of goats, camels, and skinny, humped cows.

Anok overheard Meshavilah, the eldest son, talking, and learned that they were nearing Kheshatta. They would not reach it by nightfall, but early the next day.

That afternoon, Fallon rode up next to him on her white camel. After the battle with the bandits, she had replaced her awkward sedan platform with a saddle taken from one of the fallen camels, and her riding skills were rapidly improving.

She pulled even with him and nodded in greeting.

Anok was surprised. They had barely spoken a word since the bandits, and he had wondered if she would ever speak with him again.

"I owe you an apology," she said.

"For being afraid of me?"

She squirmed in her saddle. "I am Cimmerian. We fear nothing."

A lie. But he remained silent.

"I *doubted* you."

He smiled a bit. "Do you believe in sorcery now?"

She smiled back. "There may be something to it. In fact, I wonder what I've gotten myself into, going to this city of sorcerers, or what I'll do when I get there. Just as like I'll pick the wrong pocket and end up being turned into a toad!"

"That is a danger," he agreed. "But that you had a patron."

She grinned. "Perhaps there is someone there who still has need of an old-fashioned sword." She reached over and brushed his arm, and he felt an electric tingle. "Or perhaps more *gentle* services."

Knowing her as he did, Anok could not help but laugh out

loud at the suggestion. "Don't jest with me, barbarian! Whatever else you may be, you're no whore!"

She smiled slyly. "But if one could be paid for services that one would render freely, then wouldn't one be a fool not to do so?"

He laughed again. Her straightforward manner had a way of brightening his dark moods. That gift wasn't something to be quickly forsaken.

"I'll tell you what. I've been given gold enough to rent a villa when we reach Kheshatta, and to pay Teferi as my bodyguard. It isn't much, but perhaps there is silver enough for two swords, and enough roof to go over your head as well. As for the rest—well—all else is negotiable." He chuckled.

"I'll give it some thought," she said.

Then, a moment later. "That's enough. Yes, you may have my sword—and my negotiables!"

THEY CAMPED ALONG a dry riverbed, where firewood was plentiful, and the sons of Havilah were able to water the camels merely by digging into the sandy river bottom until muddy water flowed in to fill the bottoms of the holes.

The mood, which had been somber since the bandits' raid, improved greatly. Havilah was talking of the camels he might purchase to replace those slain, and the songs around the fire were no longer merely prayers for the dead.

With the others so engaged, it was little trouble for Anok to slip away by himself. Well, almost.

He had no sooner walked down to the sandy banks of the dry river and sat down when he heard footsteps behind him.

"Is there a problem, brother?"

"No problem, Teferi. Merely delayed business to take care of." He frowned. "I don't think you'll like it though. It's magic."

"Are you ripping out hearts again tonight?" he asked dryly.

Anok chuckled. "Only very *small* magic tonight. I can wait till you leave."

Teferi considered for a moment, then shook his head. "If

I am to aid a sorcerer, I cannot continue to shy from such things. I will stay."

"Very well then."

Anok reached beneath his robe and removed a silk-wrapped bundle. He opened the silks to reveal a crystal sphere, glittering in the moonlight. "The mother of the smaller one you gave Rami," he explained.

He held the sphere in his hand, rubbing his left palm over the top of it. It was surprisingly warm to the touch, even in the chill of the desert night. It began to glow slightly, and there was a faint tinkling, like small bells. "Rami," he said, "I would speak with Rami."

The light of the crystal flickered and changed, and an image formed within the crystal, as though looking out from within a crystal sphere at some other place.

The crystal seemed to be resting on a wooden platform, perhaps a table. Around the sphere were coins, silver and gold. Beyond, Anok could see flickering candles burned quite low, and he could hear men's voices.

Then something clattered onto the table in front of the sphere with a clatter, tumbling and rolling till they came to a stop.

"Six," called Rami's voice, "I win!"

There were groans.

One of them was Teferi's. "Rami? You only said there would be magic. For magic I would stay. For Rami, I would have left."

Anok ignored him. He focused on the crystal and his eyes narrowed. "Rami! I told you not to gamble with the crystal sphere!"

There were gasps of surprise, but still nobody was visible.

"You didn't say it was magic," said a man's voice, "you just said it was *pretty!*"

He heard Rami sputtering, trying to think of something to say.

"You told us that ladies loved to touch it, and with it any woman could be won to our bed," said another voice. "But you didn't say it was *haunted!*"

A hand scooped up the crystal, and he saw Rami's face from below, looking elsewhere, a nervous smile on his face. "It's not haunted. It just talks sometimes. There's a nice little man inside. Say hello—*nice little man!*"

Anok was not feeling nice. *"Hear me! I am the sorcerer Anok Wati! This thief has stolen this orb from me, and he is cursed to die. All who do not wish to share his fate—flee!"*

There was a moment's silence, then he heard chairs toppling over, running footsteps, and men shouting. Then they were gone. He was looking up at Rami's face. He swiveled his head, looking around at the unseen room, and smiled down at the sphere. "Hey, that was a good scam! We could make a lot of—"

"We will not! I left this mystic orb with you so that we could talk at a distance. For no other reason. And I expect it to be *returned!*"

Rami laughed anxiously. "Well—sure." His smile faded, and he leaned forward so that his eye seemed to fill the entire crystal. "Where *are* you, anyway?"

"Outside of Kheshatta, five days' ride distant, which means you'll have five days to get your affairs in order if you lose this sphere!"

He coughed and nearly choked. "Hey, no, I wouldn't do that!" He leaned closer to the sphere again. "Kheshatta, huh? That's amazing. You sound like you're right here."

"Well, I didn't summon you to chat. Teferi told you I had a job for you."

"Yes, sure, but he didn't tell me what it was."

"He didn't know, and he didn't know what the sphere did either, or he probably wouldn't have carried it."

Rami grinned a little. "Playing a lot of tricks on people lately, aren't you, Anok?"

"Don't judge me, Rami! You of all people shouldn't judge me."

"Not judging, just saying: Who am I to criticize? I'm actually kind of proud of you."

Anok scowled. "Rami, I want you to keep an eye on Dejal for me while I'm gone."

"Dejal? He's at the Temple of Set. I can't get in there."

"You don't have to. The priest, Ramsa Aál, is sending him on some kind of mission. He'll be leaving the temple in the next day or two. Try to find out where he's going and if he brings anything back when he returns."

"What would he be bringing back?"

"I don't know. Maybe something big, maybe something small. Maybe a golden medallion, like the one those pirates had at the Great Marketplace."

Rami smiled. "Gold," he said, as though savoring the word.

"*Don't* steal it. Don't let him know you're watching him, and don't interfere with him unless I tell you to, do you understand?"

"Yes, yes, I understand. If I learn something, how do I tell you?"

"Go someplace quiet. Hold the sphere in your hand, focus your mind, such as it is, on it, and call my name until I answer. Really, all you have to do is *think* it very hard, but it's easier just to say it aloud. Understand?"

"Yes, yes. I'll go to the temple tomorrow and try to find somebody who knows something."

"I'll talk with you again in a few days. Just do what I told you!"

He waved his hand over the sphere, and the light faded. He wrapped it in its silks and hid it away again. He looked up to see Teferi staring at him. "What?"

"This is Rami we're talking about."

"Yes."

"I have heard an old Stygian poem. It goes something like this:

> *"Oh how I hate this wretched slave,*
> *I wish that I could sell him*
> *He never does just what I want*
> *But only what I tell him."*

12

ON THE COAST of Kush, there is a break in the coastal mountains, a gap like a broken tooth, through which the prevailing ocean winds, laden with clouds, can pass.

Along the coast there lie mangrove swamps and great, treacherous, salt marshes, where whole armies have vanished without a trace, where it is said the crocodiles are big as ocean ships, and unknown fevers can strip away a man's skin and turn his flesh to liquid in but a day.

Beyond this, the clouds give forth to support a strip of dark, forbidden rain forest that extends many days travel north and west into the interior of Kush.

Farther inland, the clouds grow thin and lean, but still sometimes offer their tears to the normally arid savanna below. When they do, the grasslands bloom, and the watering holes fill as nowhere else in that arid plain. Great and terrible beasts graze in herds beyond number, and are stalked by fearsome lions with teeth like swords. It is from this region that the famed Kushite warhorse hails, and where brave, or perhaps foolish, men perish by the score each day in pursuit of ivory.

By the time the ocean winds cross the border into Stygia, they have already given up most of their precious water, and were it not for an accident of nature, would do little to change its parched land.

But the city of Kheshatta is built in a basin, surrounded on the north and west by low mountains, which catch those winds from the distant ocean and wring from them every last drop of their remaining rain.

The rain gives life to the surrounding mountainsides, where the poisoners grow their special plants and lotus flowers, and great wizards build their castles, looming over the city. The water runs down to nourish Kheshatta, and to form Lake Nafrini, which bounds the east side of the city.

The basin is open to the south, which some call "the Mouth of the Winds." But while this opening is Kheshatta's blessing, it is also its curse. For centuries, raiders from Kush crossed into Stygia and sacked and looted the city, until finally a great wall was built, beginning in the mountains on the west and extending well into the waters of the lake on the west.

At last protected from peril, blessed with water amid the desert, located at the junction of many caravan roads, Kheshatta could have become a peaceful center of farming, trade, and culture.

Instead, the sorcerers came . . .

THE GATEWAY BETWEEN Kheshatta and the desert was a winding, sandy-bottomed canyon that had likely been the bed of some ancient river. At regular intervals along the high walls of the canyon, small, defensive towers stood, ready to rain down arrows upon raiders or bandits and to light signal fires to put the city's defenses on alert.

In this narrow passage, Anok could almost imagine himself back on the streets of Khemi, as a constant flow of caravan traffic wound through in both directions, with high stone walls surrounding them instead of buildings.

But the illusion did not last long, as the walls slanted

away, and the valley opened up, increasingly covered with low brush and other plant growth. Finally, they rounded a last bend and got their first, though limited, view of the city.

Only a slice of it could be seen trough a gap in the mountains, but it was enough to pique Anok's interest. In some ways, what he could see resembled the packed sprawl of Odji, but in general the buildings were taller, rarely less than two floors, and often four or five in the center of the city. There were also many grand buildings, temples, and towers, but unlike Khemi, where they were mostly concentrated in the walled Inner City, these were widely dispersed among smaller and lower buildings.

In the distance, he could see the wall defending the city's southern edge, an undulating affair that followed the contours of the land, broken occasionally by wide, squat towers that seemed to be fortresses in themselves, and broad enough so that war chariots could ride along its upper roadway.

But the most striking feature for the weary desert traveler was the lake that lay beyond the city, a broad expanse of shimmering silver reflecting the morning sun. The surface was dotted with small fishing boats and cargo vessels. The lake's boundaries could not be clearly seen from where they were, and it was easy to imagine it wandering away forever, curled between hills and mountain peaks. The sight of it filled him with longing. He wanted to run to it.

Havilah looked at him and grinned. He had doubtless seen that same expression on countless travelers' faces in his lifetime. "You think of swimming, perhaps? I would temper that thought if I were you. There are freshwater crocodiles, and catfish big enough to swallow a man whole." As they rode on, more of the lake came into view, including a tall, rocky spire of an island connected to the land by a narrow causeway. At the island's highest point, a tall, shimmering castle, seemingly made out of black glass, raised its sinister spires. "That," he said, "is the palace of Thoth-Amon. I do not know if he is there now or not. The Lord of the Black Ring is mysterious in his comings and goings, and for myself, I do not care to know."

"If he's not there," said Anok, dryly, "he soon will be."

Perhaps sensing something in the tone of Anok's voice, Havilah glanced at him curiously. "You do not think well of your cult's master?"

Anok said nothing. He suspected the old caravan leader understood more about his feelings for the cult than either of them was willing to discuss.

Before them, the valley widened out into an expanse of trees and dry grassland, bounded by fences, where camels, mules, and a few horses grazed. In the center of it all, a cluster of houses, barns, and large storage sheds bustled with activity, both animal and human.

"The camel station," explained Havilah. "This is where our journey ends. It is but a short distance to the city's edge, but as you can see, your journey may yet be some distance depending on your final destination. The Temple of Set is in the eastern part of the city, near the end of the causeway to Thoth-Amon's palace. Here you can arrange passage for yourself and your belongings into the city."

"It is early in the day," said Anok. "Perhaps we should walk and get to know the city."

Havilah shook his head. "This is not Khemi, where Set's power dominates all, and one who wears his robes is safe on any street. Set has enemies here, and there are places where one such as you should not go. Better to hire a cart and driver who knows the streets and can guide you safely through them."

Anok was surprised, but simply nodded. He had lived all his life under the shadow of the Great Temple of Set. To know that Set's hold could be so weak, especially within the borders of Stygia, was almost invigorating. The cult was powerful, but it was not *all*-powerful. Perhaps there was some small hope for his quest.

Havilah studied his expression, then laughed. "I sometimes forget! City dwellers think they know everything! That another city could be so different from their own—unless they have traveled, as we have, how could they know?" His expression turned more sympathetic. "I will find you a driver. Someone knowledgeable and trustworthy—as trustworthy as city men come, anyway!"

WHEN THEY ARRIVED at the camel station, workers appeared to unload and unsaddle the camels quickly and efficiently. Their belongings and cargo were taken to a holding area in one of the sheds, and the camels were led away to graze and water.

With just as little ceremony, a healer appeared to treat Moahavilah's wound.

Seeing his surprise, Havilah explained, "Despite the army patrols, there are many dangers along the caravan roads. It is not unusual for new arrivals to need the services of a healer." His eyes narrowed. "Are you sure you don't need to be looked at? You were much bloodied in the battle, and Fallon would hardly let anyone near you."

This last report surprised Anok.

Well, at least she only fears me when I'm awake.

Anok shook his head. "I heal quickly," he said, avoiding any further explanation. "So it's common for the wounded to arrive with the caravans? It's interesting that you didn't tell us this before we left. Or can we blame that on Moahavilah?"

Havilah grinned slyly. "In that, he has learned the lessons of his father well. Only a fool would think that travel is without peril—but if the fool has money, what am I to do?"

"Perhaps if we travel together again, I will not be such a fool."

Havilah reached out and clasped his shoulder. "May it be that we do. Consider well my counsel as you navigate this city." He pointed to the main building of the station. Around on the far side a line of wagons, carriages, and chariots waited. "Look for a red-painted wagon driven by a man named Barid. He will treat you fairly and guide you well. Farewell, and may Jani watch over you."

Anok grinned slightly. "I won't count on it."

As he walked to find the others, he considered the irony. Constantly befriended by gods he did not know or believe in and pledged to destroy the one he knew all too well.

He joined Teferi and Fallon, who were standing near the shed where their belongings had been stored. Teferi frowned at the shed. "They say our things are safe here, but I do not trust them."

"Well," said Anok, "we don't have to trust them much longer. I'm going right now to secure us a wagon into the city. I'll be back."

He turned and started to leave when Fallon reached out and touched his arm. He turned back. Her expression was sheepish. "There is a matter I would discuss with you." She looked away, as though her pride were wounded. "I need to borrow a bit of silver from you."

He found himself laughing. "Borrow? A few days ago, you were bragging how you had spent all your money. Why do you need money?"

"I wish to secure boarding for my camel."

"You're keeping the white camel? I was about to suggest that you sell it. It's apparently quite valuable, and what use do you have of it now that we're here?"

"I've grown . . . fond of the beast. We've known battle together. Am I to sell Fenola to some stranger who might work her to death or cut her up for skins?"

Anok couldn't help but grin. "You *named* the camel?"

She glared at him. "Please, do not make this any more difficult than it already is. Cimmerians are not in the habit of borrowing. We *take* what we want."

"Well," he said with mock seriousness, "we can't take that chance, can we? I'll give you an advance against the services of your sword, then." He reached into his bag and extracted five pieces of silver. He placed it in her palm, and as their skins touched, found he rather liked the idea of her being beholden to him. "Will this be enough?"

She looked at the coin. "For now."

"If you spend everything I pay you to feed this . . . creature, what will be left for yourself?"

She grinned slightly. "I am told that the calves of a white camel are highly prized for their strength and size, and if one of them should be white as well, even more fortune will smile on me. I expect I can make a profit over time."

He laughed. "You always find a way to turn things to your advantage, Fallon. Very well. Now let me get us a ride." He turned slightly, then hesitated, looking down at his nomad's robes. He scowled. "There's something I must do first, though."

THE CARRIAGE WAS small and solid, yet ornately painted, predominately in red, as Havilah had described it, but covered with lines and scrollwork in white, gold, and green. Anok had heard that the mixing of paints and pigments was yet another trade associated with poisoners, and this seemed to confirm it. The little vehicle had four spoked wheels, a low center floor with two inward-facing benches, and a box on the rear for cargo.

Barid was a small man, bald, his skin tan and smooth, though his beard was streaked with gray. He was tending the two mules that pulled his cart and looked up as Anok approached. He smiled, though there was an air of apprehension in it. "Good sir of Set, may I be of service?"

"My friends and I need passage into town and a guide as we seek lodging and come to know this place. Havilah sends his greetings."

The little man's dark eyes widened.

"Is there something wrong?"

Barid seemed hesitant to speak, and his expression was apologetic as he finally explained, "With pardons, sir, but while Havilah does business with everyone, as he must, he is no great lover of the Cult of Set."

"Well," said Anok, his hand unconsciously twisting the silver ring of Jani, "he seems to like me. Or have I been misinformed about the quality of your services?"

Barid glanced at the ring, then seemed to reassess Anok. "I see that you are an unusual man, for a follower of Set. My

friend Havilah knows that I have an interest in unusual people and their stories. It seems he has sent you to me as a favor. I would be honored to serve you." He looked around
Anok. "Where are these friends you speak of?"

"Back by the sheds with our belongings."

Barid gestured toward the carriage. "Then get in, please,
and we will fetch them."

Barid drove the chariot back to the sheds with the confidence of one who had done it many times before. He greeted
many of the workers and camel drivers with a smile and
wave and, following Anok's instructions, quickly found
Teferi and Fallon. He found a worker to load their belongings into the back.

Teferi watched closely, to be sure everything was put
aboard and nothing was pilfered in the process, then settled
into his seat as they got under way. "This is a strange city,"
he explained. "I think it wise to be suspicious." He glanced
toward Barid.

"Havilah vouches for him, and I trust Havilah." He
glanced at Fallon. "Is your camel taken care of?"

She frowned, and looked uncomfortable. "Yes, it is at-
tended to."

Anok smiled but said nothing more. *The barbarian heart
is not so hard as we have been told.*

The road into town was wide, well kept, and paved with
crushed stone. As they bounced along, Barid kept up a constant patter, explaining the general lay of the place, the wall,
the lake, the hills with their castles, farms, and great estates,
and the palace of Thoth-Amon. "You have never been to
Kheshatta before?"

Anok shook his head. "I've lived all my life in Khemi and
rarely ventured beyond its edge."

"Then there is something you must understand, especially with those robes you wear. Khemi is the center of
Set's power in Stygia, and Kheshatta is the ragged edge.
There are many factions here, many wizards, and many
gods. Your robe will not protect you in Kheshatta. In fact, in

the wrong neighborhood, it will make you a target for scorn, or worse."

"I thought Thoth-Amon held sway here."

Barid laughed. "That is a simple way of putting it. But yes, when he is here, which he frequently is not, his power is rarely disputed. But what power he enjoys over Kheshatta is granted to Thoth-Amon, the mighty sorcerer, not Thoth-Amon, the leader of your cult. Many things are respected in Kheshatta, wealth, power, and, above all, knowledge. But those fine robes will earn you nothing here that you do not earn yourself."

They passed along a street of strangely constructed buildings marked with many red-painted columns holding up tiered, gracefully curved tile roofs. The doorways and windows were marked with strange symbols and hidden behind ornate wooden screens carved of dark wood.

Anok caught a glimpse of one of the residents who, from the unusual tone of his skin and his narrow, strangely shaped eyes, Anok at first thought some sort of demon. A thin moustache hung from the corners of his mouth like the whiskers of a catfish, adding to his unworldly air, and his long silk robes with bell-shaped sleeves that hid the hands disguised even his human shape.

Barid laughed. "I see you have never seen a man of Khitan before. They come from the shores of the distant Eastern Ocean seeking magical herbs and objects of power. Though their appearance is strange to our eyes, they are men like any other. Still, you would be well to stay clear of them. They are followers of some nameless spider-god, and practice a deadly form of open-handed sorcery. They care little for Set or his followers."

They passed a company of foot soldiers marching toward the wall. Anok watched them pass, impressed with the precision of their march, something he'd rarely seen in the slave armies of Stygia. "Set seems to have many enemies here, yet from what I've heard, without the protection of these soldiers, the city is barely livable."

"Do you see any red sashes on the officers? These are not Stygian troops. They are a private army, paid for by the poisoners, the great sorcerers, and their ilk." He chuckled. "Doubtless you saw the many garrisons and troops along the caravan road. They protect the caravan trade, yes, but they also serve to ensure that the army of Kheshatta *remains* in Kheshatta!"

Anok nodded. "Then where could one such as I find lodging? I had hoped to rent a villa or house."

Barid glanced back. "You came to study, yes? The libraries and halls of antiquity are everywhere in Kheshatta, but there is a district near Set's temple where some of the finest are to be found. I know a man who owns several houses there. Perhaps one is vacant."

Anok opened his purse, took out a handful of coins, and handed the rest to Teferi. "Can you and Fallon see to securing us a place to stay? If this isn't enough, I'm to receive a stipend from the temple."

"That shouldn't be a problem," said Barid. "While Set's power here may not be absolute"—he grinned—"his credit is still quite good."

"Take me to the Temple of Set then. I should announce my arrival and speak with the priests. I know little enough about what they have in store for me here. Then take my friends to see after our housing."

"I'd sooner look for a place to drink," said Fallon. "It's been a long trek across the desert."

Anok smiled slightly. "First one, then the other. But be mindful, this may seem a holiday for you, but it is serious business for me."

Her expression became more serious, and she nodded.

He felt a little bad for that, but he was filled with uncertainty at the moment. As much as Ramsa Aál had seemed a constant threat back in Khemi, he had become used to dealing with the scheming Priest of Acolytes. The only certainty he had here was that things would be very different from his life at the old temple.

For a time, Anok wondered if they were going the right way. Kheshatta was a jumble, in more ways than one.

In the slums of Odji, where Anok had lived most of his young life, the people were jumbled, of many races and creeds, but the great majority of them were descended from slaves and had lived in Stygia for a very long time, adapting to Stygian ways of living.

For the most part, their dress, the construction and decoration of their homes and shops, all had been Stygian in fashion.

Here, the people all seemed to have just arrived by caravan from every corner of the world, each with their own food, their own style of dress, their own ways of building.

It was strange and exciting, but unsettling as well. Some deep part of him wished they would all conform, dress as Stygians dressed, and live as Stygians lived.

Is this my Stygian blood speaking? If so, I do not like it.

At last a great dome appeared, bulb-shaped and covered with gold, atop which a relatively humble (at least by the standards of the Great Temple of Set at Khemi) statue of Set looked down upon the surrounding city.

The temple itself was surrounded by a stout masonry wall and guarded by tall, slender towers, each topped with its own, smaller, golden dome.

They approached an arched gateway, flanked by open doors, stout and reinforced with iron bands. There were nearly a dozen heavily armed guardians of Set there, who eyed them suspiciously as they approached. Only when they had spotted Anok's acolyte robes and golden yoke did they relax their guard.

Anok jumped down onto the cobblestone street. He looked up at Barid. "I'll need you to come back for me later."

Barid nodded. "When they have concluded their business. I will wait for you here."

Anok watched as the carriage pulled away. Fallon turned and leaned over the back. "We'll save some wine for you!"

13

AS THE WAGON pulled away, Fallon waving like a fool, Anok frowned and glanced to see if the guards were paying any attention. The men were grinning, though their smiles vanished as soon as he looked at him.

Curse that woman! He liked Fallon, and part of him was glad of both her company and her sword, but he wondered if having her with him in Kheshatta was going to be more trouble than it was worth.

His was a mission of stealth and deception, neither of which seemed to be concepts she was much familiar with. Her clumsy attempt to pass herself off as a noblewoman had only lasted as long as her drunken unconsciousness. She was anything but inconspicuous.

Anok turned his attention to the waiting guardians of Set. He stepped up to the ranking man of the group, identifiable by the golden serpent pin on his sash. He was tall, dark-skinned, hook-nosed, obviously of relatively pure Stygian blood. Anok glared. "Haven't you ever seen a woman before?"

The officer looked at him uncertainly. "Rarely such as that one, acolyte."

Anok tried to look stern, but he was uncertain of his status here, both as a stranger to this temple and with the guardians. Technically, they were only answerable to the priests, but they all knew that his acolytes yoke marked him as one rising in the cult. If they angered a full acolyte today, it could well cause them trouble when and if that acolyte was advanced to priesthood.

"Well, there aren't many like her. She's a Cimmerian, a warrior born. She's my bodyguard, so see that you treat her with respect."

The officer nodded. "We meant no harm, acolyte."

He softened his expression. "I'm sure you didn't. She is striking, but be careful around her." He grinned. "Trust me, you never want to taste her sword."

The officer grinned back, "Certainly not, acolyte!"

"I'm just in from the Great Temple at Khemi, and I wish to announce myself to the priests."

"Welcome to Kheshatta, acolyte. Today is a day of study, so the priests are all over the compound, but they will be meeting with the High Priest in the audience chamber shortly. It's past the altar, to the left, and up the stairs. Shall I send one of my soldiers to guide you?"

"I'm sure I can find it. I'll speak well to them of your service."

"Thank you, acolyte. My name is Menmaat, if I may be of service."

Anok walked by, secretly pleased with his new air of authority. He was no longer a virtual prisoner within the temple but a force unto himself, with some small authority and freedom of movement.

As he passed through the gate, he felt a tingling in his left wrist, as though the Mark of Set somehow knew it was home. Unlike before, the sensation was neither painful nor uncomfortable.

In a way, it was almost pleasant. When he thought of it,

which he had to admit was not often, he was distressed at how comfortable he was becoming with the mark.

The courtyard of the temple was dominated, not by a statue of a great serpent as in Khemi, but by a great sundial, its brass upright in the shape of a rearing snake about to strike. Inlaid into the stone, strips and castings of metal marked a series of lines and circles around the upright. The hours of the day were clear to Anok, but the meaning of many of the lines and markings were unknown to him.

While the Great Temple of Set in Khemi was tall, deep, and relatively narrow, this temple was wide and, but for the great dome over its central chamber and the various smaller towers and domes projecting from its roof, no more than three or four stories tall. The wings had open galleries on every level, and he could see many doors within, suggesting that the wings were divided into numerous smaller rooms.

He passed through the main doors, flanked by a quartet of guards at attention, through the entry hall, on into the ceremonial chamber. He was immediately struck by its beauty. The inside of the dome was open, gilded with gold, then painted with great murals of Set battling and humbling other gods. A circle of small, arched windows under the rim of the dome admitted light to the room.

The altar itself was round and located under the center of the dome. A tall golden statue of Set, five times the height of a man, stood in the middle, flanked with rearward-facing snakes that leaned against his shoulders. Benches surrounded the altar in concentric circles and were spaced far enough apart so that worshipers could kneel and prostrate themselves before their snake-god.

He walked past the left side of the altar, down the aisle there, and through an arched doorway. To his left he immediately spotted a curving marble staircase and ascended to the next level. There he found a wide hallway with several doors. He had to stop a novice acolyte for directions to the proper room.

The chamber was round, with a high ceiling and a cupola ringed with windows to admit light and fresh air.

Most of the room was occupied by a large, circular table surrounded by two dozen straight-backed chairs. Four heavy tapestries hung around the room, red with gold symbols, one marked with the sun and the moon, one with a skull, one with a serpent curled around a staff. The final tapestry had two glyphs, one meaning "lead," the other "gold."

Near the head of the table, a lone priest tinkered with some unknown apparatus, an earthenware jar and some strange bits of metal.

The man was short, round of body and face, his skin pasty and nearly white beneath his dark beard. His robes and yoke marked him as a ranking priest, but the style was different than that used in Khemi, and Anok was unsure of their exact meaning.

The device on the table consisted of a large pottery jar, a lid with some kind of metal projections on the bottom, and a polished shaft connected to the lid by a flexible rope seemingly made of spun strands of copper. Anok had never seen anything like it before.

The priest glanced up at him, assessing his interest, then turned back to his work. Anok leaned closer to watch. "Master, my name is Anok Wati. I have just—"

The priest cut him off with a wave of his hand. "I'm busy here. If you're going to stay, make yourself useful." He picked up the brass rod and handed it to Anok. "Hold this."

The metal was cool in his hand. He turned it, looking at the curious metal braid connected to it.

As he was examining it, the priest dropped the lid onto the jar.

There was a cracking noise.

Something seemed to explode.

Anok suddenly found himself on the floor, his arm numb, his hand tingling and numb where he'd been holding the rod. He struggled to reach for his sword with the other hand, but he saw that the priest hadn't attacked him. In fact, he hardly seemed to notice Anok at all.

The priest carefully removed the lid from the jar and set it on the table. Only then did he look down at Anok. "You're still alive. Good."

Forgetting all protocol, Anok replied, "Your concern is touching."

The priest walked over and offered him a hand up.

After some hesitation, Anok took it.

"What was that?"

"Lightning in a jar!"

Anok staggered to his feet and shook his numb right hand. The tingling ran up his arm almost to his shoulder. "I've had some experience with lighting. It didn't hurt so badly last time."

The priest cocked his head. "Who did you say you were?"

"Anok Wati, sent from Khemi to continue my studies here."

The priest raised an eyebrow. "Ramsa Aál's pup." He reached out and grabbed Anok's left arm, pulling back the sleeve. "So it's true. The Mark of Set! Well, it didn't help you much against my lightning, did it?"

He pulled his hand back, using it to rub his numbed right hand. "Was that a test?"

"Not an intentional one, but it *was* interesting. If you plan to flourish at this temple, you'll learn that you need keen powers of observation. From observation comes knowledge, and knowledge is the most valuable commodity here in a city rich with valuable commodities."

"So what did you learn?"

"That power, even great power, is no certain shield against my lightning."

"Then if you can simply get your enemies to stand next to you and hold that rod, you can certainly administer them a powerful stinging."

The priest smirked. "This jar is little more than a toy, court magic of the sort used to impress kings and other fools. But if I could make one bigger, and learn to cast lightning as the clouds do, then I might have a useful weapon, one that could stand even against mighty sorcerers. As of yet, I do not know how to do this, but through trial and observation, I may yet learn."

Anok looked at the jar. "This is a curious kind of magic."

"In truth, I believe it is no magic at all, but an application of natural laws that we do not entirely understand. This is my special interest, the application of natural law to create devices of power, to use against sorcery, or more importantly, to *enhance* it."

Anok nodded appreciatively. "You know my name, but I do not know yours."

The priest raised an eyebrow. "I am Kaman Awi Urshé, your new High Priest."

Anok's eyes went wide. He'd made a terrible mistake. He immediately bowed and averted his eyes. "Master! Forgive me! I did not know!"

"Stand up! Stop making a fool of yourself! I am but a priest with a lofty title and little taste for ceremony."

Anok stood straight and met the High Priest's gaze. "I'm sorry, master. It's just that in Khemi, we rarely even saw the High Priest, and when we did—"

He waved his hand. "Yes, yes, I've been there. And the reason that you rarely see him is that he fears assassins. The High Priest of Khemi always has many enemies, many priests who covet his job. Doubtless, the High Priest there has lain awake many nights thinking troubled thoughts of your master, Ramsa Aál. But that is Khemi, seat of Set's power, and this is Kheshatta." He shrugged. "Few would covet my position, and there are really only two kinds of Set worshipers here, those who wish to stay for reasons unrelated to power and those who wish simply to leave. We will see which you turn out to be."

"I will try not to disappoint, master."

"And no more of this 'master' talk. I have a name. Use it."

Anok nodded. "Kaman Awi Urshé."

"Kaman Awi is fine." He gestured Anok toward a door at the rear of the room. "Come, let me show you what we do here."

Anok followed him through the door and out onto a balcony overlooking a large atrium. "Most of our priests and acolytes here are engaged in scholarly pursuits related to the study of natural law as well as magic.

"The wing to our left is where study is made of astrology, the sky, and weather. Those curious devices on the roof are used to take measurements and observations of the sun, moon, stars, and other celestial bodies.

"To the right we study alchemy and the secrets of earth, rock, and water.

"Across the courtyard our surgeons study the human anatomy, for purposes of healing, torture, and transformation." He smirked. "I assume it is located in the farthest wing so that we need not listen to the screams."

"I assume there is one more?"

Kaman Awi gave him a curious, sidelong glance. "What makes you think that?"

"There are four tapestries in the room, four sides to the courtyard, and you have mentioned only three bodies of study."

The High Priest grinned. "Very good. Yes, in the rooms below us some study of the poisoning arts takes place. The study is more limited, in that most knowledge of poisons is closely held by the poisoners themselves. We have attempted, with only limited success, to convince them to come here and join us in our pursuit of knowledge."

"Why not just buy the poisons you need?"

He chuckled. "Because my belief is that the greatest application of knowledge may be gained by the combination of various studies.

"For instance, my lightning jar combines knowledge of lightning gained by observation of the sky and the properties of metals and certain natural elixirs gained through alchemy. Neither alone is sufficient to bring it into being. If all four areas of knowledge could be combined, then forged together with our already great knowledge of sorcery, who knows what could be done?

"We could level mountains, humble armies, part oceans."

"And place Kheshatta firmly under the control of Set?"

The priest smirked again. "Perhaps, though that would be more difficult." He studied Anok for a moment.

"You have a quick and inquisitive mind, Anok Wati. I would be pleased if you were one of my students in the natural laws. But yours is another path, and such studies would be useless to you."

Anok was almost disappointed. Much as he was hoping for independence from the temple and the freedom of action that came with it, these "natural laws" interested him. "Why is that mast—"—he corrected himself—*"Kamin Awi?"*

"Such subtle studies are not in Ramsa Aál's plans for you. You carry the Mark of Set, and you are, to say it simply, a magical blunt instrument." His words had a certain tone of regret. "You are here to study the old texts for spells of great power, spells more suited to you abilities."

I will study the old texts, not to gain power, but to control what I already have. Anok felt no desire to learn more spells. He made little enough use of the ones he already knew and felt himself poor and weak in their application. The power that flowed through the Mark of Set was different, and his application of it seemed almost instinctive, in a way that was as much frightening as useful.

"How am I to find these texts? In Khemi, the temple had a great library, but I am told that here the libraries are scattered all over the city."

"We have a library here as well, and it is at your disposal, but the emphasis is again on the natural laws rather than pure sorcery. The scrolls and books you seek are mostly to be found elsewhere. Finding them is not easy, and interpreting those written in ancient and forgotten tongues even more difficult.

"Amahté Remmao, our Priest of Troves, will be here shortly, and I will make introductions. He will provide you with gold to live and to hire yourself a scholar."

"A scholar?"

"To guide you in finding texts and in reading them. It is a highly respected vocation in Kheshatta. They are as common and as valued as scribes. There are many, but you could be wise to find an exceptional one."

"Who is the best in the city?"

Kaman Awi roared with laughter. "There is one, but you will not be hiring him!"

Anok nodded. "I'm sure he demands more gold than I can afford, even with the temple's stipend."

"If it were only a matter of gold. The blind scholar Sabé cares little for the Cult of Set. If he could be bought so easily, I would have hired him myself."

"I can be persuasive," said Anok.

Kaman Awi chuckled. "I like you, Anok Wati! You do not shy from the limits of the possible!"

"I thought," he replied, "that was a sorcerer's job."

HIS PURSE FATTENED considerably, Anok found Teferi, along with Barid's carriage. Teferi seemed pleased with himself, having secured them a villa across the street from a large private library.

"You should see it! Shelves of books! Racks of scrolls that extend to the ceiling!"

"I don't suppose you know what's in any of them?"

Teferi looked surprised. "Does it matter? There are *many!*"

"Of course it matters. Knowledge is not measured by *weight*. If you wish to learn how to read and write, you'll discover that it matters greatly."

"Fear not," said Barid. "It is in a good district. Close to many libraries, and there are many friends of Set nearby."

This latter bit of news didn't exactly delight Anok, but perhaps it would be safer that way. He didn't want to spend all his time in Kheshatta fighting the enemies of Set, who might someday be his allies.

"How much is this fabulous villa costing me?"

"Fifty silver pieces a month. I talked him down."

"My brother would have taken forty," said Barid.

Anok's eyebrows raised. "Brother?"

Teferi looked annoyed. "Why didn't you tell me?"

Barid looked incredulous. "He's my *brother.* Besides, he was right there, listening!"

Anok cut them off. "Fortunately, the cult has been generous. Of course, I may have other need of my gold." He looked around the carriage. "Where's Fallon? Back at the villa?"

Teferi smirked. "She's gone to make the rounds of the nearby taverns. She promises to return with a full report, as well as food and drink for later. Should we go wait for her, or better yet, go join her?"

Anok shook his head. "Do as you wish, but I have other business to attend to."

Teferi's smile faded. "I'm here to be your bodyguard. My place is at your side."

"You act as though I need protecting."

The corner of Teferi's mouth twitched. "Who said I was protecting *you?*"

Anok couldn't help but grin. He turned back to Barid. "Do you know of a scholar named Sabé?"

Barid laughed.

Anok scowled at him. "Not you, too."

"He will not see you." He laughed at his own unintentional joke. "He sees no one, of course, he is blind. But he will not give you audience."

"He does not care for Set. So I have heard. So what if I simply do not tell him? He's blind. How will he know?"

"I have heard his senses are keen. He knows the cloth of Set's robes, the incense burned at his temples. He will *smell* Set upon you."

"Then I won't lie to him. I will persuade him."

Barid laughed again.

Anok was annoyed. "Do you know where he lives, or not?"

"Of course I do!"

"Then take me there."

Barid shrugged and urged his team onward.

They didn't have far to go. They traveled north a short

distance up a wide and busy avenue, then turned west onto a narrower street lined with a mix of businesses, small houses, and a few larger buildings that were probably libraries or museums.

"There!" Teferi pointed right, at a small, two-story, flat-topped masonry building surrounded by a low wall. "That's our villa!" He looked curiously at Barid. "I thought we were going to see this scholar, Sabé?"

Barid grinned. "We are. He lives very close. I told you it was a good area for your purposes."

They continued a block or so past the villa, turned right, then left in rapid succession and pulled up in front of a building set back from the street that looked somewhat run-down.

A man-high wall surrounded the building, but the gate was open, and a narrow flagstone path led up the door.

"This is it," said Barid, "But he will not talk to you."

"Wait here," said Anok. He climbed out of the carriage and walked up to the gate. It was open, but he hesitated, holding up his hand and slowly moving it across the opening. He could feel *something* magical there, not across the gate, but just within.

Carefully he stepped through and repeated the process. The narrow path was clear, but immediately to either side, he felt something invisible and dangerous. *So, this place is not so run-down and unprotected as it seems.*

He sensed that the small forecourt, the wall, the small windows in the front of the building, all were protected with powerful magical traps. He was certain that if a nonsorcerer stepped off that path, they would immediately be killed by some unspeakable magic.

Even great sorcerers would find themselves battling for their life. Perhaps a great sorcerer *would* have stepped off, just to test his abilities, but not Anok. He knew the one safe place was on the path, and he stayed there, wondering what to do next.

During his training at the temple in Khemi, there had been an exercise where the acolytes had been placed in a darkened room with an unknown threat, forced to use a sorcerer's innate sensitivity to magic to learn its nature. Perhaps he could do the same here.

He closed his eyes, trying to divine the nature of the unseen dangers.

Almost to his surprise, he was able to sense the size and shape of the nearest trap, a circle perhaps the width of his arm spread. He focused on that space and had a sense of a demon, but only a sense.

This is no complete spell, only the potential for one. He quickly realized that anyone entering the trap would complete the spell, summoning a demon, who would likely be ordered to attack them. The real brilliance of the scheme, he realized, was that it would be the intruder springing the trap, not the sorcerer who set it, who suffered the corruption and potential insanity that resulted from such a summoning. If the demon didn't kill them, they might end up insane anyway.

As he slowly made his way down the path, he continued to sense invisible danger all around. There were dozens of invisible traps, all different, summonings of demons, elementals, and beasts, spells that would enlarge and animate the common garden plants to attack an invader, curses of cold and fire, madness and fevers.

In a sense, this invisible garden of death was a sort of library itself, an amazing exhibit of dark knowledge, for those with the ability to appreciate it.

But the path itself was clear, and the door had no obvious protections. There was a kind of logic to it. An honest man approaching the front door was in no danger. Yet a thief, a prowler, a spy, would instantly suffer peril.

Finally, he reached the door. It was stout oak, with no window or peephole. An iron hammer hung from a leather cord, forming a knocker. He lifted the round head of the hammer and pounded it repeatedly against the door.

He waited.

Nothing. Again he tried pounding, longer and harder, but again there was no result.

He leaned forward and listened to the door. He heard nothing, and started to wonder if Sabé was even home. Yet some sense told him that the infamous scholar was there, simply avoiding him.

He pounded again. He yelled, "Sabé, are you there? I have need of a scholar." He listened again. Nothing. "I have gold. Price is no object!"

Again nothing. He had great confidence in his powers of persuasion, but they would do him no good unless he could talk with the man. He looked at the door. There was a metal lock of the type that opened with a key.

His intuition told him that any attempt to open it through magical means would trigger another of the deadly traps, but through his association with the little thief, Rami, Anok had picked up many useful skills. Though he lacked any special tools, he suspected he could open the lock with nothing more than the point of his dagger. In a city of sorcerers, would Sabé be expecting such a simple method of entry?

He ran his fingers over the cool metal. Anok was hoping that Sabé had overlooked the obvious, but was it possible that he was missing something obvious as well?

He grasped the handle, pushed the latch lever. There was a click, and the door opened.

Unlocked.

He swung the door open and stepped inside.

The interior of the house was dark. The windows were small, and all were curtained or shuttered. He saw a few candles, and there were lamp stanchions in the walls, but none was lit, and there was no smell to suggest that any of them had been lit in some time. Most of what he could see was illuminated by the light streaming through the open door.

There was no entry hall. The door opened directly into a large, central room that seemed to occupy a good portion of the building's floor space. There were desks and tables, all covered with scrolls and books, though he was uncertain how a blind man could read them. Also visible were hundreds of clay and stone tablets, stacked on stout wooden tables that seemed to have been made specifically to support their weight.

He glanced at one of them, finding it covered with unreadable symbols, both ancient and arcane. He ran his fingers over the clay, clearly feeling the impressions. It was at least clear how a blind scholar could read these ancient texts.

"It is Thurian," said an unseen voice, deep and resonant. "Or perhaps of an even more ancient race. Though the language is similar, the symbols themselves are unique and resemble the standard Thurian alphabet only slightly."

Out of the shadows stepped an old man, dressed in a tattered gray robe that seemed even more ancient than its wearer. A black cloth tie belted it at the waist, and the man wore no visible weapons. His face was narrow and angular, his nose thin and relatively flat. A fringe of unkempt gray hair surrounded the bald top of his head, but his silvery beard was neatly trimmed to a point. The most striking thing about him, however, was the band of gray cloth tied around his head, covering his eyes.

"Sabé! I'm sorry," said Anok. "The door was unlocked."

"Indeed it was. A locked door is a sure barrier against an honest man. You, sir, have given away your true nature."

Anok tensed as the man made a sudden gesture with his hands. There was a flash of light, as if someone had thrown open all the curtains at once. Anok had a brief sense of falling, as though a trapdoor beneath his feet had given way, but dropped him only a few inches.

He blinked. Suddenly he was somewhere else. It was light, and though he had a sense of being in a contained space, it was vast. He could see great pyramids and temples in the distance, peaked mountains that belched smoke and fire, and great beasts stranger even than the curiosities he'd seen brought back from the plains of Kush and the jungles of the Black Kingdoms.

He was standing on a plain, or perhaps a vast floor, as it was made of polished marble. The air was cool, and scented with banana and wildflowers. He was suddenly aware that he was not alone.

Sabé stood a dozen paces away, holding a polished wooden staff. The old man's clothing had changed, his robes were white and ornately trimmed in a style unknown to

Anok, but similar in some ways to the Khitans he had seen that morning. The man himself was different as well. His face was still old, though perhaps not so deeply lined, but now he carried himself with the strength and assurance of a young warrior.

His eyes were still covered, but by a band of hammered iron rather than of cloth. He seemed to be watching Anok, as though his vision was not impeded at all.

Anok was startled to discover that his own clothing had changed as well. He wore the simple leather sandals, silk kilt, and tunic that he had often worn in his days in Odji. His twin swords hung from his belt, rather than crossed over his back as he had taken to wearing since joining the Cult of Set.

He looked at Sabé, who seemed to be smiling at his confusion. "Where are we?"

"A place of memories and knowledge, intruder, where truths can be revealed and true strengths tested." He pulled apart the staff, revealing a long, curved sword hidden inside. "Enjoy its sights, as you will not be leaving alive!" He tossed aside the half of the staff that had formed the sheath and advanced with the blade held high.

Anok smoothly moved to a fighting stance and drew his own two blades. Even as he prepared for battle, his mind raced. He thought he knew what this was.

A war of souls!

He had seen several references to it in some of the ancient texts he had studied. It was the ultimate battle between two sorcerers, carried out on the plain of the mind rather than in the physical world. It was a direct test of mystic power, arcane knowledge, courage, and force of will.

He and Sabé circled each other warily.

"I did not come here to fight you."

"Of course not. You hoped I would be out, so that you could raid my stores of knowledge."

"I came to buy your knowledge, not to steal it."

"My knowledge is not for sale to Set, not at any price!" He swung the sword, and Anok blocked the blow with his own crossed swords. "You don't look like much of a wizard to me. Perhaps only a thief with aspirations to power, or acting in service of some hidden master."

"I serve no master but myself." But even as he said it, he thought of Parath, and wondered if that was a lie.

"I sense untruth. I *know* you serve Set! I smell his foul temple on you, hear the metal yoke of his service clanking around your neck! You are his puppet, come to torment me. Well, *it will not stand!*"

He spun, bringing the sword down on Anok with furious power.

Using both of his swords, Anok was able to deflect the blow, but the old man's sword was now changing, the narrow blade becoming a mighty greatsword, nearly as long as Anok was tall, its tapered blade cloaked in ghostly blue flame.

He wielded the mighty weapon with effortless ease, and it came down in a slashing blow.

Anok dived to one side, rolling quickly to his feet as the sword struck behind him, the ground shaking with the force of the blow, the gray marble split deeply by the blade.

He could not best this foe by force alone. *Think!*

"Where are those robes now? If I truly serve Set, then why do I not wear his colors in your arena of truth?"

Sabé seemed to hesitate a moment. "I do not know. Yet it matters little whom you serve. Your actions have made your intentions clear!" He cast aside the sword, picking up the rest of the staff, which, as he did, transformed into a spiked mace of iron.

The air whistled as he swung it over his head, and again Anok dived aside just in time. Even so, the force of the impact seemed to toss him like a rag, and he slid on his face across the floor. Stopping, he struggled to stand. He glanced over, seeing Sabé advancing on him, mace held high, its iron beginning to smolder and glow red-hot.

The old scholar had called this a place of memory and knowledge, and clearly everything he saw around him was taken from the old scholar's mind. His knowledge and experience must be vast, certainly far beyond young Anok's. How could he hope to survive, much less prevail?

Still on all fours, he scrambled aside just as the huge mace fell, the heat of it searing the hairs on body, stinging fragments of hot marble pelting his skin as the blast tossed him away.

Yet there had to be something Anok could bring to the battle from his own mind. *But what? There is no spell he does not know, no weapon he cannot best. What can I do?*

Call me!

The hissing voice startled him, seeming to come, as it did, from within his own head.

Call me and I will destroy him for you! Set my power free to smite our enemies! Call on me and I shall answer tenfold!

The Mark of Set! That was his only advantage! He could not match the old scholar for knowledge, and his will and courage had been the only things keeping him alive this far. But he could not win without power!

Let me crush him! Let me split his flesh and grind his bones! Set me free!

He raised his left hand and was startled to see his wrist, brown and bare of the mark. He blinked, hesitated. Though he could hear it, sense its power, knew that he could call that power to destroy Sabé, he hesitated. *I don't want to destroy him! I want his service, his friendship if it can be had!*

He closed his hand, clenched his fingers, curled the wrist back toward his body, struggling to control the power and push it back into its hiding place.

A wave of pain washed over him, deep, bone-cracking pain, which traveled up his left arm to his head, then back down to his feet. He gasped in agony, almost didn't see the mace swinging toward his belly.

He jumped, diving across the top of the weapon, but the force of it seemed to hit him like a wave and tossed him in a high arc through the air.

He landed on his feet, but his legs immediately gave way, and he rolled, head over heels, again and again and again, his vision fading, his ears ringing. He staggered to his feet and swayed like a drunk.

Still Sabé came at him

Free me! The voice was small and distant as though from the bottom of a well.

Anok tried not to listen, but it was so hard.

He turned to face Sabé, standing ground against his advance. "I do not wish to fight you, but I must survive. Thus I summon up that which has never failed me in the past."

Sabé laughed. "Bring on your foul power then, call up your demons and monsters. I know things that will make them all *tremble!*"

Then Sabé howled in pain, his eyes wide with shock, as a bloody arrow point sprouted from his shoulder like a spring blossom. He reached up, and with a roar pulled the arrow completely through his body. Still holding it in his hand, he turned to face his attacker.

Teferi stood, feet wide, wearing the lion-skin loincloth, feather headdress, and white war paint of his warrior ancestors, his mighty Stygian bow drawn and aimed at Sabé's heart.

"What am I doing here, Anok?"

Anok laughed. "I don't know if you are here, my old friend, but your memory lives in this place as if you were!"

Sabé tossed aside the arrow, and his robes changed shape into armor.

Teferi's arrow was loosed, too late, and clanked against the thick metal of Sabé's chest plate.

"This is not what I expected. I know not what Kushite demons you serve, but they will not stand before me!" He advanced toward Teferi.

Anok suddenly was aware of a bow in his own hands, an arrow with a flaming tip, nocked and ready. He aimed for the back of Sabé's neck, the join between armor and helmet, pulled smoothly, and let fly.

The arrow flew true, the tip splattering as it struck, spreading flame across Sabé's back.

He cried out in pain, then spun back toward Anok. "You strike me with fire, when I know that *dragons* once walked the earth?"

As he advanced, Sabé seemed to get bigger, his hands

turning to claws, his armor to shining scales trimmed with feathers, the ground shaking with each step of taloned feet. He roared like thunder, and mighty jaws in a head as big as a pony opened to swallow Anok whole.

Then something thundered between them, a flash of white and a glint of steel, and the dragon jerked back, a bloody slash across his face.

There was a whoop of triumph, as Fallon stood atop her galloping white camel, her sword held in both hands, turning for another attack.

Anok nocked another arrow, the point on this one heavy and barbed. His arms strained as he pulled the heavy bow and released. The string sang, and the arrow plunged into the dragon's neck.

Then a spear, its shaft carved with ornate Kushite symbols flew from Teferi's hand and plunged between the dragon's ribs.

An Aquilonian knight on horseback thudded by, his lance grazing across the Sabé-dragon's back. The knight turned and raised his visor, smiling at Anok.

His knees nearly gave way when he recognized his father's face. His father lowered the visor and turned for another charge.

Bring forth then! That was what he had. Family, friends, and allies. Far and near. Old and new. Living—and dead.

More camels came, Havilah and his three brave sons. Asrad, friend and Raven, who had been crushed by a wagon wheel on his sixteenth birthday. Rami appeared just long enough to throw his dagger at the dragon, turn, and run away in fear.

A tall, dark Stygian woman appeared holding a sword too large for her. She stood her ground before the beast. It turned to face another attacker, and she struck its tail, drawing blood before the tail swung and struck her down.

She turned into mist even as she fell, and only then did Anok realize who she was. A memory he didn't know he had.

Mother.

Before he could process that, thrown knives stuck the dragon's face, first one, then two, then four.

It roared, and the mighty tail swung again at their source.

The woman moved gracefully, like a dancer, stepping over the swinging appendage as effortlessly as a child jumping a rope. She tossed her blond hair and pulled more daggers from her belt, throwing them, one after the other.

Anok's breath caught in his chest. *Sheriti!*

The Sabé-dragon was surrounded by small attackers, like a bear besought by wasps, his size could not save him from their torment.

Anok took advantage of the distraction to recover his fallen swords. Careful to avoid the pounding tail, he leapt onto the beast's lower back and jammed the point of one blade in, using it as a handhold.

The dragon roared and spun.

Anok clung to the hilt of his sword, until another distraction stopped the spinning. Then he jammed his blade in even higher up the scaly spine.

Another roar, but now Anok had two handholds, and there was no dislodging him. Up he went, hand over hand, until he was able to drop down and straddle the man-beast's leathery neck. He pulled his blades free, and prepared to plunge them deep into the creature's spine.

"Enough!" The old man's voice was startling, coming as it did from the huge creature. "I yield! I see I have misjudged you!"

The bright world faded, and with it those who had come to aid Anok. At the corner of his eye, he saw his father riding away, his hand raised in salute. But it was Sheriti's eyes that he met, and watched her smile as she faded into the mists of memory.

Suddenly they were back in Sabé's study, standing exactly as they had before. Anok had the impression that only brief seconds might have passed.

The old scholar sagged, leaning his weight against the heavy table.

Anok was suddenly aware that there were tears streaking his cheeks.

"I sense," said Sabé, his voice weary and pained, "that we are both wounded by the battle. Yet in battle we are tested, and we learn much of ourselves and those around us."

"I should not have come here," said Anok.

"You came seeking knowledge, and I sense now your purpose is true. A dark sorcerer seeks only power, and in that plain of dreams stands alone, lest someone try to steal that power from him. He may summon slaves, beasts, demons, and lesser gods. But of friends—he has none."

Sabé staggered and started to fall.

Anok rushed to catch him. He took the old sorcerer's arm, surprisingly thin and frail beneath the long sleeve of his robe, and helped him to a nearby chair.

He stepped back and considered the old man. He seemed so weak and harmless. It was deceptive. "You could have killed me."

"Perhaps," he said without the least bit of pride. "We will never really know." He lifted his head, looking somewhat toward Anok, but now really blind again. "One should never seek a reason to kill a man. The reasons present themselves. One should seek a reason to spare him."

"I seek a scholar. I seek knowledge. I wear the robes of Set, but in my heart I seek to destroy him."

"Set has wronged you?"

"His followers have killed those most dear to me. Matters of my past are intertwined with secrets. I must learn the mysteries of his cult, and then destroy it."

"An impossible goal—and yet, a worthy one." He nodded. "I will aid you."

"I have gold."

He smiled slightly. "Then I will take it, for dragons are ever desirous of gold. But I would aid you were you but a pauper. My grudge against the snake-god is old and deep, and rarely, in my time, have true seekers crossed my threshold."

"When can we begin, then?"

He raised his hand weakly and waved Anok away. "I am tired. Return in the morning. We will speak further then."

The old man refused any more aid, so Anok left him there in his chair and closed the door behind him.

He found the carriage waiting. Teferi was stretched out across the back, snoring softly. Anok poked at his foot to get him out of the way.

Teferi snorted, blinked his eyes, and sat up. He looked strangely at Anok. "I just had the strangest dream."

Anok climbed in across from him. "I'm not surprised." He turned to Barid. "Take us to our villa." Then back to Teferi. "I hope Fallon has returned with refreshments. I could use strong drink, and lots of it."

He was silent for a minute, then he looked back at Teferi. "I was thinking about old friends, Teferi. When was the last time we talked about Asrad?"

14

THE VILLA REMINDED Anok a bit of his father's house in the Akhet district of Khemi. He suffered a pang of sadness as he made the comparison, but it also made him feel curiously at home in a way he'd not felt since leaving the Ravens' old Nest beneath the Paradise brothel.

It was a masonry building, flat-roofed and two stories tall. It was much smaller than his father's house, with fewer rooms, but there were similarities. Through the front door on the right side of the house, there was a small entry hall with stairs to the upper level. At the top, he could see part of a hall, with doors, where likely two or three sleeping rooms were located.

To his left was a large sitting room, with chairs, tables, and padded couches. Unlike his father's house, this room was not walled off in the rear to create the room that had been his father's study. Instead it was open from the front to the back of the house, where a row of tall doors stood open to a small but lush garden surrounded by a high wall.

He could see a wing projecting off the right rear of the building with a chimney, and wood was stacked near an outside door, likely a kitchen: there was a small structure against the back wall of the garden, probably a bathhouse. On the far side of the sitting room was another door, probably leading to the remaining sleeping room.

By the standards of Odji, it was a palace, though compared to the sorcerer's castles in the hills above, it was no more than a shack. By the overall standards of Kheshatta, it fell somewhere in the upper middle range of things.

It was not that Kheshatta seemed wealthier than Khemi, it was that the wealth seemed somewhat better distributed among the lower classes. There was little of the dismal poverty he had grown up with in Odji, and the class of truly wealthy seemed smaller. Money seemed to flow more freely here, perhaps because it was not the true path to power, and power was what people truly craved.

As they entered the sitting room, there was a sleepy yawn, and Anok saw a muscular but feminine arm stretch up over the back of a couch and wave. "I thought you would never get here," said Fallon, "so I started without you."

They walked around the couch to find Fallow stretched out on it. She sat up sleepily. "I had the strangest dream," she said.

"It seems," said Anok, "that everyone did."

In front of the couch an array of food bundles, loaves of bread, and jars had been spread. Anok's stomach reminded him at once that he hadn't eaten since breakfast.

Teferi went immediately for the beer jugs.

Seeing this, Fallon said, "I'll say this for Kheshatta, the beer is better than that swill they serve in Khemi."

Teferi looked at her like she was insane. "What's wrong with Khemi beer?"

"It's swill," she said, "I told you."

He filled a mug with the contents of one jar and looked skeptically at the amber fluid. "This looks like piss."

"It's good," she said, "drink it."

He continued to stare at her. "This isn't more of your barbarian humor, is it?"

"Oh, Crom!" She snatched the cup from his hand, took a quick sip, and handed it back to him.

He cautiously took a sip, tasted. "You're *sure* it isn't piss?"

She laughed. "Just because you don't have to strain it through your teeth? Who's the barbarian here?"

Anok poured a cup and tasted. It was similar to some of the inner city beers that had been served in the Great Temple of Set in Khemi, and he found it quite palatable.

He and Teferi had been friends for so long, shared so many things, it struck him as strange and a little sad. He realized that there were now many things that he and only he had experienced. There were things about Anok that Teferi not only wouldn't understand, they couldn't even talk about them. Time and circumstances were pushing him apart from his oldest and closest friend, and it suddenly made him feel very alone, even in friendly company.

Even now, the Mark of Set troubled him, as it had since the war of souls. It paced and growled in the back of his mind like a caged lion, but even more dangerous.

He chugged his cup, hoping to silence the danger within and succeeding only in nearly choking himself.

He hacked and coughed, and his companions looked at him with concern.

He wiped his mouth on his sleeve and, with effort, quieted his coughing. "I'm fine," he said.

But of course, he wasn't fine at all.

AFTER A NIGHT of dark and restless dreams, Anok awoke in one of the upstairs rooms of the villa, with little recollection of how he'd gotten there. He had some dim memory of staggering up the stairs with Teferi, but little beyond that. His head told him that the drinking had gone on for some time into the evening.

The room was comfortably, if not luxuriously, furnished, with a soft bed, a worktable, shelves, and a chest for storage.

His belongings were piled in the corner, and he decided he'd unpack later.

He met Teferi in the hallway, just emerging from his own room, and they found Fallon already awake downstairs, apparently having taken the large sleeping room there for her own.

She laughed at Teferi as he came down the stairs, bleary-eyed. "I thought you cared not for the beer of Kheshatta?"

He sat down, rubbing his head. "It has its charms. Gods if I can remember what they are this morning, though."

Anok poked through the remains of last night's food, looking for breakfast.

Teferi watched him, frowning. "How can you think of food?"

Anok picked up a bit of greasy sausage, which looked a bit more appetizing than nauseating, and wondered the same thing. He took a bite of the salty sausage, and Teferi turned his head away.

He glanced at his left wrist, where the Mark of Set tingled slightly. He had a feeling there was a connection. The mark had helped him to heal rapidly before. Perhaps it was helping to burn the drink from his veins as well.

"I go to see Sabé this morning and begin my work."

Teferi scowled, though it didn't seem to be about anything in particular, just the pounding in his head. "Shall I try to flag down a carriage?"

"There's no need. It isn't far, and I can find the way. There really isn't any need for you two to go with me, either."

Teferi glanced up. "We are here to be bodyguards, and I, for one, will act the part. We do not know this Sabé, or if he can be trusted, and the streets are full of danger."

"Perhaps you're right about the streets, but as for Sabé, I think I know him well enough now. Still, it might be good for him to meet you, should I ever need to send one of you to him on an errand."

"I will go, too, then," said Fallon. She grinned. "What else would I do but drink or get into trouble?"

"Knowing you," said Teferi, grinning back weakly, "little enough."

THEY FOUND THE curtains open at Sabé's house when they arrived, and the old scholar opened the door promptly when they knocked. He introduced Teferi and Fallon, and the old man greeted them cordially.

"I feel as if I know you both," he said, failing to elaborate. "I hope the room is bright enough," Sabé said, leading them into his cluttered study. "It has been some time since I've had guests."

"I'd think," said Anok, "that a scholar of your reputation would have many callers seeking his services."

"There are callers," he said, "but as you experienced, not many make it past the door, or even to it. The secrets of the ancient tablets here I mostly keep to myself.

"None besides I can read them, and I do not write my translations down. Those few that I do share are greatly valued. I earn enough to take care of my humble needs, and the importance of my translations earns me the protection of the city's most powerful sorcerers. They all vie to seek my favor, for they know that any one of my tablets could change the balance of power in Kheshatta forever."

"Then," said Anok, "I am little different. I seek to study the ancient texts and learn powerful spells that I can use against the Cult of Set."

Sabé ran his fingers over one of the tablets, his fingertips scanning down the lines to read them. "Powerful magics I have plenty. But you must know by now that sorcery corrupts the user, brings him madness, and often escapes the wielder's control. The trick is to use the magic without doing more harm to yourself than your enemies.

"That is less of a care for villains who care not how their hearts are corrupted, but I know that your heart is good and that you would wish to keep it that way."

"I fear it is not so good as you say, anymore. I have seen and done things . . ." He faltered.

Sabé watched him patiently.

"In this guise of an acolyte Set, I cannot avoid magic. I must engage in it, for their purpose, or my own. I chose that it be my own, and if a price must be paid, so be it. I only wish that I never harm my friends or lead them to my corruption." His eyes narrowed, and he looked at Sabé. "Yet you must have *some* way, or you would not have agreed to consult with me."

"A man may use fire without being burned, or hold a sword without cutting his hand, but sorcery is not like that. Long have I searched out methods to wield it for good, without harm or consequence, but my success has been limited."

"Limited, but you have had *some* success. Is this how you were able to create the magical traps around the house?"

Sabé smiled and nodded, apparently impressed. "So you sensed their exact nature, did you?"

"That you had contrived them to visit their ill effects on the intruder who triggered them, yes. Can't this method be employed in other ways?"

"To attack your enemies? No. So far as I have learned, such trickery only works on defensive magic of the most passive nature. My recent studies have been working toward using the method to create a kind of mystic armor that would protect a sorcerer from magical attack as these traps protect my home."

"Then we will aid you in that task, if we can. If I am ever to stand against Set and his followers, I will face the wrath of terrible sorcerers, perhaps even the head of the cult, Thoth-Amon."

Sabé sneered at the mention of the name. "The Lord of the Black Ring. That foul wretch. Long I have wished for his downfall. Does he contaminate the clear waters of Lake Nafrini with his presence again?"

"Not now that I know of, but I have been told he will return here soon, and I may be given audience with him."

"I do not envy you in that, then. Know that he is the most evil and treacherous man in all of Hyboria." He raised his hand and waved it before Anok. "I sense that you have already learned to cloud aspects of your true nature. What I have seen of you is not all you are, but I have seen enough to trust you and your purpose.

"Know that Thoth-Amon will try to learn all your secrets, to peel you like a grape. You face a terrible danger in his presence."

Anok was a bit mystified by Sabé's statement. He had not consciously applied any spells of concealment to himself. Perhaps it was some doing of the Mark of Set. Did Sabé know he had it, or what it meant?

He almost said something, but hesitated. What purpose would be served by revealing himself? Perhaps Sabé would even judge him tainted by the mark and withdraw his offer of assistance. Better to wait.

"Then you must help me prepare for the meeting."

Sabé scowled. "It would be better to avoid it completely."

"I don't see how that is possible."

"You can run, as far and as fast as you can. Give up this foolish notion of defeating Set!"

Teferi was giving Anok that "I told you so" look.

"You said that you'd aid me. I thought you hated Set!"

"I hate the Cult of Set as much as anyone," Sabé fired back. "How do you think I ended up like this?" He pointed to the rags tied over his eyes. "But you are paying me to advise you, and I would be remiss if I did not try to talk you out of your obsession."

"And you have done so. Now that you've failed, can we move on?"

"Teferi, can you not talk sense into your friend?"

Teferi smiled slightly. "I have tried, elder."

"And you, Fallon? Can you not use your feminine wiles, or simply club him over the head, as barbarians are fond of doing?"

She smiled as well. "I have tried both. They provide amusement, but little result."

Sabé sighed. "So be it then. We will do what we can."

"Then you still think my quest is without hope?"

"Nothing is truly without hope for those who do not recognize the impossible, be they heroes—or fools."

15

WEEKS PASSED, AND Anok took up his studies. Yet Sabé soon complained about Anok's lack of focus. Anok's mind often wandered, and some days it seemed Teferi learned more than he did. Teferi had struck up a friendship with Sabé, and while he helped the old scholar with physical labors around his house, Sabé would repay him by teaching him to read, using the old texts. At least some were written in a form not unlike modern Stygian, but he taught him some of the old languages as well.

Anok occasionally found himself jealous. He had promised to teach Teferi to read, but little had come of it after they'd bought those scrolls in the Great Marketplace in Odji.

He also wished that Sabé was as forthcoming in sharing his knowledge with Anok. But the old scholar only read to him things that seemed more like riddles and pointless stories than instruction in sorcery. Anok had one day suggested that Sabé teach him how to read the texts directly, but Sabé had rebuffed him. "You are not ready for that. Power must not come too easily to a young sorcerer such as you. Terrible things come of it."

"You teach Teferi to read the old texts."

"And perhaps one day you will be able to avail yourself of his skills, though he has far to go. In any case, he is no sorcerer to use those texts himself, and he would no more knowingly pass to you knowledge that would do you harm than I. This is dangerous knowledge I share with you, Anok. Patience! You must absorb it in its own way, in its own time."

Yet comprehension was slow in coming, and often his thoughts drifted, thinking about the Parath, or his lost sister, or the secret plans of Ramsa Aál. One day, as Sabé read to him from an ancient tablet, his attention began to wander.

Sabé stopped his recitation in midsentence. "The texts of power are not for the inattentive and weak-minded! A poorly swung blade can slay its master as easily as its enemies. If you cannot devote yourself fully to the study, you should not study at all."

Anok did not handle his criticism well. "Am I paying you, or are you paying me, old man?"

Anok was sure that if Sabé's eyes had not been covered, he would have been glaring. "I take Set's gold because it suits, me, and I have chosen to instruct you for the same reason! I could cease instructing you just as easily. I have no need of your gold. I have secret stores I have not touched since before you were born. I am not your slave, your beast of burden, that you can whip me to do your bidding!"

Something in the tone of the old man's voice told him how far he had overstepped himself.

"Forgive me, Sabé. It is I who am burdened, by the secret of my past and the mysteries of my life. Though the destruction of Set is my means, it is answers I truly seek."

Sabé's frown softened. "There are no answers in destruction. Answers come"—he gestured at the tablets spread across his table—"from scholarship, study, and contemplation. Perhaps you have chosen the wrong road for yourself."

Anok shook his head. "That is not my way. I lived for years in the streets of the Odji slum, not as a mouse hiding in the shadows but as one who walked proudly through the middle of the street. If it was easier for trouble to find me, it was also easier for justice to be served. I once heard my father say, and I do not even remember the context, but I have never forgotten. He said, 'let the wicked come,' and I do."

Sabé leaned back against a marble column and sighed. "And if I am to understand, your father no longer lives. Make of that what you will. I hope, at least, that he died well."

Anok licked his lips. Had his father died well? There was no question of his mother, who had taken up arms in defense of her child. Yet even though Anok had watched his father die, the circumstances were less certain.

For what had his father died? For what had he lived? And what of the muddled legacy he had left for his son, the burden of the Scale of Set, the mystery of a sister he had never known?

His father had taught him everything, *meant* everything to him, yet it increasingly seemed he had never known the man at all. Did he truly serve Parath? Ibis? Even Set? Could Anok really be certain of anything?

Sabé seemed to read his silence. He tilted his head quizzically. "Tell me, young master, do you wish to unburden yourself of these secrets that trouble you so?"

Anok hesitated a moment. Nothing would be easier. He looked uneasily across the room at Teferi, who sat in the corner, staring intently at a scroll he could not yet read. *Lies kept,* he reflected bitterly, *ferment into poison. And the longer they were kept, the more poisonous they became.*

The one person he could trust, and he could not share his secrets with him, and Sabé, the one person he could share his secrets with, he was not sure he could trust. Still, there might be something to be gained, a way of slipping some secrets and still keeping their nature hidden.

"My secrets must remain my own for now. Perhaps someday I will share them, but not this day. But of mysteries, I will share one. My father once mentioned something, and I have always wondered what it meant." He paused, licking his dry lips. "Have you ever heard of the Scales of Set?"

Sabé frowned slightly. "Of course. They are mentioned

many places in the old texts, sometimes not always directly." He stepped down the table, sliding his fingers along the tops of the arrayed tablets as he did. He stopped on a polished slab of brown granite near the end. His fingers scanned over the text as he read. "And Lord Set had three coins of power, yet they were stolen before they could be fully spent."

"The Scales of Set aren't coins!"

Sabé turned toward him, and Anok instantly realized that he'd said too much.

"I don't think they're coins," he added quickly. "From the way my father spoke, that is." He didn't convince even himself.

But Sabé turned his focus back to the tablets. "It's a metaphor. Many of the old texts are full of such indirect statements, which is part of why so few can understand them even if they can decode their symbols. It is said that the three Scales gave Set dominion over all the snakes of the Earth, and all the cold-blooded things that crawl, and also those that worshiped such beasts. You see, the first beings to live in this world, be they men or not-men, worshiped only those things they could see: animals, mountains, rocks, storms, the sun above, moon, the stars in the night. Only later did gods come and seek to turn those first people to worship them."

Anok shook his head. "I thought that gods came before men, that they created men."

"As I said, these may not have been true men, in all detail of body and flesh, but believe what you will. I believe they were creatures not unlike us, in spirit if not in form, and they had no gods."

"What does this have to do with the Scales of Set?"

"Some tales said he forged them himself. Some say he found them. Some say he stole them. Some say that he and two other gods each forged one, and Set took all three for himself."

Anok considered that. Could the three gods be Set, his ancient enemy Ibis, and Parath?

Sabé continued. "But there were certainly three and three only, and Set wore them on a chain around his neck. Once he had taken dominion over those who worshiped snakes and serpents, Set became very powerful indeed, and the other gods were jealous, fearing he would use their power to take their worshipers as well. For in their hubris, the gods had commanded their followers to prostrate themselves before them, to crawl like Set's beast, and in so doing, had made them susceptible to his power. So they stole the Scales and squabbled over them endlessly. No god could ever hold on to more than one for long, and they were scattered to the corners of the world and lost." He let that hang for a while.

"But this was long ago, before men. Sometimes in the old the texts I find tales that one or another of the Scales has been found, but I suspect they be just rumors. Besides, individually, their power is limited, and two are no better than one. Only with all three can they offer power worthy of a god."

Three Scales to grant the power of a god, and Anok had held two of them in his hand. He wore one of them around his neck this very minute, hidden in its cold-iron disguise. He shivered.

Anok felt a need to distance himself from the subject. "My father was a trader and traveled through many lands in his youth. Perhaps he heard tales of them somewhere in his travels."

Sabé's mouth puckered, as though he had tasted something sour. "Perhaps," he said.

THOUGH ANOK HAD a great deal of freedom from the temple, he was not able to avoid it completely. On the second day of every week he was required to return to collect his stipend, and he was also expected to meet with Kaman Awi if the High Priest was present and available.

During his next few visits, Anok was able to anticipate times when the priest would be occupied with temple business. But he knew that tactic would eventually fail him, subjecting him to the priest's scrutiny, and so the trips put him in a foul mood.

On temple day it had become their custom that either Fallon or Teferi would be waiting to escort him when he awoke in the morning. But this second-day morning the villa was empty except for Anok.

He found Fallon's bed unslept in, suggesting that, as often had been the case of late, she'd drunk the night away at some tavern. Teferi was already up and gone.

He ate a hasty breakfast of fruit and bread before proceeding to the old scholar's home.

He let himself in and, hearing voices, moved quietly into the study. There he found Teferi helping Sabé sort though a large stack of tablets. The weight and bulk of the ancient texts made storing and dealing with them a constant chore. Teferi was happy to relieve the old man of this labor in exchange for his lessons.

As Anok watched unnoticed from just outside the room, Teferi paused to read some word aloud that Anok did not recognize.

Sabé smiled and nodded, directing him where to place the tablet.

With a grin, Teferi then read a word from another tablet, and the process repeated.

Anok wondered if Teferi had forgotten the day, and part of him was furious at the thought. Yet his friend was clearly enjoying himself, and Anok was reluctant to interrupt. His heart twisted with conflicting emotions, Anok quietly withdrew.

As Anok stepped through the yard and onto the street, the Mark of Set again troubled him. It seemed to whisper to him, bidding him return to Sabé's house, punish his disobedient friend, and wrest Sabé's secrets from him by force. He had vague visions of terrible and painful torments that it would visit upon Teferi and Sabé.

Anok growled at himself, lowered his head, and marched away from the house. Yet even as he walked, the Mark seemed to be trying to pull him back. Each step was an effort, and he felt as though he were walking uphill through soft sand.

He turned at the corner and headed in the direction of the

temple. It would have been simple enough to flag down one of the many carriages for hire that plied the streets, or to pay a street urchin to summon Barid, but he did neither.

Certainly, it would have been a safer way to travel the streets, but walking was a distraction from his dark thoughts. Waiting for Barid would have been even worse.

Still, it was not a fine day for walking, either. Across the tilted shallow basin that formed the central city, he could see the southern wall, and above it, dark clouds advanced, bringing moisture from the southwest.

Kheshatta was a vastly different city than Khemi. The scale of the better buildings was smaller and less oppressive, the styles more diverse. Rich apartments stood only blocks from the homes of the poor.

In truth, wealth had little meaning here. The only truly distinct class line was between wizards and poisoners, those who had mystical knowledge, and those who did not.

By that standard, Sabé was a very wealthy man here, but since he chose not to use his power, it was little apparent. *Is that my fate? To end up humble and alone with nothing but ancient texts for company? What good is power if it is not exercised? And if it is exercised, do I not deserve all the rewards it can give me? Yet here I am, trudging to my masters to beg for a handful of gold.*

So lost was Anok in his thoughts that he didn't notice the group of men walking toward him on the street until he slammed into one shoulder first.

The two rebounded from each other, and Anok was startled to find himself looking into the young face of one of the strange men Barid had identified as Khitans. The man's face was narrow and angular and clean-shaven, his cheekbones high, his eyes dark, narrow slits that angled softly.

Anok looked around. The man's three companions were also Khitan, all older, though still strong and dangerous-looking, if not particularly large in stature. One among them was older even than the rest, his short, black hair and waxed beard peppered with gray. By his carriage and look of calm authority, Anok took him for the leader of the group, yet he held himself back from the others, watching the scene intently.

The younger of the man's two companions regarded him with the sort of detached disgust that one might hold for an unpleasant insect discovered in one's bed. The face of the eldest remained impassive and unreadable. Only the man he'd run into showed something more: an obvious look of anger. "Are you blind, *snake-lover,* that you cannot make way for the servants of the Jade Spider?"

Anok stood his ground, but tried to keep his temper even. "I have no quarrel with you. Our meeting was an accident. Let it pass as such."

The man glared at him with his narrow, strangely shaped, eyes. "Snake-lover, our *quarrel* with you and your foul cult is that you breathe at all! Drop to your knees and beg forgiveness, and perhaps we will let you live!"

Despite his efforts at control Anok quietly seethed. He'd endured too much already this day to humor any strange fool. The men carried only small daggers, not proper weapons. Perhaps it was time that they learned what such weapons looked like.

He took a step back, and in one swift motion drew his swords from their scabbards on his back. As he held their polished steel before him, the reaction from the aggressor was not what he would have expected.

The young man laughed. "You draw steel against the servants of the Jade Spider? Your ignorance is appalling. I, Shi Bai-ling, will show you how foolish you are!"

The man suddenly struck a strange pose, feet apart; knees bent akimbo, arms and hands raised into a curious pose, his hands rigidly flat and open. It looked more like a dance than an attack.

Yet Barid had said something about their "open-hand sorcery," and the remembrance of that gave Anok a moment to prepare.

Abruptly, balls of glowing energy materialized under the Khitan's palms, and he moved, almost too fast for Anok's eyes to follow, launching that energy at his swords.

The blades were ripped from his hands, flying through the air behind him.

Instinctively his mind flashed on a *spell of summoning*. He reached out with his power, and before the swords could fall to the ground, he had them.

He felt them with his mind as they reversed their course and spun back toward him. He plucked them out of the air, letting their hilts slap into the palms of his hands, then returned them to their scabbards as quickly and cleanly as they had been drawn. "It is well I know your name now, Shi Bai-ling. My name is Anok Wati, son of Khemi, and I would not wish to strike down a man unless we had been properly introduced!"

Then he held up his own hands, ready to match sorcery with sorcery.

Bai-ling's smile faded as he realized he faced a more formidable adversary than he anticipated.

"I say again," said Anok, "I have no quarrel with you or your cult. Perhaps you should not be so quick to judge a man by his appearance." Anok noticed that Bai-ling's companions were standing back, and the eldest of them frowned with obvious disapproval.

"Then" said Bai-ling, "I'll judge you not by your appearance but your mettle!" His arm shot forward with blinding speed again.

Anok's defense against the attack was total reflex, there being no time to think. He placed his right hand out to deflect the attack, and Bai-ling's spell of force met one of his own.

The two energies met in the arm's length between their outstretched hands with a ringing crash. The force of the blow was so sudden and great, that Anok thought his arm might shatter. He gritted his teeth, pushing back against the attack, but they were deadlocked.

After several moments of struggle, Anok raised his right hand, tapping just the barest beginnings of the Mark of Set's power. He gestured with his right hand, adding that power to his spell.

Bai-ling was thrown backward into his companions'

arms, his spell shattered. He threw off his companions and was preparing to leap back toward Anok, when the eldest man laid a hand on his shoulder. Bai-ling hesitated, and the man leaned forward to whisper something into his ear.

Bai-ling frowned. He flinched, and seemed to draw his anger back into himself. "It is a lucky day for you, snake-lover! My master Dao-Shuang tells me that Thoth-Amon has returned to his castle on the lake. Though we have no love of your kind, and you have transgressed against us, even we would not make war with such a powerful sorcerer as he. By his shadow, even a gnat such as you can be spared!"

He stepped back, and three of the men walked around Anok and continued on their way. He turned to watch them go.

The eldest man, Dao-Shuang, lingered for a moment. "You must forgive my pupil. He is young, and brash. He has skill beyond his years and wisdom beneath them. Though our houses are enemies, I sense no malice in your actions, and it is written that while a man is always bound *to* his house, he is not always bound *by* it." He bowed slightly. "May we meet on better days." He walked past Anok and continued on his way.

Anok stood, his heart still pounding from the encounter, his arm still aching. Yet he stood most affected by the words, not the blows.

Was it true? Was Thoth-Amon even now in Kheshatta? Though his coming was expected, it was not welcome news. Ramsa Aál had promised he would have an audience with the great sorcerer, and he feared it was an audience he might not survive.

He continued on his way, and as he did, a warm, misty rain began to fall. He took no caution to protect himself from it, and considered again his encounter with the Khitans. Thinking back on it, the young aggressor Bai-ling had shown no signs of being a powerful sorcerer. Though his attack had been potentially devastating, its power has been in skill, stealth, and speed, not raw force.

Would that he had such skill. Again and again, Sabé had tried to teach him subtle magics, and always he had returned to the great spells of power. For all his knowledge, Sabé knew little of people, and for all his wisdom, he was not a great teacher.

Those were qualities he had admired in his father, and he had sensed those missing qualities in Dao-Shuang. Part of him wanted to throw off the yoke of Set, run after them, and beg Dao-Shuang to be his teacher.

If his life had been his own, he might have done so, but it was not. It was a mix of burdens, promises, debts, and lies. Often he had touched the medallion around his neck in remembrance of his father. Now he slammed his fist against it, as though to shatter it and make himself free.

He succeeded only in causing himself pain. The medallion was, of course, unharmed. He would not be rid of it that easily.

He might never be rid of it at all.

He thought back to when Kaman Awi had told him he was a "magical blunt instrument." It was true. He had power, but little skill, and the price of using that power was a piece of his own soul. He was like a muscular fool slinging a flail on the battlefield: a menace to everyone around him *and* himself.

That was not how Anok Wati of the Ravens had fought. It was not how his father had taught him to fight.

With swords, his strengths were speed, finesse, and misdirection, not power. Why could he not learn to use sorcery as he used a blade? If he could substitute skill for power, he might use less of it and thus avoid some of its ill effects.

It might be possible, but without teaching, without guidance, he would be like a man groping alone in the dark. He might eventually find what he was looking for, but doubtless he would fall many times before he did. Pray that a bottomless pit did not lie beneath one of those falls.

As he arrived at the temple gate, the day turned from bad to worse. The guardian officer stationed there recognized him, and told him he was to report to the chambers of Kaman Awi. Grimly, he asked for directions, and the guardian signaled one of his men and instructed him to escort Anok to his destination. He would be denied even the excuse of becoming lost or confused on the way.

The large oval room was located on the third floor, in a tower situated on a corner of the temple's inner courtyard. Though it was all one contiguous space, Anok did not see Kaman Awi as he was ushered in. The room was jammed with clutter: books, scrolls, mystic objects of every description, and others stranger still that he took to be instruments for the study of "natural law."

Only a few he recognized: a balance scale of the type sometimes used in markets to weigh gold and silver, though larger and of finer craftsmanship, sundials, knotted measuring ropes, notched measuring rods, plumb bobs, cups marked for measuring, and jars of unknown substances that might be related to alchemy.

Kaman Awi's lightning jar was there as well, sitting on a table, and Anok was careful to keep his distance from it.

Instead he picked up a polished cylinder of crystal and held it up, fascinated by the way it distorted anything viewed from it.

He was surprised when Kaman Awi appeared suddenly from behind a stack of books. "Curious, is it not? I feel there must be some use for its ability to bend the way things are seen, but what that might be has escaped me."

Anok quickly and carefully replaced the rod where he'd found it.

"I don't mind your curiosity, acolyte. I appreciate it. Though"—he gestured around the room—"in this place it can occasionally be"—he smiled slightly—"hazardous."

"I'm sorry, master."

"And I told you to call me Kaman Awi." He walked over and nudged the crystal rod with his fingertip. "Fortunately, you picked a most harmless object to examine. Still, I wonder. A crystal ball bends seeing as well. Could that relate to its ability to see mystically at a distance? I wonder if, at some level, magical law and natural law are intertwined. It's a subject for consideration, anyway."

"Indeed, it sounds interesting—Kaman Awi."

"There are other things of interest to me." His voice turned more serious. "I hear that you have persuaded the blind scholar Sabé to aid you in your studies."

There was little point in denying it. "This is true."

Kaman Awi's eyes narrowed. "For as long as I can remember, since I was but a young acolyte, the priests have coveted the old man's secrets. But he guards them jealously, and many sorcerers of great power vie for his favors. Indeed, even our master Thoth-Amon has on occasion benefited from those few trifles of knowledge the old man has chosen to release, and so we are forbidden to take action against him."

Anok listened with concern. "What action would you contemplate?"

Kaman Awi smiled just a little. "I venture that a few days with our scholars of anatomy would make him eager to share his secrets with us. But alas, Thoth-Amon does not agree, and so we have waited—until now." He leaned closer. "I don't know what you did to persuade him, but you have an opportunity. Perhaps he is finally ready to reveal his secrets. Perhaps in his old age, he seeks someone to pass them to."

He put his hand on Anok's forearm, and something about it made the hairs on the back of his neck stand up.

"You must do whatever it takes to gain the old man's favor, and whatever you learn from him, you must share at once. With me. *Only* with me."

"As you wish." He carefully pulled his arm away.

"Ramsa Aál tells me that you fear the power of the Mark of Set, that you hesitate to use it. Is this true?"

Anok licked his lips nervously. "There may be some truth to that. Great magic has its price, as you know."

"The so-called *corruption*, and madness. I understand your fear. I do. Madness is an infirmity of that which I value most, the mind. Long have I fought to keep my mind free of madness. Yet know that madness, at least in the long term, can be avoided by many. That you have been able to use great magic so far without madness, this is an encouraging sign."

"And what of corruption, master?"

The corner of Kaman Awi's mouth twisted up, and his eyes narrowed to slits. "What of it? This is something a sorcerer of Set should not fear. This *corruption* is nothing but a release from those *hobbles* that bind the mind of man, from those petty moral concerns meant only for lesser men than we." He looked at Anok, and the priest's stare, his eyes glinting darkly deep in his shadowed sockets, gave Anok chills. "Do not fear corruption, Anok Wati. *Embrace it.* It will set your mind free to do great things. Impossible things."

It was then that Anok fully understood that Kaman Awi had gone to the well of corruption and drunk deep and long. Only now did he see his true nature.

Such a man would not hesitate to kill, torture, or maim in pursuit of his treasured knowledge, and Anok now stood directly between Kaman Awi and something he wanted very, very, badly.

AS HE LEFT the temple, Anok found the whispering of the Mark of Set maddening. Was this the corruption he feared or the beginnings of madness? He couldn't be sure.

So intense was his distress, he found himself standing on a street corner just outside the temple slamming his wrist against the edge of a wall, again and again, until his wrist was bruised and swollen. Only then did the whispering fade to a distant murmur.

Upon returning to Sabé's home, Anok contrived to send Teferi and Fallon out to purchase food for them. He wanted to talk with the old scholar alone. He reported his conversation with Kaman Awi and expressed his concern over the twin threats of corruption and madness.

Sabé listened, then sat carefully in a chair to think. "Well it is that you are concerned about these things. This is the riddle of sorcery, to use it without its destroying the user. Yet sorcerers have their ways. It is why cults such as yours exist."

"But the cult exists to worship Set."

Sabé chuckled. "Set is real. Most of the gods worshiped

by men are real in some form, or so I believe. But what they are is perhaps beyond our understanding. Demons seeking to deceive humans for their own purposes perhaps, or powerful beings fallen from the celestial spheres. Perhaps there are gods. Who am I to say? But of cults and temples, though they may serve the purposes of gods, they are built by men with their own purposes in mind."

"I don't understand."

"As an acolyte, you have doubtless performed the rituals and chants of power for your masters."

"Of course. In my early days as an acolyte, we did little but."

"And as you did, you and your fellows visited some small measure of madness and corruption on yourselves, though you might not have known it. Such power flows to your masters, and it is you, their students, who bear the price."

Anok thought about it and realized that it was true, that it explained the strangeness he had felt in himself, and seen in the others, after these ceremonies. "Is that all acolytes are to them, food for their power?"

"And tell me, who does most of the common sorcery for the priests, those lesser spells needed every day around the temple?"

He saw what Sabé was getting at. "The acolytes. It's considered an honor to serve one's masters thusly and to have one's abilities judged."

"So they would have you believe, but as such, you acolytes are little more than useful slaves to them. A wise sorcerer seeks to possess most powerful magic, and yet, *not* to use it. He holds those magics in reserve until he has no choice but to use them, or until his purpose requires spells more powerful than his followers are capable of performing."

"A powerful sorcerer remains powerful by *not* using his magic?"

"No matter how great a warrior he is, a great general does not fight a war with his own sword."

"Sorcerers are not generals."

"Not precisely, no, but like generals, many have their foot soldiers."

Anok frowned. "Then what is a lone sorcerer, without followers or lackeys, to do?"

"There are other paths for restoration that can forestall the inevitable: rituals, meditation, and the healing of deep sleep, which can restore the mind. Yet sleep becomes difficult for powerful sorcerers, and it is said that some of the most powerful no longer sleep at all." He studied Anok's face and seemed to judge that it was time to offer some scrap of hope.

"You have no followers or lackey from whom to leech power, but you do have friends who may help restore you from its exercise. Choose where you use your magic wisely and hope your friends can bring you back from the edge of the pit."

It was Anok's turn to sigh.

Sabé smiled grimly. "You see what a difficult path you have put yourself on? With my knowledge, I venture that I could be among the most powerful sorcerers in Kheshatta, but I know too well what the use of that knowledge would do to me. No man exercises the power I hold and remains himself."

Sabé's wrinkled hands tightened into fists, like someone facing a terrible truth. "I value my sanity more than I value power. That is the difference between me and someone like Thoth-Amon. Each time he uses the great powers at his disposal, he risks everything, and he does it with abandon."

"That's all there is, then?"

Sabé's lips pressed together into a thin, bloodless, line. "With great magics, there are methods by which the sorcerer can choose their poison, trading madness for corruption, or corruption for madness. Thoth-Amon and his ilk, they embrace corruption as a virtue. You," he said grimly, "must decide which you will choose."

ONCE AGAIN, ANOK'S dreams were troubled.

He dreamed himself in the courtyard of the temple at Khe-shatta, talking with Ramsa Aál and Kaman Awi. Their words made no sense to him, but he was fascinated nonetheless.

Hearing a commotion, he turned to see Teferi and Fallon being dragged into the center of the courtyard, where a pair of altarlike platforms made of stone awaited them. They were tied to the platforms and called to Anok, but he could barely hear them.

Then Kaman Awi finally said something he could under-stand: "Here come the surgeons."

A line of priests marched single file from a doorway and proceeded toward his bound friends. They carried a terrify-ing assortment of instruments, saws on long poles, knives, metal-tipped prods, needle-sharp spikes, all polished and gleaming in the sun.

Ramsa Aál looked to Kaman Awi. "Do you think they will last long?"

Kaman Awi nodded. "Days. Their deaths will be long and terrible. Unless . . ." He turned to Anok. "You could kill them, acolyte."

Ramsa Aál nodded. "Use the Mark of Set. That is why I gave it to you."

Kaman Awi frowned. "He found it. It's his."

"It is, I suppose. It is on his wrist."

Anok rubbed at his wrist. "I don't want it," he said. "Take it back!"

Ramsa Aál smiled. "It's yours now. Oh, look, they're beginning!"

Anok turned to see the surgeons closing around his friends.

"Bring down the lightning," said Ramsa Aál. "I'd like to see that."

Teferi and Fallon began to scream in pain.

The Mark of Set seemed to come to life on his wrist. The head of it turned and spoke to him. "Let me bring down fire. It will be quick, and the surgeons will die, too!"

"We'll all die!" Ramsa Aál smiled broadly. "Yes! Kill us all! End our pain!"

The screaming grew louder, but somebody said his name in a surprisingly calm tone of voice.

The ground shook, and he saw a mountain looming over the city, a volcano with fire and smoke belching from its peak.

"Fire," said Kaman Awi, clutching at his arm. "Let it be fire!"

"Anok!" The voice was louder now, and he woke with a start, staring into the darkness. Something glowed with a dim, yellow light, and he looked for the source of it. He realized that the crystal ball on the table behind him was glowing.

"Anok, are you there?" The voice was coming from the crystal, and he realized that it was Rami.

He climbed out of bed, reached over to grab the crystal sphere, and sat back down on the blankets. He looked into the crystal and saw the face of the little thief dimly illuminated by a flickering candle. "Rami, I'm here. I was sleeping. You have news for me?"

"I wondered if you would answer. Talk quietly. I don't want to be discovered."

He immediately wondered where Rami was, but decided he would find out soon enough. "What have you found? Where is Dejal?"

"He is back in Khemi now. Several weeks ago he led a caravan with about thirty camels and went into the desert. With him were five other acolytes of Set. They had digging tools, supplies for a long stay, and arms. There were many laborers and guardians of Set who traveled with them. Today, they returned to the temple."

"Did they bring anything back with them?"

Rami smiled. "This is the part I knew you would want to hear. They had many heavy bundles, wrapped in cloth, and I could not tell what they were at first. But know I know. They unwrapped their bundles at their temple and began to assemble those parts into a whole."

"A whole *what*, Rami?"

"They brought back something amazing, the skeleton of a giant snake! It looked petrified, like it was made of stone!"

Anok blinked in surprise. *The bones of Parath?* It was Set who supposedly exiled the lost god to the desert. Why would followers of Set bring him back from that place? Then he started to wonder.

"Rami, how did you learn this? Do you have a spy inside the temple?"

His grin widened. "I'm a thief. How do you think I found out? I broke into the temple and saw it myself!"

"Rami," he said with growing alarm, "where are you *now?*"

"Still in the temple, deep in the air shafts, where none can hear, if you'll just keep your voice down! Do you want me to go back and see what Dejal is doing now?"

"No! You're in great danger! Didn't you see the skeletons?"

"I saw some bones, yes. It's a temple of sacrifice. You'd expect to see bones."

"How did you think they got in the air shafts, Rami?"

His expression turned puzzled. "I didn't think about that."

"Rami get out of there! Now!"

The image shifted, shaking wildly. Anok caught glimpses of Rami's face, his hands, and the dim outline of the air shaft as he moved along it. Then, abruptly, he stopped.

"I hear something."

"What?"

"A rustling noise ahead of me, like leather rubbing on stone."

The fingers of Set! The little albino snakes would eat him alive! "Rami! Turn around. Move away from the sound, as fast as you can! Your life depends on it!"

The image spun, then began to move again. "If you don't mind," Rami's voice was tinged with fear, "what is it that I'm running from? Not knowing makes just makes it worse."

"Small white snakes, thousands of them. They travel together, eat flesh, and they can strip the meat from your bones quicker than a man can finish a hard roll."

Rami coughed. "Maybe knowing wasn't such a good thing after all. If I keep moving like this, I'm going to give myself away, or be forced out into a room where I'll be discovered."

"If that's what you must do, do it. At least then there'll be some hope of escape. Perhaps I can talk to the priests through the crystal, come up with some story that will cause them to spare you."

Again, the movement stopped.

"What are you wanting for, Rami? Get going!"

"I heard them in front of me, Anok! I hear them, and there's no way out!"

Anok thought frantically. How could Rami save himself? He was suddenly aware that the Mark of Set was itching. He clawed at it with his fingernails, trying to keep his mind clear. "Which way is the sound louder?"

In the crystal, he saw Rami look one way, then the other, his eyes wide with fear. "In front of me," he said.

Anok put his hand over his father's medallion, which still hung around his neck. Even through the iron, he could sense the shape of the Scale of Set within. If only he were there, he could use it to command the little snakes away from Rami. But Rami was in Khemi, many days' travel away. If only he could travel as easily as his words, as easy as these images did.

"Anok! *What should I do!*"

The magically linked crystals somehow served as a conduit for those images, their words. Could they act as a conduit for magic as well?

"Anok! Help me! I hear them! They're *close!*"

If it were easy, sorcerers would do it all the time. To give one's minion a crystal through which he could cast one's spells from afar, it would be a very useful thing. So it was not easy, or he would have heard of it.

But that did not mean it was impossible.

The mark itched on his wrist, reminding him that he had at his disposal more power than most sorcerers could dream of.

"Anok!" Rami was practically sobbing. "I don't want to die!"

He knew too well, now, what the price of using that power could be. Yet unless he chose to act, Rami was doomed. The little thief had never been the truest of friends, but he had been an ally for many years. He did not deserve the fate he now faced. He wouldn't be facing it at all, were he not acting on Anok's instructions.

"Anok!"

"Rami, you must not panic. I want you to hold out the crystal toward the approaching snakes as soon as you can see them. Hold it out toward them, and *do not move!* Do you understand me?"

"I'm afraid!"

"Do what I tell you, Rami! *Do what I tell you!* It's your *only* chance to survive!"

"Yes. Yes. I'll do what you say."

"Are they close?"

"I can hear them, in the darkness. Very close!"

"Hold out the crystal!"

The image moved, then he could see little in the smooth surface but darkness.

But he could hear.

The dry, papery movement of countless scaly bodies, rubbing against each other and the ancient stone.

He could hear Rami, blubbering in fear, the image shaking with his hand.

Then he saw—something—a paleness in the dark.

A wave that came out of the darkness, a wave of moving white, countless squirming snakes, hungry for flesh.

Rami whimpered.

Anok clutched the medallion containing the Scale of Set, focusing on its power to command serpents, drawing upon it, letting it pass through himself, through the Mark of Set, and out through the crystal.

Nothing happened.

The snakes came ever closer.

He clutched the crystal tightly in his left hand, as though trying to crush it, focusing on the Mark of Set, letting its power flow.

The mark began to burn, but he ignored the pain.

The crystal began to glow more brightly in his hand, until the room became bright as daylight.

He could hear the Scale of Set ringing through his mystic senses. His arm trembled with strain as he held out the crystal.

More power!

He bit into his lower lip until he could taste his own coppery blood.

The ringing of the Scale screamed in his ears.

"Anok!"

His whole body shook with strain, his muscles knotted. He could feel power running from the medallion in his right hand, through his body, and through his right hand into the crystal.

It seemed as though he could feel every pace, every foot of distance between him and Rami, every mountain, every bush, every grain of sand. *So far!*

Still he strained, eyes clenched closed. He saw stars, flashes under his eyelids.

Even though it seemed hopeless, he fought on. Not since he had brought down lightning to destroy the lair of the White Scorpions had he tried so hard, and yet it didn't seem to be enough.

"Anok! Anok!"

Rami's voice seemed small, and far away.

"Anok, they've *stopped!*"

Anok opened his eyes.

His body seemed to unclench. He could feel the power flowing freely through him, like a rushing stream in its rocky course. He could feel the Mark of Set tingling. It almost seemed *happy* to have its power unleashed.

He felt drunk, giddy. He was sending his magic half a country away! What other sorcerer could do such a thing?

"Anok! What do I do now?"

He thrilled to the wonder of it. Magic at a distance!"

"Anok! *What do I do?*"

His voice came out in a growl. "Die for all I care!"

No! That *wasn't* what he wanted! He had done this thing for a *reason!*

"Move, if you value your life! Get yourself out of the temple while you still can!"

"They're still all around me!"

"Do what I tell you!"

Suddenly he sounded as afraid of Anok as he was of the snakes. "If you say so." There was a pause. "They're falling back in front of me! As I move toward them, them move away!"

"Of course they do. They *fear* my power!"

"Anok are you okay? You don't sound so good."

"I have *never* been better! Don't you feel the power in your hand? Power *I* have sent you! You are a fortunate individual, to serve me, Rami!"

"About this 'serving' business . . ."

Anok had a sudden moment of clarity and realized that these last few minutes, it had been the Mark of Set talking as much as he. "Rami, move faster! You have to get out of there fast. I don't know how much longer I can keep this up!"

"Anok? Is that you, old friend, old buddy?"

Sweat trickled down his forehead into his eyes. "Hurry!"

"I'm going as fast as I can!"

Anok found his heart pounding, and he gasped for breath. He had to keep the snakes at bay until Rami was safely out of the air shafts. "How much farther?"

"Not far. I don't see them in front of me anymore. I think they went into a side passage, but they're still behind me!"

"Hurry!" His head pounded with pain, and it was suddenly hard to breathe.

"I'm at the entrance! But I'll have to put the crystal in my pocket to grab the rope!"

"Then," said Anok, gasping, "I suggest you grab the rope first, put it in your pocket, then *jump* before they can get you!"

"Yes. Yes. I can do that."

The image shook, then suddenly shifted and went dark.

Rami leapt, but suddenly Anok was the one in free fall.

When Rami put the crystal in his pocket, it was as though the circuit had been broken.

The flow of power through Anok's body seemed suddenly to snap and reverse.

His body convulsed as the crystal went dark.

He fell forward, facefirst into his bed, unable to move, somehow oddly detached from his body.

He seemed to drift, up and away.

Dimly, he could hear Rami's voice. "Anok! Are you still there! Anok!"

But he was too far away to answer, and too numb to care. He watched his body from a distance, as his spirit seemed to drift away with the winds.

RAMI SLID DOWN the rope and landed lightly on all fours. He could barely see in the darkness, but he knew that only meant he could barely be seen by anyone else. His heart pounded as he listened for the snakes, but they seemed to have stayed within the confines of the air vent. *Anok had known all about the snakes. Why hadn't he warned him?*

Of course, he'd told Rami to stay away from the temple, but when he'd heard that Anok had penetrated into its deepest heart—all that treasure—how could he have thought Rami would *not* try to sneak in? *Seriously!*

Rami froze as he heard distant voices toward the front of the building. *Guardians!*

Keeping low, he ran away from the building, the soft leather slippers on his feet muffling his footsteps. He was fifty paces away from the building when he realized that the rope was still hanging there. If the guards didn't find it beforehand, it would surely be spotted at dawn.

Bel's elbows, what had he been thinking? They'd be looking for him, and he didn't dare try to leave the inner city until daylight.

He sighed and kept running. Nothing to be done about it

now. He left the plaza, turning onto a side street, then ducked into the nearest alley, following a route he'd carefully mapped that afternoon. He turned left into another alley, right into yet another, and promptly tripped over a rat.

The rat squealed and scuttled away. Rami fell and rolled, quickly jumping to his feet, but making too much noise in the process.

He ran some more, nearly crashed into a dead end.

I missed a turn!

He doubled back, eyes straining into the darkness, tracing the walls with his fingers, counting windows and doors. He found the right passage and ducked in, following a faint smell of rotting fruit and fish heads.

At the end of the passage he found his destination, a half-empty woodshed behind a food shop, most of its contents stacked toward the front. He carefully climbed over the piled wood and dropped into a recess on the back side.

A cat hissed at him, before running away. Rami crouched in the darkness and listened for pursuers.

He listened for a long time.

Finally, satisfied he was safe for the moment, he closed his eyes, took a deep breath, and let it out through his lips. He thought of those white snakes squirming toward him, like a wave of death riding up the beach.

Suddenly he felt weak and wobbly, his heart hammering, panting for breath. It suddenly struck him how close he'd been to death. Only a miracle had saved him. A miracle named Anok.

He thought of the crystal in his pocket. Anok would want to know he was alive. If he could send magic through the crystal, maybe he could send some kind of spell of concealment, keep him safe until Rami could escape the inner city.

Rami reached into his pocket, finding the cool, smooth, crystal. To his surprise, the crystal was dark. He rubbed it with his sleeve. "Anok," he said to it. "Anok, are you there?"

There was no answer. "Anok!"

Nothing.

Perhaps he'd stepped away for a moment.

Rami slid down to sit in the cold, packed dirt of the woodshed floor. He carefully balanced the crystal on a piece of firewood projecting in front of him.

He sat there, waiting for the crystal to light, for Anok's voice to speak to him.

At some point he started to doze.

He was still waiting when the first red light of dawn found the woodshed door.

16

ANOK STOOD IN the Sea of Sand like a statue, blowing sand drifting around his feet and legs. He stood unmoving, looking at the distant horizon, for what seemed like a thousand years.

Then there was a rustling, the dry, hollow sound of bone bumping against bone, and Parath slithered into his view. The dead skeleton seemed animated by fire, its empty ribs filled with flame that flowed up through its neck, and out its gaping mouth and the empty sockets of its eyes.

The snake crawled around him, the forward part of its body held up so that its skull was far higher than Anok's head. It seemed to be inspecting him.

Anok felt nervous, fearful, but he did not move. He was a statue, as immobile as Parath had once been.

Finally, Parath spoke. "You have gained power, Anok Wati. You have stolen Set's power, as I was sure you would. Yet you resist it. Why?"

He did not speak. He was a statue.

"If you are to use it in my service, you must make it part of you! You must embrace it! Why do you fight? Why do you resist? Why do you use your power only in service to your so-called friends? Why not use it in service to *yourself?*"

The skeletal snake crawled closer, its coils leaving curved tracks in the blowing sand. It lowered its head, until Anok looked directly into its open mouth and the flaming pits of its eyes.

"Do not deny you thirst for power! Do not deny that it excites you, that you glory in it! *All* men share this thirst! *All* men can be corrupted, even the most virtuous! Do not fear it! Power has chosen you! Make it *yours!*"

Parath seemed to fade into the blowing sand, and Anok stood there another hundred years, till the blowing sand crawled up his body and at last covered his eyes, plunging him into darkness.

THE DARKNESS TOOK some kind of form, some substance, and he was suddenly aware of it covering his face and mouth like a shroud. He felt a sudden panic and realized with some relief that the power of movement had returned to him.

He thrashed wildly, and cried out, trying to tear away the cocoon that trapped him.

There was light, and strong hands pushed him back into something soft.

"Teferi," said Fallon's voice, "I think the fever has broken."

He gasped for breath, reached out, and clutched her forearm so hard that she flinched. "How long?"

She looked down at him with a mixture of concern and surprise. "Four days and nights since the fever took you." She licked her lips. She looked tired, as though she hadn't slept in a long time. "The healers could not tell us what was wrong with you. We feared you might die."

Teferi entered the room, flashing Fallon a look of disapproval as he did. "She feared for you. I knew it was just a fever, no more."

His claim rang hollow, and Anok suspected that Teferi was only trying to protect him from the truth. He had nearly died, or so it had seemed to them.

Yet even as he thought it, he knew it wasn't true. There had never been any danger to his body. The Mark of Set would heal him from any sickness. Even now he could feel its power flowing up his arm. His deathlike sleep had been one of fatigue from the great magic required to save Rami, a time of recovery and restoration.

He blinked. If they only thought he'd suffered a fever, then they couldn't know that he'd talked to Rami, or what he'd done. After a moment's consideration, he decided to keep it that way.

What purpose could be served by sharing the information with them? Teferi would only worry, as he did about anything magical, and Anok didn't know what it all meant. Why had Ramsa Aál send Dejal to bring the bones of Parath in from the desert, and had Parath truly appeared to him in his dream?

Perhaps it was just that, a dream. Or perhaps, he thought grimly, it was the first crack in his sanity, the first sign that sorcery was leading him to madness.

He sat up, feeling rested, strong, and ravenously hungry. He didn't feel any less sane, or any more corrupt, though he wasn't sure he'd know if he were. Still, he'd had far worse hangovers. *This isn't so bad. Perhaps I shouldn't fear great magic if I can recover so easily.*

He stood, found his clothes, and started dressing.

Teferi watched him with alarm. "You should go back to bed! You were near death just hours ago!"

Anok glanced at him and grinned. "I thought you said I was fine, that only Fallon was concerned for my life?"

Teferi frowned. "Perhaps I was less than truthful. You should rest!"

Anok continued dressing, noticing that Fallon had been watching him appreciatively. He caught her gaze and smiled.

She looked—not embarrassed, Anok wasn't sure if her barbarian nature was capable of it—but as though she'd been caught picking fruit from the king's tree. But after a moment, she slyly smiled back. "I think he is truly feeling better, Teferi. Perhaps you should trust him in this."

Teferi sighed. "Fine then. Do you feel strong enough to go to a tavern for a meal? I can send for Barid's carriage."

He shook his head. "It isn't far. I can walk."

Teferi frowned, but said nothing.

"Teferi, truly you are the mother I never had."

Fallon laughed, and Teferi seethed at the jape.

Anok did not care.

ANOK ALSO WITHHELD the truth about his mysterious "fever" from Sabé, but the old scholar seemed skeptical about the story as he told it on his next visit. "I am glad to have you well again, though the nature of your illness still puzzles me."

Anok continued to be evasive. "Perhaps some bad stew was my undoing, or some sickness picked up in the street. I have heard that strange sicknesses travel here from the East, along the caravan road."

He nodded. "This is true, though the suddenness of your recovery is unusual in either case. Are you sure magic did not play some role in your return to strength?"

Anok shrugged, then remembered that the old man would have no way of sensing the gesture. "Who knows? My use of magic in the past has sometimes been unconscious and instinctive. Perhaps in my fever, I may have unknowingly caused some healing spell. In fact, that must be it. How else can my recovery be explained?"

Sabé still sounded unconvinced. "How indeed?"

He let the matter pass, and got back to the business at hand, carefully laying out a series of tablets on the table before him. "In that spirit, perhaps it is time that you learned those rituals of recovery and restoration that we discussed." He ran his fingers over the top of one of the tablets. "According to the writings of the ancient Atlantean sorcerer Neska, a sorcerer can cleanse themselves of corruption by—"

"Perhaps," interrupted Anok, "we could save that for another day. Right now, I am more interested in great spells of power, spells that can be used to battle a sorcerous foe. It is said that you know spells lost to time, that no sorcerer will expect, and few can resist."

Sabé frowned. "That was not our plan. You should learn the rituals of restoration first."

Anok laughed. "It isn't as though I plan to *use* the spells. At least, not yet, and not ever except in the most *dire* of circumstances."

"I don't know—"

"Sabé, I'm paying you to help me learn to fight the forces of Set. I would get to that business first!"

Sabé took a deep breath and let it out through his nose. After a moment, he began to stack the tablets he'd just spread on the table and replaced them with the contents of another stack. "Very well then. If you insist, let us consider the writings of Marti, hermit of Vendhyan . . ."

Feeling satisfied that he was in control of the situation, Anok couldn't help but smile, and was glad the old scholar could not see.

17

LIFE IN KHESHATTA fell into a kind of routine, one that left Anok increasingly isolated from his friends. Most mornings he rose early, ate a hasty breakfast, and made his way to Sabé's house, usually with either Fallon or Teferi as escort.

There, he would begin his tutelage in the arcane and ancient spells to which only Sabé was privy. Though Teferi would often remain through much of the day, Fallon was quick to leave once her escort duties were done.

Though Anok found himself wishing to spend more time with her, her restless barbarian blood bid her to wander. She spent her time exploring the streets and taverns of the wizard's city, tantalizing adventures for which Anok had no time. More than once she returned bloodied and bruised, always with a cruel grin of victory on her face.

Teferi, though he spent time in the taverns himself, had become fast friends with Sabé. Though there remained a strained formality between Sabé and Anok, no such barrier existed between the old scholar and the Kushite giant. Teferi was happy to spend his days running errands and assisting Sabé.

Perhaps most annoying to Anok were Teferi's long-delayed reading lessons. While Anok studied the ancient texts, struggling to extract from them some crumbs of power, Sabé patiently instructed Teferi in reading not only Stygian and Aquilonian, but the barest beginnings of the ancient languages on his tablets, a secret he had shared with no man, not even Anok.

So even as he was surrounded by others, Anok found himself increasingly alone with his own thoughts, and he found them poor company. The Mark of Set filled his dreams with disturbing visions of blood, sacrifice, and death; and as time passed, those images crept even into his waking thoughts unless he was eternally vigilant.

He shared his growing dread with no one and still kept his communication with Rami a secret. The dread it only added to the festering resentment he felt toward those around him.

Only occasionally did he have a moment of clarity, when he realized that his friends were ever true, and it was he who had parted from them, headed down some dark path from which there might be no return.

Once a week he returned to the temple to take his gold and consult with Kaman Awi. He saw the High Priest's true nature now, the corruption that rotted his soul. Despite his bumbling and cordial manner, the priest was utterly ruthless in his pursuit of power and knowledge. One had only to listen to the screams coming from the surgeons' chambers to be sure of that.

Two weeks passed before he was able to contact Rami again. Each night since awakening from his fever, in the privacy of his chambers, he took out the crystal and called to Rami, but there was no answer. He had begun to think that he had rescued the little thief from the temple's flesh-eating guardians only to have him fall into the hands of its human protectors. If so, without his intervention, Rami would be long dead.

So it came as a shock when, one night, Rami's face finally appeared in the depths of the crystal ball.

"Rami! Where have you been?"

"Forgiveness, Anok. After escaping those devil-snakes in the temple, I had a case of the shakes that wouldn't go away. So I went on a four-day bender, crawling through every pub between the harbor's edge and the walls of the inner city. And then—" Rami hesitated, his expression pained.

Anok frowned. "What happened, Rami?"

Rami swallowed. "I—lost the crystal. That is, it wasn't really *lost*. I just couldn't *find* it."

Anok groaned. "You *lost* the crystal of vision?"

"I couldn't *find* it. I retraced all my steps of course. But there were a *lot* of steps, and given that most of them were taverns and brothels, I couldn't help but *avail* myself a little along the way. Eventually I found the crystal in the head-dress of a whore near the Great Marketplace whom I had spent a very pleasant evening with the week before."

"I'm sure she was very special, Rami." His voice dripped with sarcasm.

"It was very memorable," Rami said earnestly. Then his expression turned to confusion. "If only I could remember it." He shrugged, as though the whole business were nothing. "In any case, I didn't stop watching Dejal for you, though I've kept my distance from the temple."

That, at least, was good news. "What word of him, then? Are you watching him now?"

"I would be, but he's gone."

"Gone?"

"Four days ago they brought a special wagon to the temple, one with many wheels, pulled by four horses, made to carry something long and narrow. It entered the temple, and emerged later with a large bundle on top, long and thicker than a man's body, but tapered like—"

"A giant snake!" *They've reassembled the bones of Parath!*

"Like a snake. Exactly."

"You say they've taken it somewhere?"

"They formed a caravan, this wagon, many camels, Dejal, that priest Ramsa Aál, and a bunch of his lackeys, and headed west on the road toward Kheshatta, toward you.

That's why I was trying so hard to contact you. The wagon will slow them down, but they could be there within a few days, I imagine."

Anok blinked in surprise. Ramsa Aál and Dejal were coming to Kheshatta, and they were bringing Parath with them! What could it possibly mean?

DESPERATE FOR INFORMATION, Anok planned his regular second-day trip to the temple in hopes of meeting with Kaman Awi, not avoiding him as usual. Clearly, the High Priest and his strange scholars of natural law were part of Ramsa Aál's plan, though Anok could not divine exactly how.

He awoke earlier than usual, but to his annoyance Teferi was again up already and missing, presumably gone to Sabé's house. It seemed he could hardly wait for dawn to begin his studies with the blind scholar.

Fallon's room was empty, and though it was difficult to tell, as she never made her bed, Anok suspected it was unslept in.

He stuffed a bag with bread and dates to eat on the way, then headed out the door. Halfway down the walk, he met Fallon, who staggered into him, singing some song, off-key and in Cimmerian. She draped her arms around his neck and hung on him, her breath strong with drink. She grinned. "Anok! What are *you* doing here?"

He frowned at her. "I live here."

She looked around. "So do I!"

"Where have you been all night?"

She looked surprised. "Where I am *every* night! Out getting *information!*"

"Is that what they call it now?"

She pouted at him. "No! No! I talk to people! I *know* things!"

"What things?"

She frowned. "Well, just tonight I heard *two* important things! *Two!*" She hung limply onto his neck, and her eyes seemed to glaze over.

"Fallon?"

She started, blinking at him. "Anok! Wati!" She giggled. "Wati, Wati, Wati!"

"You said you knew important things."

She held up three fingers in front of his face. "*Two* important things!" Her eyes glazed over again.

"Fallon! What things?"

She frowned, trying to remember. "This thing. I heard. It could be important!" She frowned, struggling. Then she grinned. "Spiders are poison!" She giggled and slumped into him. "You feel nice," she murmured.

"That was very useful, Fallon. And what was the other very important thing you had to tell me?"

She looked up at him, serious. "Wait. I remember this one. Somebody is here."

"Who is here?"

She looked at him seriously, then cracked into giggles. "Somebody!" She continued giggling.

"I have to go to the temple."

She blinked, her expression turning serious. She pushed herself away from him, swaying unsteadily. "Wait! I'll go with you!" She pointed at the front door of the villa. "Let me get my sword."

He frowned. "You're *wearing* it, Fallon."

She looked surprised, then glanced down at her sword belt in shock. "Where did that come from?" She looked up at him and started laughing again. She staggered back against him and began clumsily groping him. "Stay here!" She laughed. "I am *so* drunk!"

He pushed her away. "Go fall down, Fallon." He walked toward the street.

She watched him go, a look of confusion on her face. Then she nodded and pointed at the house. "I'm going to go fall down." Then, as though noticing it for the first time, "I am *so* drunk!"

As he walked away, he wondered, in those last words had he heard a tinge of sadness in her voice?

His mood had improved little by the time he reached the

Temple of Set, wet and chilled. Menmaat, the guardian officer he'd met upon first arriving at the temple was there. He greeted Anok pleasantly, but Anok responded only with a glaring glance and a grunt.

"Anok!"

He looked up at the sound of his name and blinked in surprise. He had been hoping to meet Kaman Awi. He hadn't expected the High Priest to be waiting outside the temple for him.

The priest stood in front of a line of five golden chariots pulled by white Stygian warhorses, fierce, proud beasts freshly groomed. Elaborate banners of Set flew from staffs on each chariot, and each was driven by a guardian officer in light ceremonial armor and colorful dress silks.

Foot soldiers in similar dress stood at attention near the chariots, and a number of acolytes and priests stood waiting as well, all dressed in robes of finest silk.

Anok approached Kaman Awi, bowing as he came close. "You summoned me, master?"

"Yes, yes! Stop bowing! Let me look at you." He took a step back, and looked Anok up and down. "You're a mess!" He turned and looked at the waiting acolytes. "You!" He pointed at a surprised young novice. "You look the right size. Give him your robe!"

The novice looked shocked and just stood there.

Kaman Awi grabbed an ornate wood-and-metal staff from where it leaned against the chariot. He pushed a catch in the middle, and a golden ball on the end of a metal rod emerged from the end with a snap. In one quick motion, he touched the ball against the back of novice's exposed hand.

There was a crack, a flash of blue, and the novice yelped and jumped back, shaking his hand.

Kaman Awi grinned broadly. "*Listen* when I talk to you, novice!" He leaned close to Anok, and said in a whisper, "I've been working with my lightning jars. Do you like my toy?"

Anok watched as the novice frantically yanked off his immaculate outer robe and handed it to Anok. Anok removed his yoke and shoulder bag and changed robes, handing his dirty one to the novice. He felt somehow conspicuous displaying the scabbards on his back, normally hidden by the robe, but by now most at the temple were used to the eccentricity.

Kaman Awi looked disdainfully at the novice. "You look terrible! You stay here."

The confused novice turned and skulked through the arched doorway back into the temple.

"Pardon, Master Kaman Awi, who are we going to see?"

He glanced back at Anok and arched an eyebrow. "What makes you think *you're* going to see anyone?"

He gestured at the line of chariots. "I could also ask if there is to be a parade."

Kaman Awi grinned but said nothing.

"Clearly the intent of all this is to impress. You are concerned about my appearance, so obviously I am to impress as well. The middle chariot has a lockbox chained to the floor, a sign that we carry something of value. The guardians, then, serve a triple function, to impress, to protect us, and to protect whatever is in that box. I assume, then, that we are not simply out to impress the people of Kheshatta with our finery. We bring something of value to someone we hope to impress, perhaps in hope of gaining favor, or perhaps with the intent to buy or trade for something, also of value."

Kaman Awi smiled broadly. "Excellent! Deduction and reasoning. I like to see that in my acolytes!"

Anok shrugged. "It seems obvious enough to me."

"You'd be surprised how many novices we see here who would fail that simple test. They seek power like a moth seeks flame, and all movement, all thought, lies along that single line."

Anok considered his words carefully. "Don't you seek power as well?"

"We all seek power, Anok Wati. We are all but moths before its flame. But the secret is to fly close without getting burned, and that path never lies along a straight line. That way offers only two possibilities, to move ever away from power or straight into the heart of destruction. To see and simply move is the way of a fool. To *think* one's way before taking a step, that is the path of power."

"I will keep that in mind," said Anok.

"See that you do. Get in the chariot." Unthinkingly, he tapped Anok on the shoulder with his staff.

Anok jumped, but nothing happened.

Kaman Awi smiled sheepishly. "I'm sorry. After each sting, it must be reloaded by a device hidden in the chariot floor, which in turn is supplied by the motion of the turning axle."

Anok climbed carefully into the chariot next to Kaman Wati. A pair of soldiers squeezed in next to them, but Anok tried to keep his distance from the lightning staff. He watched as the priest pulled a lever on the side of the staff, retracting the ball and rod back into their hidden recess, then pushed the base of the staff into a nook in the floor where it stood on its own. As it locked into place, he heard a small *snap,* and smelled burning air.

Kaman Awi noticed his attention appreciatively. "Only a toy, right now, but imagine the city wall with a hundred of these, each a hundred times bigger, a thousand times more powerful! Imagine if the Cult of Set could rain lightning down at will on bandits and raiders! Our power over Kheshatta would again be absolute, as it rightly should be, as it was in days of old. Can you imagine it, young acolyte, what it would be like to rain down lightning on your enemies?"

Anok said nothing, but he did not have to imagine it. He remembered his first, great spell and the smoking ruin that had been the lair of the White Scorpion gang in Khemi. That spell had nearly killed him, though, nearly driven him mad. Sorcery had its price, and perhaps that was all that saved the world from being reduced to such ruin.

Kaman Awi planned to loose such power with the flick of a catch, to loose lightning as casually as a man might set in flight an arrow. What then would save man from his own madness? How then would the world survive? He shuddered. There were greater evils still than spells of power and ancient gods.

The High Priest made a hand signal, and the chariots rumbled into motion, around the temple forecourt, through the gates, and out into the streets of the city.

As they passed, people turned to look, some with wonder, some with fear, and some with anger. Sometimes things were thrown at them, rotten food, rocks, things less pleasant scooped from the street, but each time the projectile would stop short of the chariots and bounce back, as though off an invisible wall.

"A simple spell," explained Kaman Awi, "performed by the acolytes in the front and rear chariots. These are not our true enemies. The rabble in Kheshatta chose up sides, like spectators choosing a favorite camel in a race. None of our true enemies would dare attack us so directly for so little reason. They know the reprisal would be great."

"Why do we have so many enemies here? Does not all of Stygia belong to Set?"

Kaman Awi chuckled. "That is part of why I have brought you, Anok, the other being that I would have your power at my side. It is time you learned how things work in Kheshatta, and this errand will be a good lesson."

They rolled north through the streets, toward the looming mountainsides, covered in forest. "This place is a crossroads, Anok, of many caravan roads rich with trade. It is lush and fertile for the growth of the poisoners' plants, and the deserts surrounding this place are rich with ancient temples and ruins, where objects of power can be found. The hills themselves have veins of metals—brass, copper, iron—from which weapons can be made. And the place itself is rich in potential for sorcery. Things can be done here that can be done nowhere else. Things can be *undone* here that can be undone nowhere else."

"So everyone wants this place?"

"Every cult, every faction, every army, every nation, and since all covet it, none can truly have it. Though it lies just within the borders of Stygia, it is barely Stygian at all. But neither is it Kushite, or Shemite, or Keshan. We share it, as we guard it from each other." He gestured toward the mountainsides. "Today, we go to strike a deal with another of those factions, the poisoners."

The city houses were beginning to thin, giving way to walled estates surrounded by trees. The air was damp and cool, filled with the smell of water and exotic plants. Rivulets flowed along channels on either side of the now-winding road, and often they crossed small bridges over larger streams. Birds called from the greenery, and insects buzzed past, occasionally bouncing off the procession's magical canopy.

"I've heard much of the poisoners," said Anok, "yet I feel I know almost nothing."

Kaman Awi snorted disdainfully. "The Lord Poisoner we go to meet, Sattar, is typical of their type. He is hereditary owner of his plantation and defends it by force and coercion. He is a thug and a fool, who values gold over true power."

"But you said the poisoners had knowledge that you desired for your temple."

"Those that tend the special plants, who mix the sacred herbs and brew their potions, those we value, but they are little more than livestock to the likes of Sattar, to be used and killed at his convenience and pleasure."

Like your acolytes and followers? But Anok held his tongue, thinking only that anyone who tried to deny ultimate power to the Cult of Set could not be entirely bad.

The trees became thicker, and the road switched back and forth as it climbed the increasingly steep mountainside. They passed trains of pack mules, some bearing bundles of dried plants, others sealed pots and bottles, all accompanied by armed and armored guards on horseback.

At last they came upon a high wall of native stone and traveled along it a way until reaching a heavy iron gate watched by many armed men. The guards swung the gates open for the chariots and waved them through.

In the distance through the trees, Anok could see a great palace jutting out of a cliff. Doubtless it offered spectacular views of the city and lake below. One could probably even see across the border into Kush from here, perhaps offering early warning of bandits or raiders.

Something buzzed past Anok, an angry insect perhaps.

Insect?

He grabbed Kaman Awi's sleeve, but the warning came too late. The driver of the chariot slumped over, as well as the guardians who flanked them. Without the pull on the reins, the horses slowed to a halt.

Anok looked ahead and behind. All the guardians were down. Only the priests and acolytes remained. He reached for his swords, as Kaman Awi crouched down behind the shield of the chariot, his face red with anger. "The lazy bastards of Ibis! I told them to maintain the spell till we were at the palace!"

Suddenly the trees and shrubs around them all seemed to rustle and part at once. Armed men, rough, dangerous men, emerged from every side. They were surrounded by a hundred or more soldiers, swords drawn. One among them, a tall, dark man with a pointed beard and shaved head, stepped forward and sheathed his sword.

He smiled up at Anok. "I am Sattar, Lord Poisoner of Orkideh Plantation. I bid you welcome."

18

KAMAN AWI PEERED over the shield of the chariot, his eyes blazing at Sattar. "What is the meaning of this? We come on business, in good faith, and you strike down my guardians with your trickery, for no cause at all!"

Sattar chuckled, a rumble deep in his chest, like the stirring of a volcano. "No, there was purpose, just as there was purpose in you coming in golden chariots, with fine silks and flags flying to your beloved serpent god. You hoped to make an impression." He smiled slyly. "But I *know* I have made an impression on you!"

"By killing my soldiers?"

Sattar laughed. "Stand like a man, priest. We will not harm you. This was but a demonstration."

Kaman Awi cautiously stood, casually raising his hands as he did.

"Your great magic will not work here. An underground river runs under this place, and salts dissolved in it drain most of the magical energy from it down to the lake far below. It is ironic, that the very thing that makes you so weak here may be part of what makes your master Thoth-Amon so powerful in his stronghold."

Anok's eyes widened. He could *feel* that it was true. Even the Mark of Set felt cold and dead upon his wrist. Only the slightest of magics would work here, and that meant that the acolytes had not been careless in their spell. The magic had deserted them when they entered this place. No wonder the Lord Poisoner's ancestors had chosen to build their palace here.

Sattar grinned. "Ironic, also, that this stream and its salts are the source of the rare elixir that you seek." He signaled his men to put away their weapons. For the first time, Anok noticed a separate class of soldiers who stood behind the others, Kushites, thin as posts, and taller even than Teferi. They had no obvious weapons, other than a long shaft of polished bamboo decorated with feathers on the end and a leather bag that man each wore around his neck.

Sattar stepped up to their chariot, carefully reached up to one of the fallen men, and plucked a tiny bronze dart, terminated with a tuft of feather, from the man's neck. He held it up for them to see. "My special brew. These men will awaken in an hour or so, refreshed, rested, and happy. If you wish, you may then whip them for their failure." He made another signal, and a soldier stepped up to each chariot. "My men will drive you the rest of the way to my palace and tend to your guardians until they awake. Have you eaten? My people have prepared a breakfast for you."

THE INTERIOR OF the palace was a surprise to Anok. In most of Stygia, wood was rare and expensive. The homes of the wealthy were made of stone, those of the very poor of mud-bricks and stucco, and those in between of fired brick and cast blocks. Wood was used for doors, shutters, decoration, reinforcement where nothing else would do. Bamboo was rarer still.

Here, the entire interior was covered in rich hardwoods and bamboo, all oiled and polished to bring out the beauty of the grain. Through every window, vistas of green could be seen, and pots filled with strange and exotic plants lined each windowsill, stood in every sunny spot, and hung from hooks on the ceiling. No castle, no temple, had ever struck him as being quite so splendid.

A banquet had been spread for them on a long table, strange and colorful fruits and vegetables were artfully sliced and arranged on trays, a rainbow of green, yellow, orange, and red.

Blank-faced servants stood behind the table with fans to shoo away flies and insects. In fact, most of the servants Anok had seen on their way into the house had the same vacant, blissful expression. They looked drugged, and Anok suspected that they were.

The servants of Set looked curiously at the array of food, but none was willing to partake.

Sattar looked at them for a moment. "Are you not hungry?"

Kaman Awi stared at him. "You are a *poisoner.*"

Sattar roared with laughter. He pointed at one of the acolytes. "You, pick something from the table, anything, and I will eat it. Go on!"

The acolyte glanced at Kaman Awi, then picked up a chunk of melon and handed it to Sattar.

Sattar examined the orange chunk for a moment, then tossed it into the air and caught it in his mouth, chewing greedily and swallowing. He grinned. "There, you see?"

"Perhaps," said Kaman Awi, "you have an antidote."

The grin faded. He looked at the acolyte who had handed him the fruit. "If I wanted him dead, the poison would have been absorbed through your skin. You would be dead already."

Eyes wide, the acolyte examined his fingertips, then frantically wiped them on his robe.

"Surely, if I wanted you dead, you would already be dead a dozen times over. You have come to do business. There is no profit in killing you. Are none of you brave enough to sample the fruits of our plantation?"

Anok reached down to a platter of green, star-shaped

slices, dripping with juice. They were the least familiar items on the table. He took a slice and put it into his mouth carefully. The flesh was firm, tart, but not unpleasant. As he chewed, the flavor turned sweet and musky. It was an interesting experience, and so far at least, he was not dead.

He realized suddenly that the Mark of Set's healing powers would likely be useless to him here. If there were indeed poison in the fruit, he had no defense. Still, he was certain Sattar was telling the truth. If he had wanted them dead, they would be dead. "Very good," he said to Sattar. "The flavor is complex and unusual."

The others watched him, then, one by one, took polite samplings from the table. Anok noticed that only Kaman Awi himself refrained from sampling the fare.

As soon as it was apparent that they were through eating, Sattar signaled them to follow him through a door to their right. "Come. You are not my first visitors this morning. It is time that you met the others."

They climbed two steps, and emerged into a much larger room, with many arched doors opening onto a veranda looking out on the lake and the lands beyond. A towering fir tree was artfully situated to block the view of Thoth-Amon's island stronghold, as though it were a blight on the landscape.

They walked out onto the veranda, and Anok noticed a cluster of bamboo armchairs facing away from them. Several men sat there, dressed in colorful clothing of silk embroidered with gold. They wore round, flat-topped caps, and their dark hair hung down their backs in neat braids. Anok studied the symbols embroidered into their clothing, and though he could not read them, they were familiar. The hair on the back of his neck stood up.

Hearing them approach, the men stood and turned. Their faces were well-known to Anok. Two were Dao-Shuang and Bai-ling of the Jade Spider Cult, the others the same members of their cult who had been with them on the street.

Dao-Shuang met Anok's eyes, and he tilted his head slightly but said nothing.

Kaman Awi's face turned red. "First you poison my

guardians, and now you bring me here with these"—he sputtered like a boiling pot with the lid on, looking for words—"these *outlanders!*"

Sattar tried to look innocent, though it was obvious that he was enjoying himself.

Anok was beginning to doubt Kaman Awi's conclusion about Sattar's appreciation for power. It was his observation that the Lord Poisoner valued power greatly, gloried in its use. It was simply not the same kind of power that Kaman Awi valued or understood. In the poisoner's world, the priest of Set was clearly outclassed.

"You came here to offer a transaction on an item, as did these honored visitors from the East." The faintest trace of a smile crossed his lips. "Interesting that you should both come seeking the same item. Sadly, there is only one bottle in all the world, and my brewmasters have been years in making it."

Kaman Awi glared at Dao-Shuang. "What use have you for the Elixir of Orkideh?"

"Curiously, I have no real use at all. Perhaps I will use the bottle to decorate my study. Perhaps it can be used to improve the flavor of fish. I have heard only that your cult desperately desires it for use in some grand scheme of power, and I therefore wish to deny it to you. We have doubled your offered price."

"Then," said Kaman Awi, "we will double it again!"

"We are not a rich people," said Dao-Shuang, "but we will also offer double."

Kaman Awi chuckled, smiling with renewed confidence. "The coffers of Set are deep. We will outbid you then, whatever the price!"

Sattar looked from one to the other. "There are other considerations."

Kaman Awi frowned at him. "What considerations? Our bid is highest. Our offer was made first, was it not?"

"The Jade Spider Cult's gold, however, was here first." He bowed to the men in a gesture of false humility. "A humble farmer such as myself, I could not risk offending either of your powerful cults by choosing one over the other." He looked at Kaman Awi. "What is gold, if I will not live to spend it? You must settle this matter between yourselves."

Kaman Awi looked aghast. "There can be no settlement between us. We must have the elixir, and there can be no other satisfaction."

"Well," said Sattar, in a way that suggested he had been expecting this outcome, and probably hoping for it, "then perhaps you can settle the matter through a contest, perhaps one of magical ability."

Dao-Shuang looked at him quizzically. "Magic does not work here. You have demonstrated that to us."

Anok wondered if Sattar had pulled anything as audacious on the Jade Spiders as his attack on the guardians.

"Great magic," said Sattar. "Some small magics still work here to a degree, and what I propose is a test of skill and concentration, not a sorcerous battle to the death."

Dao-Shuang glanced at Kaman Awi, who scowled back. "That might be acceptable. Who would engage in this contest?"

"I don't know. Perhaps Kaman Awi and yourself, as leaders in your cults—"

"Perhaps," interjected Dao-Shuang, "we should test the young warriors of our cult against one another. My student, Bai-ling is quite capable, and I'm aware that your acolyte, Anok Wati, has great promise."

Kaman Awi glanced sharply at Anok, obviously curious how the Jade Spiders knew his name. "That might be acceptable, then, if the contest offers no clear advantage to one side or the other."

Sattar smiled. "Oh, it is my contest. Trust that there will be no favoritism." He gestured toward a stairway leading down onto the grounds. "You have chosen your champions. Now, let me show you my garden of pain!"

19

THE PROCESSION, LED by Sattar, followed a path that wound through the palace grounds, past landscaped fields of fragrant flowers shaded by fruiting trees, then down a stairway to a flat shelf of land below, perhaps two hundred paces wide, where an assortment of more utilitarian stone and wooden buildings huddled against the mountainside.

There were still many plants here, but the beds seemed as much functional as decorative, neat rows of exotic flowers and shrubs, some protected by metal and wood fences. The tallest of the buildings seemed to be barns, storehouses, and drying sheds, where various plant materials were collected for processing.

Through the open doors of the nearest shed, Anok could see large bundles of brown leaves, each as long as a man was tall, handing in rows from the rafters. A strange, peppery smell came from the shed.

Rows of long, low buildings, their roofs and sides made of some translucent fabric waterproofed with some kind of coating, were filling with growing plants, thus protected from the elements.

Beyond this were smaller buildings, where scholarly-looking men hunched over workbenches taking cuttings, counting seeds, or grinding and mixing various leaves and roots. In others, they stirred great copper caldrons that bubbled over wood fires, or watched strange fire-heated devices, closed pots made of rolled copper, connected with copper tubing, from which steam and strange odors hissed and dripped.

As they passed the doors on these places, Kaman Awi always slowed to look inside with a mix of curiosity and envy, but Sattar never allowed him to linger in any one place long.

They came finally to a tall, narrow, stone building, windowless, and guarded by a locked door. Anok noted that the roof was peaked and covered by the same translucent material as the growing houses they had already passed.

They stepped inside into a dark hallway, then up a flight of stairs that opened onto a long balcony surrounding a bright, central chamber that ran the height of the building. Light streamed in through the translucent roof and down to a tangle of waxy, dark green and red shrubbery growing below. The leaves, he noted, had irregular edges sprouting what seemed to be spines.

At the level of the floor under their feet, the chamber was crossed by stout bamboo poles, evenly spaced about an arm's length apart from one end of the chamber to the other.

As they stood at the railing, trying to divine the nature of Sattar's contest, several dozen of the Lord Poisoner's guard followed them up the steps, each carrying a long staff of bamboo, and arrayed themselves evenly around the railing. Their mood was jovial, as though they knew what to expect and anticipated enjoying it.

Sattar called for their attention. "As I said, I call this place the garden of pain. Its primary purpose is to grow the rare shrub you see below, a plant known as fire weed. It is exceptionally rare, and in fact it no longer exists in the wild, having been eradicated by man wherever it was found. The spines are poisonous. On touching the skin, they cause agonizing pain, as though the exposed part had been plunged into fire. Most interestingly, the pain does not fade with time, and for exposure to an extremity, amputation was once the only solution."

He smiled, surveying the expressions on his visitors' faces. "In fact, the affected persons were generally glad to perform the amputation themselves, even gnawing off the extremity, if no other option were available to them. More extensive exposure inevitably resulted in death, not by any physical cause other than ultimate pain."

"This," said Dao-Shuang, "is barbaric."

"Diluted, the poison has many applications, including relief for the pained limbs of the elderly and the treatment of certain fevers found only in the jungles of the Black Kingdoms. Of course"—he grinned—"there are those who will still pay for the undiluted poison, and occasionally the antidote. It is not my concern what purpose they put it to."

Anok looked intently at Sattar. "You intend to test us with pain?"

He laughed. "Only, perhaps, for the clumsy." He snapped his fingers. A rectangular tray was brought out and attached to the railing before them. On it were two engraved metal disks, each the size of an eating plate.

Sattar looked up at them. "You recognize these devices?"

They were smaller than the one Anok had spun to destruction at the Great Temple at Khemi, but there was no mistaking their purpose. "Wheels of Aten," he said.

"Very good," said Sattar. He glanced at Bai-ling. "You have seen these as well?"

"I have, but I fail to see their purpose here. Surely there is not enough magical energy here for a proper contest of will, and why two instead of one, as they are generally used?"

"The flow of our underground river is reduced in the dry season, and we keep these here to test its ability to weaken magic. If they can be turned too readily, then we know we must be on guard for sorcerous attack. In the years I have ruled this plantation, it has never happened; still, one cannot be too cautious. But there is always enough magic here to allow one of your ability to make them spin. Here . . ." He spun one of the disks with the flat of his hand. "Bai-Ling, this is yours. You have but to keep it turning." He spun the other. "Anok Wati, this is yours."

As he spun the disk, Anok reached out with his will, feeling the spin and helping it along. It required a surprising amount of focus for such a trivial task, but it was not difficult for one of his training and experience.

The two disks spun side by side on the little platform. "Now," said Sattar, "we will test your powers of concentration." One of Sattar's men took each of the two competitors by the arm, and led them to the far ends of the chamber. Each of them was handed a bamboo rod, and a small gate opened in the railing in front of them."

Sattar grinned. "I would suggest removing your sandals. It will make it easier to keep your footing on the bamboo."

Reluctantly, Anok slipped off his footwear and stepped out onto the nearest bamboo pole crossing the room. He teetered there for a moment before straddling the gap to the next pole, making it easier to keep his balance, then looked back as the gate snapped shut behind him.

Across the room, Bai-Ling joined him on the bamboo.

An excited murmur came from Sattar's men, who leaned across the rail, their long poles at ready. Anok now understood that their purpose was to keep the contestants away from the edge, where they might be able to lean against, or catch themselves on the railing.

Suddenly, in the back of his mind, he felt his wheel of Aten wobble and concentrated to bring it back to speed.

"Concentrate, young friends," said Sattar. "The first to allow his wheel to fall will be the loser. *That,* is the contest. There are no other rules."

Bai-Ling eyed Anok from across the room, then spun his bamboo rod like a staff. Though the rod was light, it still was enough of a weapon to send an opponent falling to the agonizing doom waiting below. He moved toward Anok, stepping lightly from pole to pole with catlike grace and balance.

Anok moved warily, trying to watch his opponent, his footing, and concentrate on the wheel all at once. It was like trying to pat one's head and rub one's belly at the same time, only one degree harder.

He felt the first taste of fear. Though Sattar had said neither of the two would have an advantage, Bai-Ling's training clearly included a degree of balance and agility that Anok could not match.

The student of the Jade Spider seemed to sense weakness. He smiled slightly, then lunged forward, stabbing the end of his staff at Anok's face.

Anok ducked to one side, causing the staff to miss, but in the process threw himself off-balance. He tripped, jumped heavily to the next pole, and struggled to keep the wheel turning.

Bai-Ling moved rapidly past him, crossing one pole, two, three. He swung his staff by the end, low, trying to cut Anok's feet from under him.

Anok jumped just in time, the staff striking his toes painfully as it just passed under him. He landed back on the pole with a thump, jumped to the next, trying to balance, then became aware that his wheel of Aten was wobbling.

It would have been so easy to let the wheel fall. The contest would have been over, no one hurt, and Ramsa Aál's master plan, whatever it was, would be thwarted.

Bai-Ling grinned wolfishly, circling him.

Let it fall! End this! His mind spoke, but his heart denied it, and his pride would not allow him to lose.

Anok watched Bai-Ling. The Jade Spider was always on the move, never off-balance. Then, overconfident, he stepped too close to the rail.

A cheer went up, as one of Sattar's men jammed the end of his bamboo rod between Bai-Ling's shoulder blades, and *pushed.*

Bai-Ling staggered, ran three steps down the pole, then turned to glare at his attacker.

Realizing that his opponent was distracted, Anok swung his staff at the back of his head.

Bai-Ling ducked at the last instant, shifting his weight so that he stood on one foot and swung the other high, leaping through the air to land two poles farther away from Anok.

Instantly, the Jade Spider began to move back toward him.

One pole, two poles.

Bai-Ling swung his staff two-handed down on Anok.

Anok blocked with his own staff.

Bai-Ling reversed the staff, striking again.

Again Anok blocked him, but he was forced to move one foot back to keep his balance.

Again, Bai-Ling struck.

Anok moved.

Attack.

Move.

Too late, Anok realized that he had been pushed too close to the railing.

Two bamboo poles poked into his right side, jamming painfully against his ribs as he was shoved back toward the center of the chamber.

His feet squeaked on the polished bamboo poles.

The room whirled. He saw the look of alarm on Kaman Awi's face, the cheering of Sattar's men.

He struggled to keep his balance, staggering from one pole to another, his foot almost missing. He was going to fall.

Unless.

He threw the bamboo staff away from his chest as hard as he could, providing just enough push to keep him standing on the pole. Quickly, he regained his balance, remembering as he did to spin up the wheel of Aten.

Bai-Ling laughed, stepping lightly along the length of a pole, several over from Anok, twirling his staff. Anok was unarmed now, easy pickings in the garden of pain.

Anticipating how he would be distracted by the impending attack, Anok tried to spin his wheel as rapidly as possible. The faster it spun, the longer it could endure his inattention. But the magic was so weak here he could hardly spin the wheel at all.

Then he had a thought. This contest could not be won by

making his own wheel spin, only by making Bai-Ling's fall.
He reached out with his mind, feeling Bai-Ling's wheel as
well as his own. Unlike the one at the temple, the engravings
on it allowed it to spin in one direction only. He could not reverse it, could not slow, it, but he could *feel* it, relative to his
own wheel.

Bai-Ling stepped closer, still spinning his weapon.

Anok had a memory, of a time when he and the other
Ravens were little more than children in the Great Marketplace at Odji, and they played a game they called "monkey."

They would steal a piece of fruit from a particular vendor's stall. He would chase them, but they would run to a fish
vendor's stall nearby. The fish hung drying from long poles.
They would leap up, swing around the poles onto a nearby
wall, then run away to safety.

It had been a long, long time since Anok had played
"monkey." He hoped he hadn't forgotten how.

He stepped toward Bai-Ling, who raised his staff to attack.

Anok leaned backward as he stepped forward. His feet
missed the pole and he started to fall down between them.

His wheel began to wobble, more and more.

He reached up, caught the pole with both hands, swung
his body under, his feet brushing just above the terrible
spines below.

His wheel wobbled more, slowing. He felt where Bai-
Ling's wheel spun, fast and steady.

As his body swung, he pointed his toes, jackknifed his
legs upwards toward Bai-Ling's stomach.

As his wheel threatened to topple, he did not spin it. He
pushed, felt his wheel spiral drunkenly across the little platform toward Bai-Ling's.

He caught Bai-Ling unaware in both fields of battle. The
air was forced from Bai-Ling's lungs as Anok's feet caught
him in the belly, and his wheel of Aten struck Bai-Ling's just
as Anok spun it up to speed.

With a *clang,* Bai-Ling's wheel was sent flying off the
platform, falling between the bamboo poles to land in the
shrubbery below.

Bai-Ling, stunned, fell backward, his staff flying, banged his head against a pole and fell through, barely catching himself with one hand.

Anok fell gracelessly across two poles. It was far from an elegant landing, but a solid one.

A cheer went up.

He could see Kaman Awi pumping his fist into the air in triumph.

He could see the look on Dao-Shuang's face, of concern for his student.

Anok rolled over, trying to grab Bai-Ling's wrist, but his fingers slipped before Anok could get to him.

He fell into the stinging plants, flailed about madly, and began to scream.

Anok quickly removed the tie to his robe and formed the end into a noose, which he dangled down, and tried to loop over Bai-Ling's wrist. Dao-Shuang's student was too maddened by pain to assist in the operation, but Anok managed to catch his arm anyway.

As he tried to pull Bai-Ling free of the thorns, he was aware that the other Jade Spiders were there with him, making similar loops from their own clothing. One carried several of the bamboo rods, which he placed between the poles to provide something of a platform from which to lift Bai-Ling.

Working together, they were able to hook both of Bai-Ling's wrists and pull him up.

As they got him across the makeshift platform, a laughing Sattar tossed out heavy leather gloves to them. "Do not touch his skin," he cautioned. "He is covered with poison."

"We must tend to him," said Dao-Shuang.

Sattar shrugged. "There is little purpose. He will be dead by nightfall. You could do him a mercy by slitting his throat now." He grinned. "The blood nourishes the plants."

Anok glared at him. "You said there was an antidote."

"I said there *was* one. I did not say that I would offer it to any unfortunate who fell into the garden of pain."

Dao-Shuang jumped onto the railing, grabbing the front of Sattar's coat. "Give him the antidote!"

He was instantly surrounded by Sattar's men, knives drawn and held to his throat.

"I couldn't give the antidote to the loser, without offending the winners of my contest."

Bai-Ling's scream echoing in his ears, Anok stood defiantly before the Lord Poisoner. "*Give him the antidote!*" So great was his rage, that even the Mark of Set was wakened from its slumber. *Perhaps there is magic enough in this place to kill just one man!*

Something in Anok's stare caused the brash poisoner's resolve to falter. He frowned in concern. "It is—very expensive."

Anok's gaze did not waver. "We will pay!"

Kaman Awi gasped. "Anok!"

"We will pay any price," said Dao-Shuang.

Sattar frowned, then made a signal. One of Sattar's men disappeared and returned quickly with a sealed bottle, which Sattar handed to Anok. "Give half by mouth," said Sattar, "then pour the rest over him to neutralize the poison."

Using their makeshift ropes, they dragged Bai-Ling over the railing onto the floor. Anok uncorked the bottle and carefully poured the red liquid into the Jade Spider's screaming mouth. The foul, stuff sprayed everywhere, but at least a part of it went down his throat, and immediately, he seemed to experience some relief.

Anok poured the rest over his hands, feet, face, and neck, where the exposed skin had been punctured by the terrible spines.

Bai-Ling's thrashing slowed, his screams became less frequent, and, finally, he dropped into blessed unconsciousness.

Anok stood and threw the empty bottle over the railing into the plants below. He stepped toward Sattar. "The prize," he said firmly, "belongs to the Cult of Set. And since you and your men have had your entertainment today at our expense, you will take the initial price offered to you by our cult. No higher!"

Sattar stared into his eyes for a moment, started to speak, then faltered. Reluctantly, he nodded. "That is acceptable."

He glanced down at Bai-Ling. "The antidote," he said, "is a gift. Perhaps we can do other business in the future."

Anok scowled at him. "I hope not."

Sattar sighed. "That, too, is a satisfactory outcome."

Two of the other Jade Spiders formed a stretcher from two coats tied together and carried Bai-Ling down the stairs. The other spectators began to make their way down as well.

As Anok waited his turn, a muscular hand fell on his shoulder. He turned as Dao-Shuang leaned close to his ear. "You have bested us in the name of Set, and that cannot be a good thing. You may yet have cause to regret it." He paused. "But it will not be I behind it. I am in your debt. If there is honor this day, it is yours, and yours alone."

THE RIDE BACK to the temple passed in silence, Kaman Awi clutching the bottle they had purchased tightly to his chest.

It was barely noon, and yet Anok felt they had been gone from the temple for a month. He felt weak and shaky. The Mark of Set buzzed and tingled on his wrist, restless from having been tempted with such rage and still having its power denied.

Dao-Shuang had said he might regret his victory, and already he did. He had delivered to the cult some important part in their evil scheme, and he had done it for nothing more than pride.

The one thing he did have now, was more information, for all the good it did him. He had to wonder, what kind of great spell would require an elixir made from water that leeched magic?

As their chariot stopped in the temple's forecourt, Anok noticed a number of camels tied up near one end of the building but thought little of it. Though most caravans stopped outside the city, private caravans containing heavy goods sometimes continued on into the city, and he had seen camels at the temple before on occasion.

He had barely passed through the front door of the temple

when a familiar voice called his name, a voice that made his stomach knot. "Anok! How fare you, brother?"

He turned to see an acolyte walking quickly toward him across the marble floor, an elaborate magical staff in his right hand.

It was Dejal.

The former Raven walked up and embraced Anok, who could only stand stiffly and endure the foul touch.

Dejal released Anok and stepped back, a smile on his face. "Our caravan traveled into the night and arrived here last evening. I was told you were staying away from the temple and received directions to your lodgings. I was about to go there and summon you at Ramsa Aál's request."

Kaman Awi stepped up next to him, glancing at Dejal curiously. "The Priest of Acolytes is here?"

Dejal bowed his head. "Yes, master. I just saw him a moment ago."

Anok tried to act surprised, though Rami had given him notice. Only the speed of their arrival was unexpected.

Dejal held up his chin proudly. "He is Priest of Acolytes no more, master! He is now promoted Priest of Deeds, charged directly with fulfilling the plans of our master, Thoth-Amon.

Anok blinked in surprise. This was more than a minor promotion, even greater than a High Priesthood. There were only a few dozen Priests of Deeds in the cult, and they were attached to no individual temple. The temple High Priests, the temples themselves, and all the resources of the cult were at their disposal, as Thoth-Amon willed it. In truth, they answered only to him, or to the designated High Priest of the cult while he was traveling abroad.

"You said that Ramsa Aál had summoned me? For what purpose?"

"A Priest of Deeds needs no purpose, acolyte," said another familiar voice behind him, "nor need he explain himself to anyone but Thoth-Amon himself."

Kaman Awi bowed his head in respect. "Ramsa, congratulations on your ascension. It is well deserved."

Ramsa Aál suddenly noticed the bottle he carried. "You have the Elixir of Orkideh. Excellent!"

Anok cringed. He wasn't ready for this, but he would have to make the best of it.

He bowed to Ramsa Aál, who he now noticed wore a golden yoke decorated with jewels, a mark of his new office. "Master, it is an honor to serve you again."

"Is it really? I am told by the priests here that you have been enjoying your new freedom and spend little time at the temple. Perhaps you do not wish to be an acolyte at all."

He glanced at Kaman Awi, hoping for some show support after turning the day's mission into a success. But the High Priest said nothing, apparently hoping to keep all the glory for himself.

Anok tried to look wounded. "Master, I have been hard at work studying the ancient texts of power."

"Under the tutelage of Sabé, long known as an enemy of our cult."

"And a keeper of ancient knowledge, denied to the cult, master. I have won his trust, and I will bring this knowledge to those who can rightfully use it."

Ramsa Aál looked at him skeptically. "Yet Kaman Awi reports that you have brought him little but crumbs from those ancient tablets of Sabé's. Where are these spells of power of which you claim to know?"

"The old texts are arcane, complex, and difficult to translate, even for Sabé. He writes nothing down, and so the texts must be translated anew each time. It will take time for me to learn the great spells, but learn them I shall."

The priest considered this for a moment, then nodded. "Very well. I am satisfied, if not well satisfied. Long have we coveted Sabé's secrets, though it suited us well enough merely that others did not learn them to use against us."

Others like me.

He continued. "But perhaps you will wish this day that you had studied harder and learned quicker. For today, as I promised you sometime back, is that day of your audience with Thoth-Amon!"

20

ANOK'S MIND RACED. Things were happening far faster than he had ever imagined, and he was ill prepared. His greatest concern was his father's medallion, which he wore under his robes, and the Scale of Set hidden within. He wished now that he had, as in Khemi, found a secure hiding place for it, or at least entrusted it to Teferi.

But, in his heart of hearts, he knew the real reason he hadn't done these things was that some part of him wanted the Scale of Set close to him.

The part that covets its power.

But it was too late now, unless he could slip away.

"Master, I did not come today expecting to see you, much less our master Thoth-Amon. My clothing is dirty and rumpled. Let me return to my dwelling for fresh robes."

Ramsa Aál smiled slightly. "Thoth-Amon does not care about your clothing, acolyte. Your value to him is in your knowledge and power, and on those you will be judged." He gestured Anok to follow him. "Come, his personal chariots should already be awaiting us by the side entrance."

Dejal looked at him and nodded, and as he did, casually

tilted his staff in such as way that the top of it tapped Anok's shoulder. Anok noted the touch, but his concerns were elsewhere and far more pressing.

Dutifully he turned and followed Ramsa Aál. As they walked, Anok mentally reviewed everything he'd ever read or heard about spells of deception and disguise. There had been a great deal of it, as sorcerers were always trying to smuggle some object of power or to hide one from their enemies so it could be used in a surprise attack.

Yet even as he thought his way through those spells, he dismissed them one by one. They would succeed only in attracting the attention of a master sorcerer like Thoth-Amon, and he would immediately know that something was being hidden.

They walked through an arched side door onto a portico, where two chariots and their guardian drivers waited. Anok's first impression was that each chariot was pulled by a team of two white stallions, much like the ones he'd ridden earlier.

Only when one of the huge steeds turned back and looked at him with flame orange eyes and bared its pointed teeth, did he realize differently. In a flash he reexamined the "horses" and noticed all the details that were wrong: the too-pointed ears, the hairless tails tipped with sharp spines, the cloven hooves.

He looked at Ramsa Aál questioningly. "Demon-horses?"

The priest nodded. "Strong, fast, and tireless, though temperamental. They eat only fresh meat, with a preference, I am told, for human flesh."

The sight of the frightful creatures filled him with dread. Not fear of the beasts themselves, but rather the casual use of great magic that they represented.

"But master, for such a brief journey, surely regular horses would serve as well. The temples regular chariots are already harnessed in front of the temple. Why use these?"

Ramsa Aál smiled as he stepped onto one of the chariots. "They are here to be seen. Our master is contriving every excuse to send them out across the city on errands. They serve notice to all who see them that the Lord of the Black Ring, the High Priest of Set, the mightiest of all sorcerers, Thoth-Amon, has returned to Kheshatta, that his magics are unmatched, and all must yield before him."

This, Anok realized, *was* a parade, a show of power for all who saw them pass on the streets.

Anok wondered what abominable hell-pit these creatures had been summoned from, and what unspeakable power it had taken to bring them here. Suddenly his elemental magic seemed poor indeed. How could he hope to best a man who wielded such power? How could he even hope to hide his secrets in the presence of such a wizard? If the demon-stallions were intended to cause fear in Thoth-Amon's enemies, Anok had to conclude that in his case, it was working quite well.

He walked forward and climbed onto the other chariot next to the helmeted driver, who looked rigidly ahead. The driver behind them yelled to signal his readiness. The driver of Anok's chariot shook the reins, and the great beasts threw back their heads to make a noise. Not a whinny, but something more like a scream.

They began to trot, their cloven hooves striking sparks on the cobblestones as they pulled the chariots rapidly around the front of the building and out the front gate. They turned onto the street beyond the temple, and immediately every passerby stopped to stare and watch the chariots pass. Those in the street shrunk back, some women and children even running in terror as the frightful procession passed.

They traveled north for a time, passing within a few blocks of Anok's villa and Sabé's house, then turned east onto a wide boulevard leading down to the lake's edge. Down its length, Anok could see the causeway, stretching out into the green water, and the rocky island on which Thoth-Amon's palace perched.

The demon-horses began to gallop, leaving a fading trail of fire behind their hooves as they ran.

Anok held tightly to the ornately carved and gilded railing across the front of the chariot as they rumbled and bounced down the street. Wide-eyed people scattered out of their way, horses, mules, and camels bolted as they passed, and still the chariots moved ever faster.

Anok again considered the medallion around his neck and its hidden contents. A spell of deception would only draw attention to it. The cold iron of the medallion provided some measure of disguise, but he doubted that would fool such a great wizard as Thoth-Amon. There had to be something he could do.

He thought of the leeching effect of the waters of Orkideh, and it caused him to remember a spell in one of the old texts, a spell of *transference*. Its purpose was to drain all the power from a mystical object and temporarily transfer it to sorcerer's body. Without its magic, the Scale of Set was nothing but a decorative lump of gold.

Of course, the magic would be just as detectable in Anok, perhaps even more so. But his body was already infected by the Mark of Set, and since the magic of the Scale also had its origins in Set, perhaps one would serve to disguise the other.

They were getting quite close to the causeway, and it was the only idea Anok had. He recalled the words of the spell, written in a nearly forgotten language from before the time of man. Anok had memorized the words, without actually knowing their meaning. That was known only to Sabé.

He whispered quietly, *"Komoal, anek-et, presoss, tuk-willan, martay-et, sotow-et-ek—"*

With his inner senses, he could hear a whistling sound, like wind blowing through a narrow cave, and felt the magic of the Scale diffuse through his body like warm water, making his skin tingle and the hairs on the back of his neck stand up.

He felt a strange sensation in the Mark of Set, as though it were being rejoined to something from which it had been sundered before the beginning of time. It was strangely intoxicating—and *enlightening*.

The Scale of Set's power had never seemed proportional to the importance the cult attributed to it. Now, for the first time, he had a sense that there was far more to it than a simple toy to command snakes.

Now he understood why the priest desired to have all three Scales.

Suddenly he desired them for *himself*.

So intoxicated was he by the thought that he barely noticed as the chariot again turned onto the narrow stone causeway out across the lake.

The dark clouds continued to roll in, almost touched by the highest tower of Thoth-Amon's dark citadel, and a cold wind whipped across the lake, raising waves tipped with white froth.

Halfway across the causeway the chariot slowed to a halt for no apparent reason. The air in front of them seemed to turn momentarily to fog, then instantly back to clarity, revealing an open wooden drawbridge operated by a guardhouse on the far side.

Anok blinked in surprise, realizing the bridge and guardhouse had been protected by a cloaking spell of great power and subtlety. Any attackers rushing toward Thoth-Amon's lair would have plunged headlong into the deep, dark waters between.

As Anok looked down, a great catfish large enough to swallow a man broke the surface, rolled, and regarded them hungrily with a dead, milky eye. He shuddered as the great body slid past, slime-covered and gray-green, at least fifteen paces long, then vanished with a flick of its man-high tail.

An arc of spray flew through the air and struck Anok in the face, making him start like a man awakened from a dream. He shook his head, trying to clear it, as, with clanking chains, the bridge creaked down. The end of it landed on the pier in front of them with a thud.

The chariots charged forward, rumbling across the bridge and onto the stone cobbles on the far side. Even as the second chariot was clearing the bridge, the guardians began to winch it open again, groaning with effort as they turned the great wooden wheel that wound the chain.

Anok looked up at the looming black towers of Thoth-Amon's keep with growing dread. He was trapped now, on the wizard's island keep, and it was very likely that he would never leave. He felt certain Thoth-Amon would immediately see through his deceptions. When that happened, he would be tortured to death, slowly, as only a black sorcerer could.

21

TEFERI CARRIED THE stack of slate tablets from Sabé's storage room and placed them carefully on the heavy wooden table. The ancient tomes were fragile and easily broken. A few were already repaired in places using a sticky black mortar that Teferi could not identify.

He glanced down at the one on top, puzzling at the row of large characters across the top. One by one he parsed them out, and it was with a mix of pride and concern when he realized it read, "Beware, he who reads this cursed text."

Sabé walked up next to him and ran his fingers over the same line. "Did you know you make a little sound when you are unhappy, my friend? It is a low rumble, deep in your throat, that few would notice."

Teferi glanced at him in surprise. The old scholar's perception continued to amaze him. Who else could *hear* a frown?

"Is it this text that concerns you? You need not worry. Some souls are drawn to magic, and some are anathema to it. You are one of the latter. You could read aloud the darkest texts till the end of your life and not raise enough magic to turn over a grain of sand."

"Should I take that as an unkindness?"

"You should take that as a compliment, my friend. But that it were true for me as well. All my life my mind, with its thirst for knowledge, and my soul, with its thirst for power, battled for supremacy. That war, I fear, will end only in my grave."

"May it be, then, a war without end."

Sabé smiled sadly. "I know you mean well, Teferi, but I am very old and very tired. Perhaps that is why I have finally shared my knowledge with you and Anok. In the twilight of my days, I grow trusting, or perhaps just eager to unload my burdens."

The clouds that had covered the sky all morning parted for just a moment, and shafts of light shone down through the high windows at the front of the room. With surprise, Teferi noted the angle of them. It was far later than he had realized. "Where is Anok? He should be here by now."

Sabé frowned. "Anok? This is his day at the temple. I assume Fallon is with him."

"Fallon was off drinking last night and never came home. This is my fault. I was so eager to come here and study that I forgot the day."

"Perhaps," suggested Sabé, "he is waiting for you at your villa."

"I think not. He would have come and gotten me. More likely he has gone off on his own."

Sabé held up his hands and waved his fingers, then stuck out his tongue as though tasting the air. He immediately frowned. "I feel something is wrong," he said grimly. "Go quickly."

Teferi took his sword off a peg in the wall and headed for the door. He muttered, "I am a poor friend, indeed."

Though he didn't expect to find Anok there, Teferi made his way back to the villa, just in case. He found Fallon in the front room, facedown and snoring on a couch.

He poked her shoulder and she groaned and flailed for the

sword lying on the floor at her side. She still had not found it when she looked up, bleary-eyed, and recognized Teferi. "There is an old saying," she said. "Let sleeping Cimmerians lie."

"Wake up, you drunkard!" He regretted his words even as he spoke them. Escorting Anok had been his responsibility, not hers. "Anok has gone off to the temple alone."

She plopped her face back down on the couch. "Anok can take care of himself."

"Perhaps, but the streets of this city are fraught with unknown dangers. It is our charge to look out for him." He hesitated, then continued. "Sabé thinks there may be danger."

The mention of Sabé's name seemed to goad her into motion. She groaned and pushed herself up off the cushions, her long, dark hair falling over her eyes. Teferi studied her with disapproval. This situation *wasn't* her fault, but it didn't excuse her recent behavior. Where had the proud Cimmerian warrior gone?

She sat on the edge of the couch for a moment, then snatched up her sword. "You are right. I have found too much comfort in spirits of late. I gave my word that I would protect Anok in his journeys, and that is my bond."

They stepped out into the street just as the rain began to fall again, hard and warm, and they were quickly soaked. Fallon looked especially miserable. Teferi glanced down at her. "What is wrong with you lately?"

She did not meet his eyes, and simply scowled. "There can be no excuse. I am troubled by demons of my own, Teferi. I proclaim proudly my Cimmerian birth, but ever I run farther from its dark woods and somber hills. Where will I run next? Into the Eastern Ocean? Off the edge of the world itself? Or merely into the bottom of a jug? I do not know."

He wanted to chastise her, yet her words cut too close to his heart. He had lived his whole life in exile from the land of his forefathers. Even now, its cursed border lay only a day's march to the south, yet he did not go there.

Could not.

Would not.

So they trudged on in silence and did not speak of it again.

They had traveled only a few blocks when Teferi spotted Barid's carriage driving by and flagged him down. The little Vendhyan hunched on the driver's bench under an oilskin cloak that protected him from the rain.

"We're going to the Temple of Set to look for our friend Anok. He slipped out this morning without escort, and we're concerned for his safety."

Barid frowned. "Well you should be. My brother saw him not an hour ago, on a golden chariot pulled by unnatural steeds, crossing the causeway to the palace of Thoth-Amon!"

Teferi groaned, and Fallon met his eyes with a look of alarm. Teferi looked away, casting his gaze up toward the gray sky, drops of rain running down his cheeks. "Anok, we have failed you."

22

ANOK AND RAMSA Aál were led by a pair of guardians through a great entry hall lined with cabinets full of ancient relics: small statuary, tablets, jewelry, pots painted with tableaus of forgotten gods, colorful crystals, and the mounted bones of strange and horrible creatures.

All were protected behind doors framed around glass; clear, nearly free of ripples, in itself worth a king's ransom. There was more glass than Anok had seen in a lifetime, all in this one room.

There were large statues as well, the largest ones sitting directly on the polished marble of the floor, others raised on ornate marble pillars. None represented the human form.

There, carved in marble, granite, and even silver were the forms of unnatural creatures, winged demons, horn-headed fiends, monstrous elementals, many-legged dragons, and faceless ghouls.

Amid the cabinets and statues, grim-faced guardians stood at uneasy attention, clearly as worried about the objects they guarded as any interlopers.

Yet though this collection would humble any of the museums Anok had seen in kheshatta, he sensed that it represented only a hint of the dark-master's magical stores, only those items too trifling in their power to be worth Thoth-Amon's immediate protection.

They proceeded deeper into the bowels of the palace, along dark corridors draped with heavy tapestries that swallowed every footstep, until they reached the circular foundation of the great central tower, where they proceeded up the largest spiral staircase Anok had ever seen, wide enough for six men standing shoulder to shoulder.

Anok looked up. High above, he could see a semicircular landing in the gloom. Through the open center of the shaft hung a heavy chain, and iron chandeliers hung with oil lamps were strung every thirty feet or so, like beads on a necklace.

With each marble step his dread increased. Each step took him farther from even the slimmest chance of safety or escape.

The climb seemed subjectively to take hours, but at last they reached the landing and took a final flight of stairs up through the chamber's ceiling.

Into the private hall of Thoth-Amon.

The tower flared out at the top, so the diameter of its chambers was at least thirty feet wider than the shaft through which they had ascended. The hall ran east to west, from one side of the tower to the other, curved at each end, where one could look out through white pillars at the lake and the lands beyond.

To the east, one could see the whole expanse of the city, the wall to the south, and the hills where the palaces and plantation of the other wizards and poisoners perched.

Doubtless, Thoth-Amon liked to be able to keep an eye on his subjects, and his enemies, at all times. The sides of the chamber were straight, with many heavy doors leading to smaller side rooms.

One door in particular was as heavy as a palace gate, bolted with iron bars and chains. A tiny peephole at eye level was covered by a locked and hinged iron cover.

Anok did not care to learn what demonic horror the Lord of the Black Ring might keep imprisoned there.

They proceeded to the eastern end of the room, where they stepped out onto a wide balcony that lay beyond the pillars. The balcony was unprotected by an overhang, but the stone there was dry, and the wind that churned the lake below into whitecaps could not be felt. It was the same sort of spell that had protected Ramsa Aál's chamber windows back in Khemi, but on a much grander scale.

The guardians retreated back inside, leaving Anok and Ramsa Aál alone on the balcony. They waited silently for several minutes.

"I do not see our master," said Anok, trying not to let his voice sound hopeful. "Perhaps he is engaged in other, more pressing business, and will not see us today."

"I am never seen," said a deep voice, so close behind Anok that it made him jump, "unless I wish to be seen."

Anok spun to face the voice, even as Ramsa Aál calmly turned and bowed his head, left hand held under his forehead.

Anok had been trained in the protocol for meeting the highest of high priests, but in the moment, it was forgotten. He stared blankly at the imposing figure of Thoth-Amon.

He had somehow expected a small, old, wizened figure of a man. But Thoth-Amon was tall, towering over Anok, nearly as tall as Teferi, and broader of shoulder. As he stepped toward them, he carried himself gracefully, having neither the swagger of a warrior, nor the hesitant gait of an old man.

He wore long, flowing robes of red and black, elaborately embroidered with gold thread, and on his seemingly hairless skull, he wore a skullcap of mirror-polished metal. His face was angular and deeply chiseled, his nose long and hooked, his skin dark and gray, like cold ash from a fireplace. A pointed goatee framed his lipless mouth, and eyes like black marbles glinted from deep and shadowed sockets.

He smiled, and it was a terrible thing.

Suddenly, Anok remembered himself, bowing his head in salute to the High Priest of Set.

"Rise," he said. "Stand and face me, my servants." His

voice was deep and resonant, but there was a hissing under-
tone that reminded Anok of a serpent. Thoth-Amon turned
his attention first to Ramsa Aál.

"It has been long since we last spoke face-to-face, my
pupil. We have matters to discuss, but"—he glanced at
Anok, as though that should have some hidden meaning—
"detail can wait for its due time. Now, I need only that things
go as they should."

Ramsa Aál looked around nervously. "Can I speak freely
here, master?"

"This place is warded well with the darkest spells of power.
None may hear our words—no wizard, no demon, no god."

Ramsa Aál nodded. "Then all goes as planned, master.
Protected by my magics, my underlings have recovered the
old bones from the desert at great peril, assembled them,
and brought them here. Set does not even suspect that his old
rival is missing."

Anok listened intently, trying to keep his face emotion-
less. Ramsa Aál and Thoth-Amon conspired against their
own god? How could that be?

Thoth-Amon arched a narrow eyebrow. "You presume to
be privy to the knowledge of gods?"

Ramsa Aál smiled. "I still live, do I not?"

Thoth-Amon grinned. "That you do, and it is true, surely
Set would not suffer such a heretic to live. That is why you
must bear the weight of this plan alone. Even our conversation here puts me at risk. If you succeed, you will hand all
your stolen power to me, and I will share it with you. But if
you fail, you and you alone shall suffer Set's wrath. Is that
understood?"

"Of course, master. I never would have proposed this
brazen scheme otherwise. I humbly take great risks in your
service, master."

Thoth-Amon waved his hand in annoyance. "*Lies!* You
seek power, as I do. You are too weak to do this thing alone;
otherwise, you would take everything for yourself and kill
me in my sleep."

He held up his left hand, fingers wide, showing a heavy

ring of dark metal and polished obsidian, decorated with black diamonds. "Remember that whatever happens, you are ever bound to me. With but a twist of the Black Ring I could stop your beating heart in your chest, and there is no place in the world you can hide from that power!"

Ramsa Aál looked pained, an act that did not fool even Anok. "I would never betray my master!"

"That is right. You never will!"

He turned his attention to Anok and took a step closer, looking him up and down. "So this is your new pet?" He reached out suddenly, his fingers, powerful and clawlike, grabbing Anok's left arm and pulling back the sleeve to examine the mark around his wrist.

"So it is true. The Mark of Set!" He looked up into Anok's face and scowled at what he saw. "I am mystified why the Mark of Set would choose this one. He is weak, small, and tainted by foreign blood." The pointed nails of the High Priest's right hand dug into Anok's wrist, as his open left hand waved before Anok's face. "He has not even embraced the power of the mark! This one fears *corruption!*" He nearly spat the last word.

Then something made him hesitate. He waved his hand over Anok's chest, then grabbed the golden yoke around his neck, lifted it, and pulled open Anok's robe to expose his chest.

He grabbed the medallion there, then pulled his hand back as though burned.

"Cold iron!" His face slowly formed a smile. Then he laughed. "Cold iron! You think this will protect you from corruption?"

He leaned back, brushing his hands as though he had fouled them.

As he straightened his robe and yoke, Anok realized with a small sense of triumph that he had, at least in this, fooled the master sorcerer.

Thoth-Amon had not sensed the Scale of Set within the medallion, nor did he seem to sense its magic, temporarily housed in Anok's body.

Thoth-Amon leaned close to Anok's face. His breath smelled of cloves and garlic. "Let me tell you something, acolyte. I can tell that you fear me, and you should, for I am powerful and ruthless. I could crush you with my magics and give it no more thought than eating a grape at breakfast.

"But I have not always been such. A sorcerer's power is inconstant at best, his fate uncertain, his enemies legion. In my long life I have been pauper and king, High Priest and, more recently than you would imagine, slave."

He held up his left hand for Anok to see. "But I was nothing until I found the Black Ring and made it mine. It *called* to me, and I answered.

"You have been chosen by a mark of power, and unlike mine, it can never be taken from you! You cannot imagine how jealous that makes me! If it were possible, I would take it for myself, but I cannot, so I must help *you* use it in my stead."

His tone became one of sympathy, almost pity, and the hairs suddenly rose on the back of Anok's neck.

"Understand, then, that there is no malice in what I do now. It is simply what must be done, and I do it with no more anger than a man feels when he swats a gnat."

Then Thoth-Amon turned, as though taking his leave, and began to walk away. After only a few steps, he spun, his eyes wide, his hands held high, and instinctively Anok knew what was coming.

He reacted just as instinctively, his hands raised, palms flat, visualizing in his mind an ancient glyph of protection.

An instant later, the attack slammed into him like a powerful wave. The air around him crackled with lightning, and though he was braced, his feet slid several paces back along the smooth floor.

Then it was past, and he felt a sudden sense of relief.

He had braced for the attack, and weathered it well.

Was this the best the Lord of the Black Ring could offer?

But Thoth-Amon only smiled when he saw that Anok was unharmed. "Your reflexes are good, acolyte, as is your mastery of the basic spells. Now, prepare yourself for the real test!"

Again Thoth-Amon raised his hands.

Again Anok responded, but this time he had a moment to think about it, and remembered the techniques of the Jade Spider cult. If Thoth-Amon hoped to goad him into tapping the power of the Mark of Set, perhaps there was a way he could avoid that, using not power, but cleverness.

If the attack was like a wave, then his response must be like something that can cut through a wave. Again, he imagined the glyph of protection, but doubled, and in his mind placed them side by side to form a point, like the prow of a ship.

The attack came, twice as powerful as the last, yet Anok's pointed defense halved it again, and deflected it to either side.

Part of it splashed away and caught Ramsa Aál off guard. He was thrown back against the railing before he could raise a defense.

Thoth-Amon glanced at Ramsa Aál. "I would say, my servant, that you should stand clear. You could be injured."

Ramsa Aál's eyes were wide, as he backed away against the far southern railing of the balcony and crouched.

Thoth-Amon turned back to Anok and frowned, his black eyes narrowing. "You think yourself clever, acolyte? Perhaps you are, but that will not save you here!"

Again, he lashed out.

Anok tried his defensive trick again, but this attack was much stronger. He staggered back, rattled to his bones.

He tasted blood in his mouth.

Thoth-Amon's head tilted as he looked at Anok. "Did that hurt?"

He held up his hand. "No. Let me imagine it." He straightened his head.

"My next attack may destroy you. I do not fear corruption. I do not fear at all. Who knows what my limits may be?

"If you wish to survive, I would suggest that you strike me first."

Anok's eyes widened. Was this a trick? Was he being goaded into justifying his own murder? Perhaps Thoth-Amon had never been fooled by his ruse. Perhaps they would simply kill him and take the Scale of Set.

And yet, if that were so, why would Thoth-Amon need an excuse? He had made it clear he would kill without hesitation if it served his ends, and here, in Stygia, in the heart of his own stronghold, who would dare question him?

No, this was a test, nothing more. Yet even as Thoth-Amon tested him, he was tested against himself. He knew the consequences if he drew on the Mark of Set. He had resisted it so long, but its hold on him was growing constantly.

Now that he had mingled it with the power of the Scale of Set, who knew what could happen? Perhaps he even had enough power to crush the dark lord of Set.

Perhaps he could cut off the serpent's head, and at last have his revenge against Set, for his father, for Sheriti!

You have the power! Destroy him!

Anok's eyes went wide. The words had come from inside his head, but they were not his. *I deny you! I deny your power!*

No, he would strike back, but without the power of Set, without the dark spells the Mark of Set had compelled him to gain knowledge of. He had learned many other things in his studies at the temple. They would have to be enough.

He did not say the words aloud, lest he give Thoth-Amon warning, only thought them.

In the name of Lord Opp, the ancient, I summon forces of chaos, order from nothingness, and will my enemy—shatter!

A bolt of power leapt from his hands and swept toward Thoth-Amon like a swarm of angry bees. It enveloped him, pink fire dancing around his body. His wrinkled fists clenched, his arms strained, elbows flexing out, and the energy was broken, pieces of it fluttering away and sputtering out of existence.

Thoth-Amon drew himself to his full height. "If that is the best you can do, acolyte, then you must not want to live very badly."

Again he lashed back at Anok, the effort seeming almost trivial, and yet Anok was nearly blown off his feet, his defenses shredding like papyrus from an old tomb.

He felt his body ripple, bones creaking, his very skull trying to change shape. The agony was blinding, yet he did not fall.

There had to be a way out of this.

He looked up through eyelids that fluttered with the effort of staying open. "I—yield—to my master's superior skill."

Thoth-Amon seemed almost surprised. "You don't *understand,* acolyte. This is not a contest! This is a *duel* between sorcerers. This is kill or be killed! There is no yielding save *death!*

"Now, strike me, or you *will* yield—by default!"

Anok realized he had no choice. He had to call on the Mark of Set, and perhaps even the power of the Scale. If crushing Thoth-Amon was the only way out, then that was what he would have to do!

He tensed his body, summoning up the powers that waited—no—*begged* for release! Thoth-Amon had lived by the power of Set. Now let him die by it!

Lightning seemed to fire from his left fist, lightning and fire. Around the room, mirrors shattered, furniture was tossed against the wall, and everything that was breakable was broken.

Thoth-Amon seemed to sag, as though he might collapse, but then he pushed himself back up. Now there was pain in his face.

Pain, and *anger.*

He lashed back, catching Anok unaware. In a way it was no more than a magical slap in the face, but shielded as he was, Anok took the full brunt of it. He dropped to his knees, clutching his gut, feeling his insides twist and tear like rotted rags.

Far below the balcony, he could hear shouts of alarm.

Thoth-Amon stepped toward him. "That was impressive acolyte, but not what I was looking for. You have pained me for *nothing,* and for that you will surely *die!*"

Anok knew that the Lord of the Dark Ring was a man of his word. He knew the death blow was coming.

But he still had the Mark of Set, the power of the Scale.

And he had more.

Ancient spells, dark and forbidden, from before the time of man.

Give them to us! Channel them through us! Let us multiply their power a dozenfold! Let us shatter the Black Ring! Let us make its holder bleed!

The words came to his lips, in a language lost since before Atlantis sank beneath the waves. "Idnyc-ahk ozark lisab du sandrab et!"

It was as though his body had been struck by lightning, his limbs thrown akimbo by the force of its passage through him. It left him as a translucent ball, rolling like a boulder down a hillside.

It swept over Thoth-Amon and tossed him like a dry leaf. The priest flew five paces through the air before landing on his knees and crumpling facedown.

But Anok was in no condition to gloat. He staggered and dropped to his knees. Inside, he could feel the Mark of Set healing him, feel it knitting his torn insides back together, but he was anything but well.

He trembled and shuddered, his whole body spasming. He wanted to vomit, but even the muscles of his stomach failed to work properly. He had used the great magic of old, and now he was paying the price.

Without relief, his body would tear itself apart no matter what the Mark of Set did to restore it. At best, it would only prolong his agonies.

Yet through this, a sound attracted his attention.

He looked up, to see Thoth-Amon rising to his feet. The Lord of the Black Ring seemed to pause for a moment to compose himself, then strode purposefully toward Anok.

As he drew closer, he reached beneath his robe and smoothly extracted an ornate sacrificial dagger.

All Anok could do was watch.

Thoth-Amon grabbed his hair, yanked his head back to

expose his throat, and he felt the razor sting as the sharp edge of it just sliced into his skin.

He leaned very close to Anok, so that all Anok could see were those inky black eyes. "Let me share with you, acolyte, a lesson I have learned through pain and hard experience.

"No matter how great the sorcerer, his magic will eventually be depleted. And then—" He smiled an acid smile. "And then, a sorcerer can fall to the sharp edge of steel like any other mortal!"

Anok waited for the quick jerk of the blade, the hot rush of his own blood.

It did not come.

Instead, Thoth-Amon dropped his head, stood, and walked away.

Running footsteps approached, and a half dozen guardians and household servants charged up the stairs. They stopped and surveyed the destruction. "Master," said the eldest of the servants, "we heard noises and came at once. May I be of assistance?"

Thoth-Amon smiled. "Yes," he said, "yes, you may!"

He stepped toward the servant, glancing back at Anok as he did. "You see, you see, acolyte, your power is spent. As is mine, but—"

Thoth-Amon moved so quickly the servant never suspected until it was too late. In an instant the bigger man was behind him, had yanked his head back, and drawn the blade hard across his throat.

The servant made a gurgling sound, clutched his throat, and fell, his eyes wide as he watched torrents of crimson spray between his fingers. His lifeblood ebbed away in time with his fading pulse.

The other servants drew back, but were too frightened even to run.

A spatter of blood crossed Thoth-Amon's chest. He dipped two fingers in, and delicately raised them to his mouth. When they were sucked clean, he turned again to Anok. "You are spent, and you see that my power is easily restored by the sacrifice of blood. That is because I am not afraid."

Anok groaned in agony and tumbled to his side on the cold marble floor.

Thoth-Amon walked over to Anok, and knelt beside him. "Now," he said, "you must pay the price, one way or the other. Corruption, madness, or death. *Choose!*"

Anok said nothing, but in his heart, he had chosen.

Thoth-Amon studied him for a moment, then a look of contempt crossed his face. "You have chosen poorly!"

He stood abruptly and walked away.

Ramsa Aál finally dared step away from his hiding place. "Master, what shall I do with him?"

Thoth-Amon did not look back as he disappeared through one of the side doors. "Dump him at his residence. He may yet one day be of use to me. *If* he lives. And *if* he is ever sane again."

Anok heard the words, even though he could barely understand them. His whole attention was focused on a rivulet of the servant's blood, that was slowly was snaking its way across the floor toward him, closer, tantalizingly closer.

He reached out a trembling hand, and could almost touch it, when strong hands grabbed his ankles and began to drag him away.

23

ANOK LAY ON a couch in the front room of his villa. Teferi and Fallon were there, too, but he did not look at them. His eyes were fixed on the solid carpet of scorpions climbing slowly up the far wall.

"He was like this when I found him," said Teferi, "dumped by the guardians at our front gate."

"He does not move. Is he injured?"

Fallon leaned in front of his face, and he shifted to one side, so he could look around her and watch the scorpions, which had now nearly reached the juncture of wall and ceiling, shiny black bodies packed together like cows in a herd.

"There are signs of injuries, but they are already healed. He burns as though with a fever, but I do not think he is ill. This is very bad magic."

Fallon drew back, then caught herself and tried to look nonplused. "This is beyond the ken of such as you and me, Teferi."

"I've sent a boy to fetch Sabé," he said grimly. "Until then, may Jangwa guard his mind, wherever it has gone."

The scorpions were on the ceiling above them now, their

ranks dividing and twisting, forming ancient glyphs of power whose meaning Anok could only guess. They made him laugh.

"Oh, Anok," said Teferi, "this is my fault!"

"It is not his fault, it is yours! He's a better friend than you deserve!"

The voice, so familiar, so long unheard. He turned to see him sitting next to the couch, hunched forward, his fingers intermeshed, a look of anger wrinkling his brow. Anok's eyes went wide. "Father?"

His father shook his head sadly. "What have you done to yourself? Did I teach you nothing? You cannot live among snakes without growing scales!"

"I'm sorry, father."

"Who is he talking to?" asked Fallon.

Teferi shushed her.

"I am *dead,* and nothing will undo that! This mission of revenge is folly. I gave you one simple task, and in that you have failed utterly!"

"If indeed I have a sister, father, I cannot find her. This medallion, it is *so* heavy."

"Better it be lost than delivered into the hands of our enemies."

"I have kept it safe!"

"You have brought it to our enemies' doorstep, and the day is still young! Set is patient, as are we. You are but a thread in a tapestry that runs back fifty generations. If it runs fifty more, so be it, but it must not be ripped asunder!"

"I only tried to serve you, father!"

He looked away. "You would have served me better by throwing the medallion into the sand, finding a wife, and giving me fat grandchildren. Your sister would have found you in time. Now you have doomed yourself and my legacy as well. How will a *madman* protect the Scale of Set?"

"I am not mad!"

"Yes you are," said Fallon.

Teferi glared at her. "Shut up!"

"She is not a bad woman," said Sheriti. "She speaks what

is in her mind. If she is lacking in grace, she is also lacking in deception. She lies only to herself."

Anok smiled to see her fair face again, her golden hair radiant in the light from the window. "Oh, beautiful one! You've come back to me!"

Fallon looked shocked. "Is he talking to me?"

Sheriti reached out and caressed his cheek.

"You should be talking to her. She has a strong spirit, stronger than she knows. You need her as badly as she needs you. You are two broken people who could help each other. Did you ever hear the joke about the one-legged man who fell in love with a one-legged woman?"

"No."

"They walked to the altar together." She smiled, pleased with her joke, then the smile faded as she looked as his face. "You don't understand, do you? Poor Anok. You never did." She seemed to melt into the sunlight, until only the sunlight was left.

The door opened, and a Kush boy of perhaps nine years led Sabé inside. The old man slipped him a coin, and the boy quickly vanished.

Teferi started to take him by the arm. "He's here. I'll show you."

Sabé shrugged off his hands. "No need! I am blind, but I can feel the heat of him, sense the stench of dark magic. He is like a beacon to me." He stepped over and sat down next to Anok, putting his hand on his forehead. The old fingers were leathery and cool. "Does he speak?"

Teferi nodded. "He speaks to people long dead."

"That is very bad. The madness is deep upon him. He has used a very dark spell, drawn power from the unspeakable black pits of ancient gods."

He frowned, and shifted his hand on Anok's forehead. "There is something familiar here, though I have never detected it like this before. Something that has hidden itself from me. But I cannot say what it is." His forehead wrinkled above the cloth covering his eyes. "Something is happening. I think a spell is ending!"

Anok could feel it, too.

The power of the Scale of Set, which he had transferred to his body, began to flow back to its golden home, and as it did, it took something with it. The madness flowed from his body, like venom sucked from a wound.

He looked at the old man. "Sabé? What has happened?"

"But that I understood it myself. You have used great magic, young Anok, and brought madness on yourself. Why the madness is so great I cannot—" Then a realization seemed to hit him.

He grabbed at Anok's left arm, shuddering as he touched the mark around his wrist. His expression turned to rage. "The Mark of Set! Why did you not tell me this?"

Anok did not like his tone. "I am entitled to my secrets. How did I know I could trust you?"

"I, who have entrusted you and your friends with my own long-hidden secrets? How could you keep this from me?"

"What difference would it have made had you known?"

"Well, I never would have tempted you with the ancient texts of power. Never would I have taught you spells like the one you used! The Mark of Set craves such power, feeds upon it. It must ever be denied, lest it consume your soul! A normal sorcerer might use such a spell and recover from the madness or corruption it brings. But one who bears the mark—" He shook his head sadly.

Anok could not accept what he was saying. He pushed himself up off the couch so quickly that Sabé scrambled off his seat and jumped backward. "What do you know of it anyway? What can you possibly know of the Mark of Set?"

Sabé's face reddened. "What can I know?" He yanked back the tight cuff of his sleeve to show the skin, smooth and pink as a child's, and there, a mark identical to Anok's own.

Anok shook his head. "That can't be. The texts say that the Mark has not been granted for five hundred years!"

"The texts do not lie. Surely you have seen how the power of the mark can restore the flesh. For five hundred years it has kept death from my door, until even the Cult of Set had forgotten my name. Long I have resisted that cold embrace, hoping I might yet be free of this curse before going to my funeral pyre."

"But you knew all these magics as well. You have read every text I read and a thousand more. How is it that you have resisted their temptation? Why are you not corrupt or mad?"

Sabé's mouth twisted in emotion, his lips struggling to form words through his anger. Finally, he said, "You fool! I've made my mistakes! I've paid the price! You think me an old, blind man." He reached for the knot binding the cloth around his eyes. "Well, in a sense I am blind, but not for lack of eyes to see!"

He yanked away the cloth.

Fallon gasped.

Teferi's mouth opened in a silent, "Oh!"

There, hidden by the cloth, the wrinkled skin around his eyes became puckered and crusted over with shining, green, scales. And, surrounded by those scales, were the eyes, large, round, and yellow, the pupils vertical black slits.

Anok knew them well. He had seen eyes like them before, on the great temple snakes of Set.

"This is the price I paid for my dalliances with great magic! To have the cold, inhuman eyes of a serpent of Set! To see in human flesh only something warm to be *slaughtered* and consumed. Eyes that paint each image only in shades of evil, eyes that corrupt the mind and the soul!" With each word, his voice changed, becoming darker, more sinister.

Suddenly, Sabé threw up his hands and turned away from them, struggling to regain control as he tied the cloth back into place.

When it was done, he slumped down onto a chair, his head hung low, not facing them, panting to catch his breath. "Now," he said finally, "you see. My last secret is yours as well. You see why I have helped you, young Anok, in your schemes against the Cult of Set. But it is I who am the fool. Blind, I could not see the mark that would destroy you."

"I'm sorry," said Anok. "I didn't understand."

"I need not your pity. What I have done, I have done to myself. Let it not be your fate, though I am not sure how we can spare you."

"But the madness is past! And I swear, I will never use great magic again!"

Sabé turned their way, his expression contemptuous. "Do not make promises you cannot keep. And as for the madness, do not think you are free. I do not understand how you are free of it even now."

Anok quickly explained his ruse in taking the magic of the Scale into himself and how it had drawn the madness from him.

Sabé shook his head. "A Scale of Set? How many more secrets do you have?"

"A few," said Anok.

Sabé sighed. "This is but a respite. The madness will return. You have, at best, days."

"Then I will repeat the spell and use the Scale to cleanse myself."

"And each time you do, the Mark of Set will draw more power from the Scale, growing stronger until its corruption consumes you as it nearly did me. That is no answer."

"I am doomed then?"

Sabé's mouth twitched. "There may be one other hope. For all my years I have searched the ancient secrets for some answer to my own plight. In those years, I have found but one thing of promise. It was too late to help me, but it may offer you some small hope."

Teferi stepped forward excitedly. "What is it then? Tell us!"

Sabé frowned. "There will be great peril."

Fallon grinned. "Peril again. There is always peril in a fighter's path. How else will they gain glory? How else will their stories be worth telling?"

"Perhaps there was never hope for me, Anok. But I had not friends such as these in my time of need."

Anok met the eyes of each of his friends in turn, exchanging a silent acknowledgment. Then his attention went back to Sabé. "Then what is this hope of which you speak?"

Sabé opened his mouth, then stopped. "We are being watched," he said. Then, raising his voice, "Show yourself!"

A curtain parted, and Dejal stepped into the room. "Forgive me, but is there room for one more old friend on your quest?"

Anok's eyes widened. Dejal. The betrayer. The *murderer! What is he doing here?*

As if in answer, Dejal touched the crystal ball at the top of his magical staff. "I touched you with this as you left the temple, so as to establish a connection. That, plus our long association, allowed me to follow you even into Thoth-Amon's lair and observe your ordeal. I could not hear you there for his spells of concealment, but I could still see."

"You spied on me!"

"I was concerned for your welfare. I have heard tales of those who have had audience with the Lord of the Black Ring in his chambers. Some never return, and few return unchanged, as I see it is with you."

He was in no mood for false pleasantries. "You care for none but yourself."

Dejal smiled slightly. "There is some truth, that I value my interests over all. But my interests are intertwined with those of others as well. Especially yours, brother.

"Much of my rise in the cult has been through my association with you. I admit, I have little of my own to offer. My father is rich, but not as rich as many, and I am but a poor magician, leaning on my staff of magical trinkets in more ways than one. If you are not loyal to Set, what of it? That is not my concern. But so long as Thoth-Amon and Ramsa Aál remain convinced you may be of some eventual use to them, it will serve me as well."

Anok sneered. "And if I crush your precious cult, what then?"

Dejal laughed. "You may entertain such delusions. I do not share them. In that sense, you are a problem that will, sooner or later, solve itself. I need only stand back and watch. In fact, I suspect that without my aid, your grand schemes will end here and now."

Teferi looked at Dejal, a frown on his face. "Though it pains me to admit it, Anok, he may be right. We may have need of a wizard, and for you to use more magic is only to speed your downfall. He will serve us, as long as it serves his own interests as well."

Anok grimaced. Dejal might indeed be useful, but Anok was just as sure he couldn't be trusted, and he couldn't tell Teferi why. So long he had kept the truth of Sheriti's murder from his friend. The secret had festered, and to tell it now might lose him his ally just when he was needed most.

"Very well. Let us hear the task Sabé has set out for us, then we will decide if we need your aid."

Sabé looked unhappy. "I do not like this. This one cannot be trusted."

Anok nodded grimly. "I know that too well. But he already knows too much, so we have little choice but to keep him close to us."

Sabé sighed. "Very well." He paused and gathered his thoughts. "For countless years I have seen scattered references in the texts to an ancient sorcerer named Neska. Most texts suggested that he was Atlantean, though I suspect that may merely have been a land where he dwelled. Truthfully, he may not even have been fully human. But the texts said he worked great and powerful magics, and that he was a wise, good, and just man."

"From what we know," said Teferi, "that is a contradiction."

"Indeed," said Sabé, "and so I searched for more.

"I found that he had escaped Atlantis when it sank and come to the land that would later be known as Stygia; but all accounts said his power was greatly diminished. I later learned it was because a pillar had fallen on his left arm as that ancient land sank, and he was forced to cut his limb off with his own sword in order to escape."

Teferi grimaced, but said nothing.

"Still, it is said that he sent many Atlanteans to a place of safety, built a city in Stygia, and watched over it until his death. The people built a pyramid in his honor and buried him there. But he could not save them from the unknown horrors that would later sweep over Stygia. The city was abandoned and lost to the sands."

Anok saw something crawling up the wall. A solitary scorpion. He looked away, shook his head, and it was gone. "This is interesting, but I don't see how that helps me."

"Patience. I said he used magic without corruption or madness, and I eventually learned how. It is said that he forged two bracelets that would counteract the ill effects of sorcery and allow it to be used for good. One was lost with his hand, but the other was buried with him."

"Then that bracelet could cure me, free me to use the Mark of Set to punish those who deserve it?" He glanced up and saw Dejal watching him.

"With only one bracelet, and with your spirit already infected by dark magic, I do not think so. But it could provide a firmament, an anchor, so that a strong man could pull himself back from madness and corruption. Even with the bracelet, it will not be easy."

Anok paced. "What choice do I have. How do we find this tomb?"

"I suspect it is not far over the mountains into the desert. Sorcerers come here because this is a natural place of power, and so it was then. Many have searched the sand and found nothing. But I have found an ancient spell of guidance that will guide one to the tomb."

"Then tell it to me, and we will be off."

Sabé remained silent for a time. "I fear it is too soon for you to do magic. You will only hasten the return of the madness."

Dejal smiled. "So, it seems that you do have need of a sorcerer, brother."

"And the temple . . ." said Sabé. "It will not be unguarded. Who knows what great Neska may have left to guard his tomb?"

"This," said Fallon, drawing her sword and holding it out, "would be the part of this that involves peril."

Teferi hesitated only a moment before drawing his sword and laying his blade across hers. "We are together in this, then."

Anok looked at them. "Be sure you know where this road leads. These are not bandits or pirates or guardians we will face. This temple is doubtless guarded by supernatural creatures. In my time with the cult, I have read of things, even seen things. There are creatures more unnatural, foul, and terrible that you can imagine."

"I can imagine a great deal," said Teferi. "Let us have at them."

Yet Anok suspected they really didn't know, didn't understand.

Nobody did, until they first looked into the dark abyss with their own eyes.

24

THEY LEFT KHESHATTA before dawn the next morning.

The poisoners and great sorcerers who kept their estates and plantations in the hills north of Kheshatta jealously guarded their privacy, and so the four travelers, Anok, Teferi, Fallon, and Dejal, steered their mounts carefully up the well-marked caravan road into the low mountain pass.

They rode camels, three hired for the trip, and Fallon's white camel Fenola. The beasts looked singularly out of place as they wound their way up through the lush hills. But as they moved away from the city basin, the terrain began to dry out, the flora consisting mainly scrubby brown grass, leafy flowering cactus, and an unfamiliar brush with waxy, bluish leaves and bright green berries.

As they crested the pass, they had a clear look at the land beyond, red-rock badlands, bone-dry riverbeds, and shifting dunes of sand that threatened to swallow it all.

Perhaps one day they would.

They were careful to follow the established road as it wandered down the steep and treacherous hillsides amid loose and fallen rock.

It was difficult. The road was not much traveled. The large caravans used the narrow pass to the west, where Anok had entered the city, then circled north from there. It cost them half a day's travel, but the going was easier on both the riders and the camels.

Anok didn't have half a day to spare. He could hear the imagined voices always, like a ringing in his ear, and the little scorpions were always at the edge of his vision. He might have been amused by their antics if he hadn't known the encroaching madness they represented.

He saw his father and Sheriti occasionally, too, though usually at a distance, and they did not talk to him. They passed his mother, sitting on a rock next to the road at one point. He called to her, and the others looked at him strangely before he realized she wasn't there.

He saw others long dead as well. Hericus, the chief servant in his father's house. Asrad, the long-dead Raven, who rode next to them on a spectral camel for a while before waving to Anok and going his own way.

He saw people he'd killed: pirates, bandits, Lord Wosret and the White Scorpions. Except this time they really were scorpions: human heads on pale, low-slung bodies, running alongside the little caravan on many-jointed legs, waving their pincers and stinging tails at Anok until the trail narrowed, and they were left behind.

When at last they reached the flats at the base of the hill, Dejal moved to the front of the procession. It was time to leave the more traveled road and follow Sabé's locator spell.

Dejal held up his staff before him, the crystal ball and various magical trinkets glinting in the sun, and chanted the ancient incantation Sabé had provided.

A beam of light shone from the crystal at the top of the staff and began to sweep around the horizon. It spun a full circle, then stopped, pointing to the northeast before fading away. They turned their camels to the right and headed in that direction.

Every half hour or so, Dejal would repeat the spell, and they would adjust their direction as necessary. They left all signs of roads or trails behind, winding their way among boulders and dried patches of brush.

They saw not the slightest sign of human habitation, and Teferi soon became impatient. "How will we know when we're close? This doesn't look like the ruins of an ancient city. It doesn't look like anything."

"As we get close," said Dejal, "the beam of light should shine downward."

Teferi seemed skeptical, but he was generally untrusting of magic. "Why couldn't Sabé have just had a map? This still doesn't look like anything."

"If it were easy to find," said Anok, "someone would have discovered it long before now."

"Let us hope that someone already hasn't found it," said Dejal. "I've read of Neska's tomb in my studies as well. If I have, countless others have as well."

"Knowing of Neska," said Anok, "is not the same as knowing where his tomb is located. Sabé put together the pieces of this locator spell from a dozen different tablets that it took him hundreds of years to collect. I am hopeful that we will be the first."

They had to be, he glumly reflected, or he was doomed to madness.

It was midafternoon before they noticed a change in the beam's angle. They were entering another area partially covered with dunes, and with each mile there was more sand and less rock. The camels, seemingly happy at the change after a morning of difficult, and often unfamiliar, terrain, actually began to pick up speed.

In their haste, they missed it, and had to turn back. When they finally reached the site, it was a disappointment.

"There's nothing here but dunes," said Teferi. "Are you sure?"

Dejal chanted the spell again. The beam shot downward at a sharp angle, plunging into a large dune in front of them. "I'm sure," he said.

"If there is anything here, it's long buried, and it would take an army of laborers a month to uncover."

"This is no less then you deserve," said Lord Wosret into Anok's ear.

When he spun his head, there was no one, only a faint echo of laughter.

"There must be a way," said Fallon. "We can't just give up."

"There is a way," said Dejal. He propped his staff against the saddle of his camel and clasped a small stone figurine that hung from a silver chain. He closed his eyes and began to chant, "Wachun, shepherd god of the shifting sands, move your flock to greener lands and lay bare what once was buried."

Anok heard a ringing, though perhaps again not with his ears. For a moment, nothing else seemed to happen.

Then the wind picked up, swirling around the dune, faster and faster, forming a dust devil. Sand was sucked up into the cone of air, giving it form and substance.

The wind howled around them, though they seemed at the edge of the whirlwind's influence.

The dune began to shrink visibly as sand was siphoned off into the sky. For a time, they saw nothing. Then, a carved granite roof appeared at the top, like a small house or temple. Curiously, it was richly carved with strange fish and seashells.

As the sand continued to fall, it was apparent this was only a small structure at the top of a gigantic stepped pyramid. Though there were other stepped pyramids in Stygia, this one was unique in that the "step" actually angled down the side of the pyramid, forming a kind of squared spiral that one could use to walk from the lowest level to the structure at the top.

On the stone next to the ramp was carved a continuous tableau of pictures and writing in some unknown hieroglyphics.

"I have seen symbols like these," said Teferi, "on a few of Sabé's oldest tablets. I do not think even he knows how to read them."

The pictures seemed to tell some great story. There

were many pictures of boats, coastlines, and something that might have been an island built on the back of a giant turtle.

"I think," said Anok, "that this is the story of Atlantis. It starts at the top and winds its way down to the very bottom."

"It is the bottom we'll want," said Dejal, "from the direction of the light. Perhaps the burial chamber is inside."

The base of the pyramid was at last exposed, along with part of a stone courtyard that had surrounded it, and the end of a cobblestone road leading into the sand on the east side.

As Dejal predicted, there was an entrance to the interior of the pyramid. But it was not hidden, it was a wide tunnel framed by a stone archway, and two large marble statues of fish walking on four scaly legs.

Fallon looked at where the road vanished into the sand. "There could be a whole city buried out there, just as Sabé said."

"We don't need a city," said Anok, "we need what is in this temple. *I* need what is in this temple."

They rode down the sandy slope and tied their camels to a stone pillar well away from the entrance to the pyramid.

Teferi eyed it suspiciously. "If the entrance was ever closed, it's open now. Perhaps tomb robbers have already stripped it of its treasures."

"Remember," said Anok, "Sabé said there would be guardians. Perhaps this temple needed no door to keep out intruders."

"Oh," said Fallon sarcastically, "that bodes well."

The voices buzzed in the back of Anok's head, and he was in no mood for jokes. "No one forced you to come!"

He immediately regretted his words, but at times he felt like a passenger in his own body, simply watching what was happening, listening to the words that were said, and having very little to do with either.

He saw the look of hurt and anger on her face. "I should not have said that. I am not myself."

Teferi frowned at him with concern but said nothing. He

glanced into the tunnel. "It is dark in there. We will need to light torches."

"Perhaps not," said Anok. He reached into his bag and removed four fist-sized translucent stones.

"Are those light stones, like the one you once used. What did you call them?"

"Jewels of the Moon," said Anok, "and yes. Sabé found them in his storeroom. He said he's had no use for them for hundreds of years, but they should still serve us today."

He pulled out his dagger and drew the edge of the blade across the back of his arm, just enough to break the skin and allow a small bead of blood to rise. He smeared the first stone with a bit of the blood. As he did, it flared to bright white.

He handed it to Teferi, then smeared the blood on the next one and handed it to Fallon, who took it gingerly, seeming surprisingly squeamish about the blood.

He smeared a third and offered it to Dejal. Instead, Dejal reached out, swiped his finger across the cut on Anok's arm, and wiped it on a similar orb inset into the side of his staff.

"Keep it for yourself," said Dejal.

Anok felt his jaw clench as he noticed Dejal sucking his finger clean. "Blood is power," Ramsa Aál had once told him. Anok considered that he'd probably just made a mistake, giving his enemy power, no matter how small, but it was too late to take it back.

He shrugged and walked through the archway. "Draw your swords," he said, pulling one of his own blades, "and follow me."

The sword felt strange, almost alien in his hand. His intention to keep in practice sparring with Teferi had given way to his obsession with studying the old texts, and Teferi had taken to sparring with Fallon instead.

When danger came, he might have to fall back on magic, and he was not sure what even the smallest of spells would do to him now.

Just lighting the orbs, an act that should have required

no magical effort at all, had left him feeling woozy and light-headed.

He could feel the magic all around them, from every stone of the ancient temple, and it twisted his gut. It made him sick to his stomach, but it also made him *hungry* somehow.

It wasn't he, it was the Mark of Set. But the sensations no longer emanated just from his wrist. He could feel its cold tendrils working their way up his arm, through his shoulder, around his chest, like a claws reaching out to clutch his heart.

Dejal looked at him, but there was no sign of concern on his face. "Are you unwell, brother?"

Anok grunted, and he thought he detected a slight smile on Dejal's face.

Murderer! Kill him! Kill him! Steal the temple's power and kill him!

Anok swatted at the empty air in front of his face. "Shut up!"

Teferi slid in front of him. "Why don't you let me go first, Anok."

He did not argue, though he felt like a coward for allowing Teferi to do so. He felt weak and useless.

You have power! Use it! Use it! They only want to steal it from you! Crush them! Crush them all!

He made a guttural barking noise at the voices, a raw sound of anger. He had to be rid of this curse even if he had to saw off his own arm!

But he could feel the infection in his chest as well and knew that it was too late for that. Only death could rescue him. Only death, and if Sabé was any indication, even that might be denied him.

The air that flowed out of the temple as they walked through the entrance was not stale. It was fresh and cold, like a wind blowing through a mountain cave. Anok had the odd feeling that the air was very ancient, though, as if it had been frozen in time, from the moment of Neska's entombment until the moment they had entered.

Illuminated in the blue light of the orbs, the revealed walls of the tunnel were covered with carvings of the sea, frozen waves of marble, fish, shells, squid, and people who were half human, half fish. Fallon looked at them as they walked along. "We're in the desert. Why all these sea creatures?"

"Atlantis," said Dejal, "was an island, surrounded by the sea. This place is as much a tomb for dead Atlantis as it is for Neska himself."

They passed through a doorway into a space so large that their lights could not show them the walls or ceiling.

Then there was a rumble, a sliding of stone on stone, and a huge stone door dropped smoothly behind them.

"This," said Teferi, readying his sword, "cannot be good."

Then light flared from the four distant corners of the room. The light came from large orbs much like the Jewels of the Moon, but each was as big as a man's head, and all were mounted on ornate stone pillars at least twice as high as a man.

The room revealed was huge, as though most of the pyramid's interior were hollow. The floor was square, and the ceiling sloped inward to a point far above their heads.

Of guardians, they saw none. As with the corridor, representations of the sea were everywhere, carvings, painted murals on the walls, and statues. Around the room, stone starfish stood, their bodies raised so that they stood on the tips of their arms, almost as tall as a man.

One thing dominated the room, a marble platform with an altar, and behind the altar, a huge statue of a nautilus, a squidlike creature with many arms, fierce eyes, and a beautiful spiral shell that protected the rear of its body.

They looked up at the statue in wonder.

"Is this," asked Fallon, "the Atlantean god?"

Dejal studied the altar. "Perhaps," he said, "a sacrifice is required before we will be allowed to go on."

Teferi looked at him. "Are you volunteering, Dejal?"

Dejal grimaced.

There was another scraping of stone on stone, then many.

They were coming from all around them. A motion caught Anok's eye. "The stone starfish! They're moving!"

Teferi charged toward the nearest one, sword held high. "We have found the guardians!"

He brought the blade down, and it struck one of the starfish's arms, high, near the body. There was a crunch, and the blade sank in only a few inches, dust crumbling from the crack, but the creature kept coming.

Teferi backpedaled, struck again, his blow unerringly finding the same spot.

Another crunch, then a cracking noise, and the leg fell off.

Still the starfish advanced on its remaining four legs.

Teferi swung again.

Again.

Again.

Another leg fell free, and the starfish toppled over.

But it did not stop moving. And worse, at the point where the legs had been severed, new ones were forming, small but perfectly formed, growing as they watched.

Fallon stepped into the fray, nimbly staying clear of the swinging arms, hacking away the limbs until they fell.

But already, the first starfish that Teferi had crippled was starting to rise, and a dozen more approached them from every corner of the room.

Worse, hacking at the stone was wearing away at the blades of their swords, grinding the sharpened edges down to nothing. Soon, their weapons would be useless.

As useless as I am. Anok could only stand and watch. His smaller swords all but useless against their stone foes.

A starfish caught Teferi unawares, and one of its thick arms touched his sword arm. Instantly it stuck to him, and slowly the thick arm curled around him. Just as it was about to close on him, he roared, and managed to yank his arm free.

But not without cost. His arm was raw and bloody where the thing had grabbed him. He gasped and shook his arm in pain. "Cursed thing took half my skin off!"

But it only distracted him a moment, before he was back hacking again.

Anok looked at Dejal. "They're wearing them down. Do something!"

Dejal stared at his staff, seemingly taking inventory of the magical objects attached to it. Then he reached into his pocket and drew out a metal rod as long as his hand. He turned the staff to expose a brass cylinder of about the same length.

"Listen unnatural fiends, music of destruction, hear now the bell of thunder!" He struck the rod against the brass bell, but there was no small ringing.

There was thunder.

Deafening thunder that made Anok grab his ears, that thudded hollow in his chest and made his bones hurt.

The starfish nearest Teferi shattered into chunks no bigger than a fist.

Dejal turned to where Fallon was hacking at two of the things.

Struck the bell.

Thunder, and they crumbled, one turning to powder as Fallon's sword struck it.

Dejal seemed to laugh, though Anok could only hear the ringing in his ear and the ever-present voices in his head.

He struck the bell. Another temple guardian fell.

Again, he seemed to laugh.

Anok saw something at the edge of his vision, turned.

"Look at him," said Sheriti. "He thinks he's winning. This is only the beginning."

Then she was gone.

One by one, the starfish were destroyed, by swords and magic: those that survived were driven back.

No.

They were *falling* back.

The others seemed to realize it even as Anok did. They stopped their attacks and watched as the starfish scuttled back near the walls and froze in their original positions.

Dejal held his staff high in triumph. "I beat them!"

"We beat them," said Fallon, stepping over to examine Teferi's injured arm.

Anok looked warily around the room, feeling the magic there. "No," he said quietly.

Dejal's smile vanished, and he stared at Anok.

There was a noise. Wet, liquid, and it came from the direction of the altar.

Anok turned to look at the great statue of the nautilus. It was *changing*.

As he watched, the blind, stone eyes became black, wet, and translucent, the dozens of stone tentacles turned into greenish-gray, leathery flesh, and the stone spiral of the shell turned the color and transparency of fine ivory.

There was a stench in the air, like fish left too long on the dock.

A hiss of air blasted from the fleshy funnel next to the thing's head.

It began to move.

"Get back," yelled Anok.

Tentacles reached for Teferi, and he swung his sword.

The leather skin was like leather armor. The blade struck with a thud, leaving only a small, bloodless cut.

Still, the cuts seemed to hurt, as the injured arm drew back.

Tentacles arched out on either side of the head, reaching down to push against the marble platform. With a rumble, the great shell slid forward a few paces.

Anok stepped in, just outside what seemed to be the thing's reach, and hacked at the tentacles with his two swords, hoping he could do some damage near the tips, where they were thinner.

But again the thing pushed itself forward. The sword was yanked from his left hand, and instantly it was turned and used against him.

Blade clashed against blade, and he suddenly realized this was no mindless brute that attacked them. Those eyes, each as big as a shield, looked down at him with a murderous, inhuman intelligence.

Anok swung his blade two-handed, snapping the sword held by the tentacle. The broken weapon was immediately tossed aside, and the creature resumed its original means of attack.

Anok ducked as a tentacle whipped over his head.

Teferi cried out as one of the arms wrapped around his ankle and lifted him, upside down, like a stuffed doll.

Fallon rushed forward, tried to pull him free, and was herself caught around the waist. She cried in pain as the arm cinched tight around her.

Swords would not stop the thing.

Magic!

He turned to Dejal, who just stared at the thing, frozen, by fear or wonder he could not tell.

"Dejal! The thunder!"

Dejal's head snapped toward him, like a man awaking from a dream. He swung the metal rod at the bell.

Thunder!

The thing flinched, tentacles yanked back away from the pain.

Thunder!

Teferi and Fallon were dropped to the floor, where they struggled to rise and get away from the flailing arms.

Thunder!

A huge eye looked down at Dejal, filled with hate.

A tentacle whipped out, so fast it was like lightning answering the thunder.

Dejal shrieked as the staff was snatched from his hand.

The tentacle raised it high, then it came down upon the top of the altar.

Wood shattered to splinters, metal trinkets smashed, stone and crystal broken, the crystal ball at the top smashed to powder.

A gasp of horror escaped Dejal's lips as he saw his precious staff, object of so much labor, source of all his power, destroyed before his eyes.

He stood frozen, even as the great shell slid toward him.

Again.

Again.

Tentacles reached out to crush him.

Let him die! Anok heard the voice in his head. *Let the bastard die!*

The tentacles reached for Dejal's throat.

Anok shouted, "No!" He raised his hands, acting on instinct. "Thunder!"

It came, twice as loud as before.

The walls shook.

Dust fell from the ceiling.

The altar cracked and crumbled.

The beast drew back, away from Dejal, and he scurried to safety.

And in that moment, Anok realized he had been wrong.

The voice in his head just then had not been the Mark of Set.

It had been his own.

The Mark had tricked him into saving Seriti's murderer.

He felt ice-water tendrils growing in his chest, heard the voices in his head rise up, like a chorus in song.

The great nautilus turned away from Dejal, who struggled to rise from the floor, toward Teferi and Fallon.

Anok roared in anger, but the damage was done.

His friends were still in danger, and thunder would not be enough.

His mind raced, trying to ignore the voices, the imaginary gnats that buzzed around his head, trying to remember some spell, any spell, that might drop this monstrosity.

The thing turned, and the light shone off the side of its shell like pearl, like polished bone.

There was a spell, not to kill a monster, but to fell an army.

It would have to do.

He raised his hands. The words of the great spell were in an ancient tongue, one of the few he knew well, but even as he thought of them, he translated them into Stygian. "Enemy, strong of arm, legions against our few, your strength undiminished, yet useless without bone!"

The power flowed from the Mark of Set, and he let it. It screamed in triumph.

The nautilus pulled itself toward Teferi and Fallon, shell scraping across stone.

But then shell turned to powder.

All of it, the great spiral of it, turned to powder and collapsed to the floor. The creature shrieked. It seemed much smaller now: most of the shell had been empty space. What was left behind the head was a soft, pulpy, shapeless body that sloshed wetly as it moved.

Fallon immediately sensed the weakness. With a whoop, she charged, leaping on top of an arched tentacle, diving over the thing's head, plunging her sword hilt-deep in that soft and defenseless body.

The monster screamed, trying to reach her with its arms.

Teferi rushed past them in that moment of distraction and plunged his own sword deep into its flesh, then *ripped* the blade along its length.

Bluish fluid that might have been blood or bile gushed out.

The tentacles waved and twitched without purpose or intelligence, then fell lifeless to the floor with a leathery slap.

They all froze, watching it for any sign of movement.

"It's dead," gasped Dejal. Then a laugh. "It is *dead!*"

Anok's father looked at him. "You killed it," he said.

"You killed it," said Sheriti.

Scorpions swarmed up the side of the altar and across the dead monster. Teferi and Fallon didn't seem to see them.

There was another sound, stone on stone.

They all flinched.

Anok struggled to focus his eyes in the direction of the sound. A door in the back wall of the chamber, formerly hidden behind the monster's shell in the wall behind the altar, was now revealed, and it was sliding open. Perhaps it had been held shut by the same spell that had animated the creature. Now that it was destroyed, the door opened. More light orbs illuminated within.

Dejal smiled. "The tomb of Neska. We have found it!"

The human-sized scorpion with Lord Wosret's head scuttled up next to Anok and smiled. "Too late for you, madman! Now we can play together—forever!"

The tail drew back, curved black stinger dripping venom, and struck deep into Anok's chest.

He screamed and held up his hands, trying to defend himself.

But the stinger rose and fell.

Plunging into him.

Again.

And again.

And again.

25

ANOK LAY GASPING on the floor of the pyramid, Fallon cradling his head as Teferi looked down at him with a look of grave concern.

"Poor Anok," said Sheriti, crouching down next to him and brushing her soft fingers across his sweating brow.

The Wosret scorpion scuttled up behind her.

Anok's eyes went wide. He tried to call out a warning.

Sheriti glanced back and saw the scorpion. She turned and waved it away. "Shoo," she said, "shoo."

Wosret scowled and crawled back into the shadows.

Teferi and Fallon seemed not to have noticed him at all.

Sheriti looked at him seriously. "I'll keep him away as long as I can. You have to hurry."

Anok struggled and sat up. "The tomb—"

Teferi reached down and took his hand. "Can you walk?"

Anok coughed. Every breath was agony. The Mark of Set tried to heal him, but he fought back against it. "I can walk," he said. "Help me."

Teferi pulled Anok to his feet. He tried to stand, but his legs threatened to buckle. Teferi caught him, gasping.

Anok felt a wet stickiness against his skin, and realized he had fallen on his friend's injured arm. There was nothing he could do about it.

"Come," said Teferi, "let us find what it is you need here."

Dejal stepped in front of them. "I have him," he said, taking Anok's other arm.

Teferi did not move.

"I know what we're looking for and how to use it to help Anok. I can get us in and out quickly. There may be other guardians, and we need you two to cover our retreat."

Teferi let his breath out through his teeth, then released his hold on Anok. "Hurry," he said.

Anok leaned against Dejal, who carried Anok's remaining sword. It was their only defense now that Dejal's staff was broken.

The tunnel was narrow and sloped steeply down into the bedrock beneath the pyramid.

Anok could see the Wosret scorpion watching them from the shadows.

Sheriti walked along behind them. She doubled her pace to walk in front of Dejal. She studied him intently.

"For some reason," she said, "I don't trust him."

A gaping gash opened up in her throat, and blood began to flow down the front of her silk gown, trailing along the floor as she walked. "I don't trust him," she said, livid bruises appearing on her beautiful face, "I don't know why."

As they entered the burial chamber, more orbs illuminated. On another day, Anok would have been struck by the wonder of it.

The walls were covered with gold. Not gold leaf, but sheets of solid gold. Alcoves and shelves were jammed with items of gold and silver, chests of jewelry overflowed, gemstones of every color and description glittered from the floor, scattered like pebbles, riches enough for a dozen kings.

Today, Anok glanced at it and dismissed it just as quickly. He sensed no magic in any of it. The most humble stone in the temple above held more interest to him than an emerald the size of a goose egg down here.

No, this was only a distraction, fool's gold for the greedy.

The true treasure of Neska lay in the center of the small room, on a burial platform of common sandstone, among the dry bones of a sorcerer dead since long before Stygia even had a name.

Anok pushed himself away from Dejal, stumbling and catching himself against the cool stone of the platform.

The bones were so ancient they were nearly black. It was the size and shape of a tall and broad-shouldered man, but there was a *wrongness* to it, some *oddness* to the ribs, fingers, and especially the shapes of the eye sockets and the skull, which suggested that this was not truly a man.

It was some other creature, a demon, a thing from before man, or perhaps from one of the cursed worlds from beyond the arch of the night sky.

Yet, in one way, it was exactly what Anok had been expecting, and when he saw that, he knew that it was truly Neska.

The skeleton had only one arm.

Any clothing, any decoration that might have been on the body was long turned to dust, save a few bits of metal on the remaining arm. On the first and third fingers of the hand, there were two heavy rings of gold, and on the wrist, a simple band of some silvery metal that Anok could not identify.

The band was small, wrapped tightly around the bone, and Anok found it hard to understand how it had fit around the living arm of the sorcerer.

"Quickly," said Sheriti, her features beginning to decay and putrefy. "You must act quickly!"

The bracelet seemed to be all of one piece. He reached for it, trying to find the clasp, but as soon as he moved it, the bones within turned to black dust.

He lifted the bracelet to examine it, feeling *something* tingling in his fingers, an energy, not magic, but something like *contramagic*.

No, said the voice in his head, this time certainly not his own. *No, no, no!*

Dejal stepped in next to him, but he turned away, keeping the bracelet to himself.

As he held it closer to examine, there was a click, and the bracelet sprang open from some hidden catch.

"Quickly," said Sheriti, the decayed flesh falling in chunks from her skull.

He held the bracelet up next to his right wrist for comparison. It was far too small.

Suddenly, it snapped closed.

He gasped as it bit into his flesh, tighter and tighter.

There was sizzling, and the flesh beneath the metal began to boil away like ice on a fire. He screamed in agony as the metal sank into his arm, until it finally snapped shut around a bare twig of muscle and bone.

Then the flesh began to close, flesh and tendon restoring itself, skin stretching across the gap and knitting together.

The pain faded, and tentatively, he flexed his right hand into a fist, then wiggled his fingers.

He rubbed his wrist. He could feel the bracelet there beneath the flesh, a smooth circlet close to the bone. He could feel it inside as well. Even if his eyes, his senses, his mind lied to him, the band of Neska was eternal, unchanging, a point of reference that never varied, a point of leverage that never shifted.

With this, he could *fight!*

He felt the tendrils of the mark in his chest.

He felt them, and he pushed!

The Mark of Set moaned in his mind.

The tendrils pulled back, shriveling.

He fought them, inch by inch.

Back into his shoulder.

Back down his arm.

Back into the Mark of Set itself.

He gasped and slumped against the platform.

He bumped Neska's skull. It rolled off, fell to the floor, and shattered into dust.

It was done!

Sheriti stepped in front of him. Restored. Beautiful. Perfect. She leaned into his face, looked deep into his eyes.

"Good-bye," she said.

Her lips brushed softly against his.

Then they were gone.

He let out a shuddering breath.

"Brother," said Dejal, a strange elation in his voice, "are you better?"

Anok nodded. "I—"

The words hung in his throat.

The two gold rings that had been on Neska's hand were gone.

Dejal wore one on each hand. He held his arms wide, clenched his fists, and smiled. "Good luck to you, brother, to find a way to hold back the darkness. Bad luck to you that you have not, as I, chosen to embrace it." He held his hands out before him, to admire the rings. "I am not as gifted as you in sorcery, Anok. I built my little staff of power, and these last months I have spent my time searching the ancient scrolls for clues to other magical objects. Objects that might bring me power and favor with my masters. Favor such as you have been given, and *squandered!*"

He turned toward Anok and smiled a terrible smile. "Imagine my delight when, in spying on my enemy, I learned he was going to the tomb where two of the greatest of those objects lay hidden, objects I could otherwise never have dreamed of finding, the Rings of Neska!" He held them out for Anok to see. "Why do you think he needed those wrist bands, Anok? He had created the two greatest magical weapons ever created, and he feared to use them! So he made his bands to tame their evil. But *I* do not fear them! I spit on the Band of Neska! My magical staff is broken, but with these, I have no need of it!"

Anok struggled to stand unsupported. The preceding magical struggles had left him drained, and the struggle to suppress the Mark of Set even more so. He was in no condition for another battle. "You have your power. Leave us then."

Dejal laughed. "I will leave. After I have killed you, and your barbarian whore, and that worthless Kushite trash you call a friend! I will leave satisfied that I never have to hear your mongrel name again! I will leave and claim the respect of Thoth-Amon that I so richly deserve!"

He seemed to have a new thought. "Perhaps I will even slay him, take his place, and follow through on Ramsa Aál's plan to rule all of Hyboria!" He cackled to himself.

Anok considered what to do next. He was weak, but he was not helpless, and his ability to use magic had been restored. He marshaled his will, calling up a bolt of magical power.

Dejal sensed something was happening, but too late.

Anok raised his hands, a bolt of energy leapt from his palms, and shot toward Dejal.

And past him, up the shaft, into the pyramid, past Teferi and Fallon, and into the stone seal that blocked the entrance to the pyramid.

With his magical senses, Anok felt the magic merge into the stone.

He whispered, *"Shatter!"*

From above, there was a crack, a rumbling noise, and the sound of falling stone.

Anok yelled up the shaft, "Run! Get out of the tomb!"

Dejal cried out in anger. A blast of force hit Anok, threw him up the shaft to land amid the rubble on the pyramid floor.

He sat up, giving the Mark of Set just enough freedom to heal his cracked bones and bruised flesh. He grimaced as he felt his flesh knit.

A noise made him turn, and behind him, he could see Teferi in the now-opened tunnel, obviously trying to decide if he should stay or go.

Anok locked eyes with him. "Run for your life! Don't wait for me!"

Teferi hesitated one more moment, then ran.

Just in time.

Dejal appeared walking slowly out of the shaft from the

burial chamber. Glowing bolts of power danced around his hands, like elfin fire around a ship's mast, a look of insane rage on his face.

Feeling a calm he had not known in months, Anok pulled himself to face his attacker. He took a deep breath.

"Those rings may be powerful, Dejal, but *you* are weak. You're like a child who picks up a sword and imagines himself a warrior. Kill me—if you can—but do not *ever* threaten my friends again."

Anok felt something growing inside him, formed out of the raw ore of rage toward Dejal he had so long suppressed. But it was not rage that emerged.

It was sadness for a friend long lost.

Pity for a spirit too weak to stand on its own.

It was the grim determination one feels when slaughtering a faithful dog gone rabid.

It had to be done.

It would be done.

Anok called on the power of the Mark of Set as he never had before. Without fear or hesitation he slammed down a bolt of raw power against Dejal.

The walls of the pyramid convulsed.

The orbs of illumination toppled from their pillars and rolled across the floor, casting crazy shadows as they tumbled.

Blocks of stone, as big as horses, dropped from the ceiling.

Dejal was tossed violently backward, but then seemed to catch himself and stopped, *floating* in the air. He began to laugh manically. "Is that the best you can do, Anok? The Rings of Neska have been resting, building their power for thousands of years! Your Mark of Set is spent, as are you." He settled lightly on the floor and threw his arms wide. "Do your best! Wear yourself out, so it will be easier to slaughter you!"

Anok did not hesitate to respond to his invitation. He lashed out with a spell of pestilence.

Dejal's eyes remained fixed on him, even as his face crusted over with boils. He *smiled,* and just as quickly, he was whole again. "I see I have not protected myself well enough. The rings still have untapped power with which to ward off your spells."

The rings were strange to him, but Dejal was learning fast, and Anok realized that the longer he waited, the less likely it was that any of his spells would work.

"Lightning!"

Bolts of lightning flew from Anok's fingertips and covered Dejal in a sheath of crackling blue fire.

But when it cleared, Dejal was unharmed.

"Fire!"

A spectral figure of flame flew from Anok's hand and leapt at Dejal.

Dejal waved his hands, and the flame spirit was dispersed before it could even touch him. He laughed, raised his left hand, and flicked his fingers at Anok.

Anok was thrown backward. He smashed through one of the stone starfish and pounded into the wall behind. Again, he willed the Mark of Set to heal him, but this time it was not without cost. He could feel its tendrils growing out into his arm again, and he had no time or will to force them back. The Band of Neska helped him to fight back against the mark's evil, but it offered no immunity.

He looked at the other starfish around him, and, with a gasp, raised his still-healing arms, the bones crackling as he moved. "Animate!"

The stone starfish began to move as before, slowly shifting to surround Dejal.

Dejal laughed hysterically. "These things could not defeat me before, Anok, and I had not a hundredth of the power of these rings!

One of the starfish reached out an arm and grabbed Dejal's wrist. Grinning, he tightened his fist, and the arm shattered to powder. He gleefully allowed the starfish to close in around him, touch him, and then he destroyed them.

For a moment he was distracted.

Anok let his shattered bones heal, then scrambled to his feet. He reached out with his mystic senses, feeling the wards that surrounded Dejal's person, like an impenetrable suit of armor. Perhaps, on a good day, with the Mark of Set at full power, and were he not himself exhausted, he might have penetrated those wards deeply enough to give Dejal a black eye or a scratch on the cheek.

On a good day.

This was not that day. Dejal was completely protected from any attack Anok could offer.

That was Dejal's mistake.

A terrible mistake.

He had focused all his considerable energies on protecting himself.

Dejal had forgotten to protect the rings.

Anok set free the last of his simmering anger, the last of his sadness for the loss of Sheriti, the last of his rage at seeing his friends endangered, and fashioned them into two bolts of power.

It was a terrible thing to do, even to a hated enemy.

"Rabid dog," he said.

Dejal's head jerked.

His eyes locked with Anok's.

He knew something was wrong.

Anok let loose the bolts of power.

Instinctively, Dejal tried to protect himself, not understanding that it was exactly the wrong thing to do.

The energy struck the ancient rings.

Joined with their own energies.

Infected them.

The rings exploded.

A wet, red mist splattered across Anok's face.

Dejal screamed. He screamed and screamed again, and he kept on screaming.

Around them the entire pyramid trembled, the one last indignity added to all the others of that day. For thousands of years it had stood unshaken.

Today, it would fall.

Anok stepped calmly forward, standing before Dejal.

He was on his knees.

His arms were gone, nothing left but charred stumps, too

burned even to bleed, that waved from his shoulders when he screamed.

"You have taken Neska's rings, Dejal. Now you know his curse, twice over! What spells will you cast now, without hands to cast them?"

Dejal managed to quiet his screams. For a moment, as loose stone and dust rained around them, he could only gasp and sob. Then he looked up at Anok, his eyes desperate and forlorn. "Mercy! Show me mercy, brother! I beg you! Kill me! Make it quick!" His body writhed, his head sagged.

Perhaps he was trying to bow. Perhaps he was simply trying not to fall down.

Anok didn't care.

"Mercy like you showed Sheriti, Dejal? I saw her body, saw the marks there, saw the torture you inflicted on her. There was no mercy there."

"It was my father's idea, not mine! It was Ramsa Aál that killed her, not I. I simply brought her to him!"

"As though that makes you less guilty? It was you who led her from the safety of her home with your lies. Did you use my name, Dejal? Did you tell her that I needed her? Did you make me part of her murder as well?"

The only answer from Dejal was to flinch, his eyes forlorn, like a whipped dog.

"If the others had their hand in killing her as well, take comfort in knowing that they, too, will die, with as much suffering as I can arrange." The temple began to collapse around them. "But we were friends once, so I will lift my hands no more to harm you. But don't look to me for mercy." He turned and began to walk away. "Death will take you, in its own time."

Dejal started to scream again. The noise echoed up the long tunnel and out the arched entrance, beyond which Teferi and Fallon waited.

Behind him, the entrance tunnel collapsed, the little structure on top collapsed into a pile of rubble, and a stone as big as a house rolled down the side of the pyramid and landed with a ground-shaking thud fifty paces to their left.

They ran, untying the camels and, leading them, scrambled up the sandy slope away from the pyramid.

As they reached the crest, a low rumble came from behind them. They turned back to see the pyramid falling in on itself, sand running back into the pit to swallow its crumbling stones.

They mounted the camels and trotted them a thousand paces or more before turning back to see.

The pyramid was gone, swallowed by sand, only a towering column of rising dust to show where it had been.

The watched it for a while, until even the dust was gone, and the dunes turned orange in the light of the setting sun.

Teferi looked at Anok. "You found what you needed?"

He nodded. "I did, and I am whole again."

"What," asked Fallon, "happened to Dejal?"

Anok gazed at the sand, took a deep breath, and let it out slowly through his nose. "He betrayed us, and he has paid the price for his betrayal."

He looked over at Teferi. "My friend, there are things we must talk of, secrets I have long hidden from you.

"But not today. After we return to Kheshatta. And I hope then, you will find it in your heart to forgive me."

He looked back at the mountains. "There is still light. Let us ride while we still can."

They made their way back across the sand. He rode up next to Fallon, looked at her, and smiled sadly. "You are going to be so angry," he said, "when you learn about the treasure you just missed."

ANOK LAY ON his blanket, looking up at the black sea of stars, and wondered from which of them Neska might have come. A falling star swept across his field of view, flared green, and was gone.

He heard a noise, someone moving in the darkness, and Fallon slipped in silently next to him, curling herself along his side.

Apparently she had forgiven him for the lost treasure.

He didn't complain, only thought of Sheriti and sighed.

If only Teferi would be half as forgiving—a quarter, an eighth—they might get through this.

That was one thing. There were many more.

He had fought back madness and corruption, and now he had a weapon against it.

But he was not free of it.

He knew now, he never would be.

But there was hope. Hope that justice for those murdered might be served. Hope that the tangled secrets of his past might finally be unraveled, his lost sister found.

Hope was all he had.

But here, under a crystal desert sky, with a good woman at his side, hope would be enough.